ECHOES OF VENGEANCE

ECHOES OF VENGEANCE

ROLAND CHEEK

a Skyline Publishing Book

Cover design by Laura Donavan
Text design and formatting by Michael Dougherty
Edited by Narelle Burton
Copy editing by Jennifer Williams

Publisher's Cataloging in Publication
(Prepared by Quality Books, Inc.)

Cheek, Roland.
    Echoes of vengeance / Roland Cheek. — 1st ed.
    p. cm.
    LCCN 2001126669
    ISBN 0-918981-08-5

      1. West (U.S.)—Fiction. 2. Adventure fiction.
    3. Western stories. I. Title.

PS603.H4465E44 2002   813'.6
                    QBI33-163

Published by   Skyline Publishing
                  P.O. Box 1118
                  Columbia Falls, Montana 59912

Printed in Canada

Dedication

To those other Western storytellers who've gone before, good and great, modest and not-so-modest; raconteurs all. Because of them, comes this tale.

Acknowledgement

It's my belief that anyone worth the powder to blow 'em to hell collects debts throughout life. Sometimes those debts are for favors, sometimes for friendships. We might owe for career enhancement or advancement, maybe for life enrichment, perhaps for insight or enlightenment.

As a writer, I've collected so many debts it's embarrassing to tell. And though their numbers are sufficiently legion that I can afford only to make note of their existence, perhaps by the doing, one or two may be sufficiently near entry to Heaven that St. Peter will allow them to squeeze inside.

Bill Kittredge is one. So is Vivian Palladin. Rick Graetz gave me early encouragement. Stan Jones and Bob Hirsch were my two greatest Arizona boosters. Norm Strung had more professional insight in one finger than I have in an entire body—and you can throw in two generations of Cheek ancestors, too. Dan Cherry belied both age and experience to burn camp candles to my benefit. And what can I say about a dozen others that would provide sufficient credit for their enthusiasm and encouragement?

I owe you.

CHAPTER ONE

It was a hell of a way to be jerked awake—staring down the stovepipe snout of a .50-caliber Sharps.

It all began when the intruder, in the half-light of breaking day, stumbled first over the discarded whiskey bottle, then the half-filled chamber pot.

"I'd drink to forget, too, if I was you," the intruder muttered, thrusting the Green River knife between his teeth and emptying the chamber pot on the sleeping man's head.

Major Calumet Cornelius Bates hurled blankets and quilts from his porcine body, spluttering, cursing, and clawing at his muttonchop whiskers with both hands. His voice trailed off when he spotted the big Sharps, its ugly snout yawning at his right eye.

"Kla-klatch." The sound of the Sharps' hammer as it was eared back split the sudden silence.

"Who are you? What do you want?"

"One question at a time, Major. When you're done, then I'll ask 'em."

The officer's jaw quivered as he clutched at the bedding. "What do you want?"

"First off, we'll talk. After that ..." The intruder shrugged.

"Who are you, dammit? What are you doing in my quarters? How did you get in here?"

"I said one question at a time, Major." There was an audible, tiny click as the heavy Sharps' set-trigger was latched into place. Now the slightest pressure would touch off the gun.

The major paled, but had the temerity to whisper, "How did you get into this fort?"

⸻ ⸱◆⸱ ⸻

He came over the wall during the dog-watch, when two patrolling sentries were least alert, huddling in their greatcoats, thinking only of the interminable time until changing of the guards. The moon was half and on the wane, shimmering intermittently between great scudding clouds. A tinge of pink touched the eastern prairie sky. Fort Pembina's palisades, barracks, stables, sutler's store, and armory cast shadows within the isolated post, across uneven patches of dirty snow.

He glided ghostlike from one shadow to another until reaching the commandant's quarters. Inside, Major Bates snorted fitfully, an arm draping from his bedcovers despite the Dakota Territory's November chill. The wraith flattened against rough bark-covered cottonwood logs, then crept to the building's door where he bludgeoned a slumbering sentry and pulled him into the shadows. The intruder abandoned the door when it creaked, turning instead for a window.

Leaning the heavy Sharps buffalo rifle against the logs, he pulled an Indian trade knife from the sash around his middle, then used it to pry the window open. It gave with a soft shudder.

Bedsprings squeaked as Major Bates rolled onto his back. The intruder melted against the wall logs, but when the officer resumed snoring, the man's face appeared above the sill. Only a faint rustle accompanied him as he squirmed inside. Even in the dim light, his mouth pinched into a thin line and tiny lights danced in gray eyes that were all the more startling because they were set in a dark face.

By now, the half-light of pre-dawn filtered into the room, falling across the whiskers, beetle brows, and ruddy face of the officer. The commandant lay with an arm across his forehead, puffy mouth open to expose stained teeth.

Then the intruder stumbled over the whiskey bottle and chamber pot, and the major's day was ruined before it even began ...

"For God's sake, move that gun!"

The Sharps never wavered.

"Who are you? At least tell me that."

"You don't remember me, Major?"

"No! Dammit, man, move that gun!"

The stranger made no sign he heard. "My name is Jethro Spring, Major. That mean anything to you?"

"No, no, no. Why should it? My God, one move and you could blow a hole ..." The major's voice trailed off.

"That's the idea, Major. To blow a hole. I worked on your post out in Montana. Fort Ryan. You still don't remember?"

The intruder was clad in buckskins, with knee-length moccasins on his feet. Bates sensed that the man was little more than a youth. "No! I don't know what it is you're after, but you'll never get away with it. You're inside a United States Army post. Three hundred men are just outside. Guards everywhere. You'll never get away with anything. Please!"

Unwinking gray eyes met the major's red-rimmed ones.

"Guard!" the major shouted. "Guard! Help!"

The shout brought only silence. The buckskin-clad stranger chuckled. "Ain't no guard there, Major. He's got a headache right now and is off takin' something for it."

The major twisted and untwisted his bedcovers. "What do you want?" he said again.

"I was just a stable hand who could speak a little Blackfeet. Not fair, I suppose, to expect you to remember me."

The major's eyes narrowed. "Now I remember," he said. "You're the young idiot who tried to tell me how to run my command."

"No, Major. I just tried to stop you from butchering an Indian village."

"And I had you thrown in the stockade."

"Now you got it right, Major."

"And for that, you follow me to Pembina, break into my quarters and hold a gun on me? You'll get the stockade for twenty years, you fool." Major Calumet Bates paused, then added, "If you touch that trigger by accident, you'll hang."

The youthful stable hand's hollow laugh sent another wave of shivers through the major. "Won't be by accident if I touch it."

"What do you want, then? Make it quick."

"I want to talk about that Indian village. Do you remember it?"

"Do I remember it?" The major's bleary eyes drifted from the youthful face and the penetrating gray eyes. "Of course I remember...."

———•·•———

Snow lay in patches, heavy and deep along the Musselshell—residue from a long, hard winter that blew in early from the Canadian Prairies. The tiny Indian encampment was pitched on a sweeping bend south of the river. High sandstone bluffs to the north provided some protection from the keening arctic winds that swept the land. The expected Chinook was slow in coming, but had arrived at last.

Reconnaissance was swift and accurate and between the hours of three and four a.m., Major Calumet Bates positioned five mountain howitzers and two hundred and fifty men in the soft, melting snow along the foreslope of the low hills south of the village. An additional fifty men of "A" and "F" Companies slipped into the brush across the Musselshell, under command of Captain Wesley Dix. All were in readiness, awaiting daylight and Major Bates' order to fire.

"Sarge, what's this all about, nohow?" Private Joshua Finster whispered to the burly man next to him. "What'd these red devils do? Is it a big village? Are they dog-soldiers down there, with bloody hands and bloody scalps hangin' from teepee poles?"

Sergeant Burke Mallory spat a thick stream of tobacco juice, staining the snow at his side. "Dunno," the sergeant replied in a whisper. "All I know is we got orders to leave no survivors. We're to kill 'em all—even women and kids if they's any among 'em."

"Must be some women, Sarge, what with that wailin' goin' on down there. Gods, don't they never shut up?" The eerie chant, begun as they moved into position, continued uninterrupted. "Why they do that?" the private asked.

"How the hell do I know? I ain't no Indian."

Farther along the line, Major Bates, lying on the muddy ground, lifted his heavy field glasses and smiled grimly. A godsend had brought this reservation-jumping band of Blackfeet within range of his command. Only a fool would miss such a heaven-sent opportunity to demonstrate military prowess. "Pink is beginning to show in the east, Lieutenant," he said.

When his junior officer said nothing, the major spat, "Damn! Why can't we see down into the village? Are the Gods hiding that infernal camp from us?"

Lieutenant James, lying beside his commanding officer, shook his head. The village would be last to receive the morning light. "We'll show clearly against the snow, sir, and easy pickings if we're discovered before we can make out our own targets."

Major Bates peered through his field glasses once more and suddenly spat, "Damn that squaw! Will she never shut up?"

The lieutenant propped himself on an elbow. "Sounds to me like a death chant, Major, sir. Leastways, it sounds something like one I heard coming from a 'Rapaho camp one time."

Major Bates chuckled. "There'll be ample reason for it soon. I wonder who it's for?"

"I don't reckon it's for any who died, sir. More'n likely it's for them who are about to."

"What? Impossible. There's been no sign of alarm. Are

you suggesting they know we're here, Lieutenant?"

"No, sir. But maybe they know they'll die. Indians have funny ways and I'm thinking, sir, that some are beyond a white man's understanding."

"Poppycock! Please inform the company officers to commence firing when discovered, or at six a.m., whichever comes first."

"Yessir." Lieutenant James rolled to the knob's far side and clambered to his feet. His lip curled to a sneer as he saluted the major's backside.

His heart thumping with excitement, Major Bates again lifted his glasses. A dog barked in the village. Bates cursed. The unnatural keening continued. Once more Bates peered to the east.

Lieutenant James skidded up moments later. "Still not too late, sir, to rescind the no-survivors order—if you've had a different thought, sir."

The major ignored his junior officer. He could barely make out a tipi—no two—through his glasses. His uneven teeth flashed through a ragged grin.

An old crone waddled from a tipi at 5:57 a.m. When she raised her skirt to urinate, a rifleman could contain himself no longer. He missed. But the hundred-odd other rifles trained upon her did not. The roar of a ranging howitzer boomed out, followed by others. The third howitzer in line scored a hit, its burst falling directly on the village's largest tipi. Major Bates shouted with glee. "See that gunner gets a commendation, James."

"Yes, sir."

A melee erupted as men, women and children burst from the remaining tipis. They scattered to the river, away from the concentrated fire blasting from the southern hills.

"Where the hell is Dix?" Bates shouted.

Just then, Captain Dix's command opened fire from

across the Musselshell, cutting a swath through the frantic Indians. Three women, a warrior, and two children fell among the ice chunks at the river's edge. Another white-haired woman staggered into the Musselshell and fell into the freezing water. She surfaced once, then sank slowly from sight, blood staining the water around her. The turbulent tide of Indians, many limping and bleeding, swept back to their demolished camp against the remorseless hail of bullets from the ridge. Dozens of dead and wounded lay where they fell between the river and camp. Others lay broken and twisted among the wrecked tipis. As targets diminished, the soldiers' fire became sporadic. Within minutes, nothing moved in the broken village and a lull fell over the carnage. Yet the eerie death chant still wafted from somewhere among the torn tipis.

"Tell the howitzers to range on the rest of the tipis, Lieutenant," Major Bates snapped. "I want that noise stopped immediately."

"Yes, sir." Lieutenant James pushed to his feet.

"I don't believe there was a shot fired in return, Lieutenant," the major said, studying the village through his glasses. "Our surprise was complete."

"No, sir. They've not returned fire, sir. But then, I don't think I've seen more'n four or five braves. The rest have all been women and ..." The top of Lieutenant James' head exploded. Major Calumet Bates recoiled in horror as his lieutenant's lifeless body sprawled across him. A puff of black smoke drifted from one tipi flap amid a rising breeze.

A voice shouted a clear command in Blackfeet. The answering roar of rifle and cannon from the hillside drowned further commands.

Minutes later, a howitzer bracketed the tipi. A burst blew mud, dirt, rocks, and snow into the thin buffalo robe shelter from one side, another near-miss fell on the other side. The tipi seemed to shudder, then collapsed as the concussions fractured supporting lodgepoles. By then, desultory fire came from the wrecked village. That sporadic fire proved remarkably accurate, however. A soldier near Private Finster sank moaning into the snow. Another, not far away, propped on one knee and firing methodically, threw up his arms and fell to one side, blood gushing from his throat. Other soldiers fell as it became the bluecoats turn to die on their exposed foreslope.

"Dig in!" a sergeant shouted and soldiers obeyed with alacrity.

Another puff of black smoke erupted from the edge of the collapsed tipi, and a howitzer gunner was slammed against his gun carriage. Again the howitzers ranged upon the Indian riflemens' hiding places. Another puff of black smoke and again a gunner fell across his howitzer.

At noon, Major Bates sent a courier for Captain Dix, ordering him to report to a command conference as soon as possible. Instead, Sergeant George of "A" Company arrived.

Sergeant George threw a salute and said, "Sorry, sir, but Captain Dix bought the farm. He's got a hole in him you could drive a ..."

"What about Lieutenant Johnson?" interrupted Major Bates. "Why didn't he come?"

"Wounded, sir. Don't know if he'll make it back to Ryan."

"What in heaven's name is going on?" the major cried in exasperation.

"They're gunnin' for the officers, sir," said the sergeant. "Damned accurate, too, if you ask me."

The major's face turned crimson. "We must do something! I want those red devils wiped out before dark!"

A towering gun sergeant stepped forward and said, "Begging your pardon, sir, but me'n the guns can do it if we can move behind the hilltop. Nobody can train a gun when he's got to jump around to keep from catchin' a ball hisself."

"You can silence them?"

"Sure enough, sir. We can wipe that village off the face o' the earth, given enough time."

"How long?"

"Before dark, sir."

"See to it, then."

By three o'clock that afternoon, the mountain howitzers began ranging on the village from their new backslope sanctuary. With spotters on the ridge and accurate rifle fire from nearly three hundred troops protected behind sheltering earthworks, the battle could go but one way. One by one, the fusillade silenced suspected pockets until spotters directed the cannonade at the Indian's last redoubt, where occasional puffs of black smoke flared.

"By God, that's got to be a big gun down there, don't it, Sarge?" Private Finster asked.

"At the least a fifty, private. Keep your head down, though, and I'll take you home to your momma yet."

Finster grinned. "Tell you one thing, Sarge. Black, red, white or blue, whoever's holdin' that gun is one I'd like to have on my side in a tight fight."

Sergeant Mallory nodded at the private's sage observation.

At five o'clock, Major Bates asked his one surviving officer for a casualty report. He bit his lip when Lieutenant Ames gave it: twenty-seven dead, nineteen wounded. By six o'clock, nearly an hour had elapsed without return fire and Major Calumet Bates ordered Ames to take a patrol into the devastated village.

Soldiers of the patrol threw away the tattered shreds of the last tipi and found but two occupants. A startled corporal exclaimed, "My God, Lieutenant, it's a white man!"

"A white man?"

"Yeah." The corporal nudged the bloody white-haired body with his toe. "Yeah, it is."

"An old squaw layin' next to him, too," a nearby trooper said. "Wonder was she his squaw?"

"All right, you men," Lieutenant Ames barked, "get to the other wreckage and see if any hostiles are still hiding."

A few minutes later, Lieutenant Ames wagged an arm back and forth in an "all clear" signal. Just as he did, the blood-soaked old white man opened his remaining eye and furtively slid the barrel of his Sharps buffalo gun forward. The roar shattered the battlefield's stillness and the heavy slug blew Lieutenant Ames around, face down in the mud.

Major Calumet Bates strode angrily into the village shortly after the patrol fired volley after volley into the withered body of the white man. Bates was livid. His losses included every one of his junior officers. He promoted his sole surviving artillery sergeant to on-the-spot field command and ordered him to take the white man's scalp for the major's very own souvenir. As the new lieutenant knelt to perform his odious task, the pepper-haired old squaw, blood seeping from her mouth, and with the last of her strength, sank a Green River knife into the fledgling Lieutenant Krachek's back.

———————

The command returned to Fort Ryan amid mixed reviews. While the final body counts were falsified to achieve more favorable impressions, the truth leaked out: nineteen soldiers wounded and twenty-nine dead, including seven officers.

An honest assessment of the Musselshell Massacre was appalling: It took a modern fighting unit, armed with five howitzers and three hundred of the latest rolling block rifles—a unit whose surprise was complete and positions insurmountable—to kill seventy-four Blackfeet Indians, fifty-five of whom were women and children. And it was whispered that few of the nineteen slain Indian men were of fighting age.

The Army reacted to preserve itself. Department of Missouri Commanding General Philip Sheridan initiated an internal investigation. In order to save face, Major Calumet Bates, as the sole surviving officer, was given a "bravery-under-fire" commendation. But his coveted promotion was side-tracked and he was shunted to isolated Fort Pembina, in the Dakota Territory, only four miles from the Canadian border.

———·•·———

"Of course I remember." Major Calumet Cornelius Bates said. He perched naked on the edge of his bed, staring at but not seeing the young man before him. "It was a great victory. Why shouldn't I remember?"

The gray eyes turned as flat and blank as a frozen pond. Finally the younger man sighed. "My pa died in that village, Major."

Bitterness exploded in the major. "A white man living with those red savages—if it hadn't been for that insane …"

"And my mother was one of those red savages. Way I get it Major, you hacked her to pieces with that sword." The intruder pointed to the regular-issue cavalry saber hanging from a nearby wall-peg.

Major Calumet Bates pulled himself together—but not without effort. He stared down in surprise at his nakedness and pushed heavily to his feet, shivering with the cold. "Get out of my quarters!"

Like taut bands snapping, the youth whipped forward shoving the officer back onto the bed with a foot. Crazy lights danced on the icy surface of his eyes. "You've got no more orders to give, Major," he panted. "All you've got left is retribution. And I'm damned well here to see you give it."

"Guard!" Major Bates gasped, recovering his breath. Just then a bugle sounded reveille. Both men cocked an ear to listen.

"You'll never escape now," the major said, struggling upright.

Jethro Spring smiled without mirth. "Didn't figure to, Major. You see, I figure to die right here. But you're goin' out ahead of me. You're goin' out with a scalp missing— just like my pa. See this rifle?"

Bates stared.

"It's a 50-caliber Sharps, Major. The same gun that you put on display at Fort Ryan. It was my pa's. I figure it rightfully belonged to me, so I took it when I broke out."

Jethro Spring pulled the Green River knife from his sash and twisted it wickedly in the clear dawn light. "And you see this knife? It was my ma's. I took it from the display, too."

Major Bates shuddered, his face turning to chalk.

"What do you suppose I aim to do with 'em, Major?"

The officer looked from the knife to the wild gray eyes. "You wouldn't," he croaked. Then he lurched forward grabbing the Sharps by the barrel.

The roar of the big gun was deafening in the confines of the sleeping cubicle. The blast hurled Bates across the bed, against the far wall.

Jethro Spring slumped into a chair, gray eyes glazing. A moment later, however, his vision cleared and his head jerked up. The Sharps clattered to the floor. He leaped to his feet, hurling the Green River knife aside. Survival, after all, became the first law of Jethro Spring. Gone his intent to scalp the major, then die in a blaze of glory. Gone the desire to die at all. He dove through the half-open window.

CHAPTER TWO

The dispirited bay plodded through pelting rain, hip bones protruding, skin sagging where flesh and muscles had once lain—a victim of hard over-use.

Its rider sat hunched, shrouded by a sopping blanket that was so filthy it belied its multi-colored Hudson's Bay origin. The blanket was belted around the rider's middle with a dull-colored sash. Moccasined feet hung below the swinging stirrups of a U.S. Army-issue cavalry saddle. The rider's face was thin and haggard and wreathed in pain, and his hatless head lolled with each stride of the listless horse.

Behind the man's right shoulder, fresh crimson seeped into crusted blood already caked upon the blanket. The man groaned and gripped the saddle pommel with boney fingers. He lurched, caught himself, opened feverish gray eyes and stared about. Night was falling on this late-January day of 1872.

"Must be in Indian Territory by now," he muttered.

"Got to be." The gaunt bay had stopped, his head hanging almost to the ground. The rider clucked to the animal and feebly drummed heels to the stark ribs with little effect. The rider reeled, flinching with pain. Then he clinched his teeth and clucked to the listless horse once more.

———•·•———

From the moment he'd dropped the Sharps rifle and the Green River knife, Jethro Spring's mind fixed on survival. After diving through the window, then leaping to his feet, he knew he could not risk the fort's outer walls and must find a hiding place within. Soldiers swarmed from the barracks. Jethro headed for the shelter of the first building he saw. Shouts rang out and a bugle sounded alert. He had but a few moments before certain discovery. A door loomed before him. He slapped up the latch and yanked it open.

Four feet inside was another, heavier door. A wad of discarded sacking string hung from a nail, a pile of burlap sacks lay in a corner. He recognized what must be the entry to the fort's ice storage room. Jethro slipped inside and eased the first door closed. A faint light crept in from a crack above the outer door. As his eyes adjusted to the near-blackness, Jethro groped for the inner door. He swung the pivot latch upward and pulled the door open. Cool, moist air met him. He felt along the wall for a piece of the sacking string he'd spotted, then chanced opening the outer door a bit. He quickly tied a release knot around the door's outside latch, ran the string over the top, pulled up the latch and closed the door. Then he jerked the sheepshank loose and pulled the string through the door's crack, nodding to himself as he heard the outside latch fall into place.

The tighter inner door and latch proved thornier. He wedged the latch upright on a delicate balance and slipped through, closing it gently behind. Twice, the latch fell before the door closed tightly into place, but on the third try, Jethro locked himself in.

It was November. Ice blocks stored during the previous winter had melted and the coming winter's ice was yet to be collected. However, by feeling his way around, Jethro discovered the storage room held melons, pumpkins, and various root crops from the soil-rich Red River Valley. He found sawdust used to keep ice as well as for fruit and vegetable storage piled deep in one corner. Groping, Jethro buried into the sawdust to remain undiscovered for three days and two nights.

The searchers missed him because no one thought to look behind two latched doors. Neither did the cooks or their helpers blunder into the hidden man during the half-dozen times they entered the cold storage for apples, onions, and potatoes.

The fugitive had a ready supply of food in his hiding place, but soon lost track of night and day. Once, he chanced a quick look just as a cook closed the inner door. Still dark, he told himself. Must be a morning meal he's fixing.

When the cook came again several hours later, Jethro judged it to be afternoon. Still, he let hours pass before emerging stiff and cold. He exercised to loosen up, then tested the inner door's latch.

"Tight," he whispered to himself. But the door gave after he bodily struck it several times. The outer door popped open with only a little pressure. Jethro paused long enough to prop the latches back into place before melting into the fort's darkest shadows.

Reasoning that pursuers would assume the killer would flee north, hoping to shelter among Louis Riel's Metis, at the time in the midst of their own rebellion against Canadian authority, Jethro Spring fled south and west across Dakota Territory on foot, moving by night, hiding by day. He subsisted for a time on a small slab of bacon and a few fruits and vegetables thrust beneath his shirt as he fled Fort Pembina. He stole a horse along the James River and rode it into the ground by the time he reached Fort Pierre. He stole more food and the tall bay from an army remount depot and continued south, riding with the wind. He crossed the White River, where he rested for a day, then forded the Niobrara and fled into Nebraska. There, he scavenged corn for both himself and his horse among the scattered stalks of isolated, snow-covered farm fields. He also competed with evening grosbeaks and cedar waxwings for late-hanging wild plums and crabapples found along creek bottoms. Once, he drove two rangy wolves from a fresh-killed range cow, kindling a smoky fire of damp buffalo chips and gorging for two days before caution forced him ever south.

Jethro crossed the Union Pacific track near Grand Island and ran into his first cavalry patrol. He escaped by swimming his bay across the ice-filled Platte. No longer under any illusions, he redoubled his furtiveness, continuing ever southward. Near Salina, Kansas, he saw the first "JETHRO SPRING - WANTED" poster. He fled again on his fading bay, living on what little food he could steal during midnight forays at isolated hamlets, homesteads, and trading posts.

Near Wichita, he caught a bullet from yet another cavalry patrol. After that, pursuit was always near at hand. Between the Arkansas and the Cimarron, he used the last of his wits and the last of the bay's energy to remain free. Now, with rain drumming down, a played-out horse, and a feverish wound, Jethro Spring was near the end of his tether.

———•◦•———

"What ees?"

Jethro opened his gray eyes. It was dark. Rain still fell. Someone raised a coal oil lantern higher to peer into his face. The big bay stood listless, head to the ground, wobbling on his feet. "Not armed," the wounded man croaked. His head sank to his chest.

He heard quick chattering in some incomprehensible Indian dialect. More jabbering and he was pulled from his horse and laid upon the muddy ground. A hand jerked the blanket from his face so that rain beat upon it. Again he opened his eyes. In the lantern's glow, Jethro saw a smooth, dark face under a head of raven hair. Black eyes bored into his.

"Ma," he said, and passed into oblivion.

———•◦•———

Daylight filtered into the cabin through the one cracked window and rainwater dripped through the sod roof as Jethro returned to consciousness. He lay quite still as he surveyed his new surroundings. He discovered he was lying on a pallet in a corner of a small one-room cabin, covered with a wool blanket and a moth-eaten buffalo robe. His clothes were gone. His right shoulder hurt like hell.

Probing it, he discovered a tight, well-placed bandage. A woman stood by a clay fireplace, humming to herself. She saw he'd awakened and said, "Who are you?"

Jethro only stared, not replying. She chuckled and Jethro saw she had a certain beauty in her round face, black hair and eyes, her slender body. He first thought her young, then wasn't sure. She came to stand over him, hands on hips. Her calico dress hung calf-length, but from the floor he could see her ankles and calves and well-shaped legs to her knees. He averted his face. Her throaty laugh came again.

"Who are you?" she repeated. When he still said nothing, her voice flattened. "You will tell me what I want to know, eh? If you do not, I will hide you no longer."

He rolled his head back to look up at her. The smile was gone. In its place, a sullen scowl made her appear years older. "Hide me from what?" he asked.

Her mouth corners drooped further and her frown deepened. "You have bullet in shoulder, ride horse with U.S. Army brand. You do not hide, eh?"

"Go to hell," Jethro said tiredly and she kicked him in the face. He jerked away, wrenching his shoulder, crying out with pain.

Her frown remained. "You name?" she asked without emotion. When he did not reply, she again kicked him in the face. "What is you name?"

"James. James Storm ..." Jethro gasped, blood seeping from his mouth. Then he thought of these Indians. "James Storm-Walker."

"Is much good. Much better." A smile replaced the frown, as easily as if someone jerked a pull-cord. "You smart man. Indian, too. Is good. But weak. Ver' weak. Not strong. Whispering Leaf make you strong again. Then we see how smart is James Storm-Walker, eh?"

"Sure," mumbled the new James Storm-Walker. "Sure. Whatever you say." And he drifted off to sleep as the Indian woman continued to stare at him, a half-smile on her lips. She began to hum.

"Oww," he moaned as Whispering Leaf shook him. It was nearly dark in the room. Late afternoon; perhaps early evening.

"You must hurry. Cavalry is come."

"Huh?"

"Jimmy must hurry. We hide. You come."

Jethro Spring, weak from his throbbing shoulder, struggled to a sitting position as beads of sweat course his forehead. "Where?"

"Cherokee have cellar. They no find. Hurry."

Jethro clambored from his pallet as she pulled the bed from the corner and threw back a tiny trap door. He staggered toward the opening while the woman gathered his bedding. His head whirled, his right arm hung useless, but his left was strong enough to let himself down the ladder rungs. His head no more than cleared floor level when the woman threw the pile of bedding down the hole and slammed the trapdoor. He heard the bed screech across the rough boards.

Jethro collapsed and pulled the buffalo robe around him with his good arm. "At least," he muttered, "there won't be snakes in February." Then he heard horses. Voices carried to his hole.

"Seen anything of a stranger, ma'am? Dark fella, wearin' buckskins and riding a big blood bay?"

Whispering Leaf's voice rang clear: "No. No stranger is here. Only Cherokee. Is such a man bad man?"

"Yes he is, ma'am. A killer. Mind if we look around?"

"Sure. You look all you want. Maybe it take you long time and you spend night, eh?"

Laughter rippled among the men of the patrol. He heard the officer clear his throat and say, "I'm sure a quick search will suffice, ma'am. If he's not here, we'll just head on our way."

"Too bad. Sometimes I lonely."

More laughter.

"Smith and Tucker!"

"Sir!"

"Search the cabin."

"Yes, sir!"

A few seconds passed, then the officer said, "No, ma'am. You just wait out here with us. The boys will not bother a thing, I promise you."

Even though the cellar was cool, perspiration ran into Jethro's eyes. *Trapped. Caught like a rat in a cage.*

Boots thumped against the floor above and he heard cupboard doors jerked open and slammed shut. Someone walked to the bed and his knees thumped the floor as he knelt to peer underneath. "Nobody in here, Lieutenant!" he shouted.

"Check the outbuildings then. The outhouse, too."

"Yes, sir!"

The tramp of boots faded. Jethro heard the men shout from a distance, but couldn't make out the words.

"Well, thank you, ma'am," the lieutenant said. "I trust we've not inconvenienced you?"

"Only by no stay longer, Capitaine."

"Yes, well, ahem. Good day ma'am."

Whispering Leaf gave a throaty laugh, then lifted her voice to the departing soldiers, "Goodbye, Capitaine! Come back soon, eh?"

Jethro heard her walk into the cabin, humming to herself. Soon he heard her at the fireplace. He tried the door, but couldn't open it in his weakened condition. He knocked and heard her laugh again. Then the bed was slid away and the trap door opened.

The woman chuckled and said, "My trapped animal wants out, eh?"

She spread his pallet and smiled as he covered his nakedness with the blanket and returned to his corner. "Hole is dirty. Bed is dirty. You are dirty. Like pig, eh?"

She stooped to run fingers through his dark hair, raking out cobwebs. "My poor Jimmy animal. We must first make you well. I bring you somet'ing to eat."

Propped against a wall, Jethro ravenously ate the hot soup. He was awkward with his left hand. After he finished, he asked for more. As she handed the second bowl to him, she asked, "Why you kill man?"

"What man?"

She did not reply. He glanced up at her. An ugly scowl stole slowly across her face. Then her bare foot lashed out and sent his bowl and soup crashing against the wall. "You will tell me why you kill that man!"

His jaw tightened. Then his face lost its tension and he said, "Someday you'll do that once too often and I'll break that leg. Or your goddamned neck."

Her face was swallowed by a smile. "Already the mouse roars with only one soup, eh? Maybe you man after all, okay?"

He shrugged, wincing with the pain.

She gave her throaty laugh and spun toward the stove. "I get you more soup."

When she returned, she knelt and handed it to him. The buffalo robe slipped from his bare shoulders; she examined his wound's dressing, fingers trailing down his bony ribs. "But you too skinny for Whispering Leaf. You get strong and fat, eh?"

"Okay by me," he said.

Her liquid black eyes were only inches from his gray ones. "I ... I guess I didn't thank you," he said, "for hiding me from the soldiers."

She pushed back and to her feet. Again the throaty chuckle. "I make them nervous, too. Like Jimmy. I know they no stay. Good trick, eh?"

He smiled. "Good trick, yes. What did you do with the horse?"

"He far away," she said, returning to the pot burbling in the fireplace. "Horse no more. U.S. Army horse ver' bad to find on Cherokee land. Cherokee bury."

Sounds reasonable, Jethro thought to himself. But a lump came to his throat when he thought of the strong bay that had carried him a thousand miles across the plains.

———·•·———

One day drifted into another at the isolated Cherokee farm where Jethro Spring lay hidden. Bit by bit, he regained his strength. Twice more, cavalry patrols rode by and Jethro retreated to his hiding place. Each time, Whispering Leaf rubbed fireplace ashes into her face and dirt and grease into her clothes before she met the soldiers outside the cabin—a slovenly squaw offering her home and body to any who had a coin and would care to stay. Each time the soldiers laughed in embarrassment and, after a cursory search, rode away.

"Where are the men?" Jethro asked one day. "The men who helped me out of the saddle, carried me into your house, buried my horse. Where are they?"

Whispering Leaf leaned casually against a cupboard.

"Men here. Men not here."

"But," he said, "you can't run a farm by yourself. Somebody plows, plants, harvests. Somebody replaces the roof sod and cleans the well."

"Yes," she said.

"Well, where are they?"

Whispering Leaf's face remained expressionless. "Sometime here. Sometime gone."

"Who?" he persisted. "Your husband?"

"No."

"Is this your farm?"

She hesitated. "Yes. Is too. Papa, he owns farm. But is mine."

"I don't understand?"

"Papa 'fraid."

"Afraid? Afraid of what?"

"Me."

"You! You're joking with me. You're just a woman."

An ugly scowl darkened her face. Seeing she was not joking, Jethro asked again, "What is your papa afraid of, Whispering Leaf?"

The corners of her mouth turned down—she aged before his eyes. "Me," she said again.

"But why is your papa afraid of you?"

"Brother 'fraid, too."

Jethro stared at her from his pallet, saw her black dilated pupils and a strange foreboding ran through him. He struggled to sit against the wall. "My clothes," he said. "I'd like my clothes."

Her face changed in an instant. She smiled and once more appeared ten years younger. "No clothes," she said.

"What do you mean? I can't run around naked as a jaybird. What did you do with my clothes?"

"We bury," she said.

"Buried my clothes? For God's sake, go dig 'em up. I must have some clothes."

"Not yet time. No buckskin. Army look for man with buckskin." She gave her throaty chuckle. "They no look for man without clothes."

"Hey, look …" Jethro struggled to his feet, pulling the wool blanket tight about him. "I'm not running around this way. I need clothes to wear."

"Why?"

"Because," he said, his voice rising, "it's just not proper. Besides it's winter—March, anyway—and it's too cold to run around without …"

"No," she said. "Is not cold. Is fire here."

"But, Whispering Leaf," he said in exasperation, "people just don't run around in the winter without clothes—not even Indians."

"No?"

"No."

She began unbuttoning her dress.

"What are you doing?" Jethro demanded.

"You say one thing. I show you something else."

"Hey, you can't go naked, too. I won't—hey! Quit it!"

"Why I can't be like you?"

Jethro started toward her. Then he backed away as she pulled her dress over her head and tossed it across a chair. The woman wore nothing beneath. She tipped her head down and shook the long black hair, then looked up at him from under her lashes, a coy smile upon her lips.

"You can't," he mumbled, pulling his blanket tighter. It's … it's just not done." He backed against the wall. "People just don't … we're not married. What'll your pa say? Or, Gods! Your brother?"

She chuckled. "You 'fraid of Whispering Leaf?"

"You're damned right I'm afraid of Whispering Leaf."

"Good. So they. They no bother."

"Well, you bother me. Put that dress back on."

"No."

"Oh my God!"

Whispering Leaf whirled to her cupboards and began preparing dinner, while Jethro watched in disbelief. She moved about with no apparent inhibitions, her slender body supple and enticing. Jethro bit his lip and slipped under the buffalo robe, averting his face. She seemed not to care in the least as she continued cooking the meal in her nakedness, humming a strange melody. Later she called to him, "You come table, eat."

Jethro started to refuse, but hunger got the better of him and, blanket clutched about him, struggled to his feet. Rigid and uncomfortable, he sat at the little table while a naked Whispering Leaf lounged across from him. He pretended not to notice while concentrating on plate after plate of steaming hot stew.

"Why you kill man?"

The question caught him by surprise. "I thought we'd talked this over before."

"So? You don't tell."

"What's to tell?"

She scowled. "Why you kill man."

"I didn't say I did."

Whispering Leaf's flat palm slapped the table. "You will tell!"

"No."

"I will make you!"

"Go ahead and try." His eyes challenged her.

Her anger subsided. "There are ways. You are mine to do with as I will."

His jaw tightened and his eyes did not waver. "I owe you a lot," he said evenly, "but I don't reckon slavery is a part of it."

A sweet smile softened her features. She leaned forward to pull the blanket from his shoulder. Then she moved beside him to look more closely at his bandage. "I change," she said, caressing him as she did.

The door opened and Jethro knocked over the chair as he leaped to his feet. She restrained him with a hand and jabbered something in Cherokee. The bandy-legged old man who'd been about to enter, mumbled a reply and closed the door.

"Who in hell ..." began Jethro, but a knock on the door cut off the question. Whispering Leaf, fully exposed in her nakedness, went to the door and opened it. The old man said something and she padded to a cupboard, taking down a can of rusty square nails. She returned and thrust the can at the man, then closed the door and returned to Jethro, picking up where she'd left off, unwinding his bandage.

"Who was that?" he stammered.

"Papa."

"Oh my God!"

＊　＊　＊

As Jethro Spring regained his health, growing stronger and gaining weight, he began to chafe under the restraint of his nakedness. When Whispering Leaf permitted him outdoors for his infrequent trips to the outhouse, he covered himself with the dirty wool blanket.

Finally one warm early-April day, Jethro watched listlessly through the window as Papa and Brother plowed under an old cornfield. He fingered his blanket, then glared at Whispering Leaf as she sat working a large churn. "I want some clothes," he demanded.

She ignored him.

He hurled the blanket away and stomped to stand over her. "You're using that to keep me here, aren't you? I really am a prisoner, am I not?"

"Me, too."

"You, too? Hell! You come and go as you please. You walk around this house without clothes because you want to walk around without clothes. You're using your nakedness to hold me, too. Why? Why am I so important?"

She stopped churning to look up at him with veiled eyes. "You will tell why you kill man, eh?"

"Dammit!" he shouted. "I'm through here!"

"No. You stay. If you do not, Army, they know."

"Damn you, woman, what do you want? What, for God's sake, could it hurt if I at least had a pair of britches?"

"You not so pretty then." She stared at him in open admiration. "You grow strong. You well soon. Then we see how much man."

He stooped and snatched up his blanket, started to wrap it about him, then threw it away in disgust. He returned to the window and stared out while leaning his hands on the back of a chair.

She padded to him. "We take off bandage, eh? Is well now I betcha."

"I don't give a good goddamn what you do."

She unwrapped the bandage, her gentle fingers probing the healing scar. The fingers trailed along his shoulders and began kneading the back of his neck. "My poor animal," she murmured. "He no like cage. Soon we must let him out to run for while, eh?"

Jethro kicked the chair. It caromed off the wall and fell on its side. He whirled, pointing an accusing finger at her. She was already returning to her churn. Her voice lashed out at him, giving pause: "You kill man. You safe here. Whispering Leaf make it so. Papa and Brother, they make it so, too."

She pointed to the door. "Out there—Army and many enemy. They know you bring five hundred dolla. More than Cherokee make in five year. Here, Whispering Leaf protect you. Out there is nobody."

"If you know I'm worth five hundred dollars, you know who I am."

"Jethro Spring," she said.

"And who I killed."

"Army major."

"Why, then, dammit, do you hound me about it?"

"I not know why you kill man." Once more her arms moved in rhythm with the churn handle.

He dropped to his knees beside the churn. "Why don't you turn me in?"

"Because," she said, "I think maybe you worth more to Whispering Leaf than five hundred dolla."

He helped her pour buttermilk from the churn. "What am I to do for you that makes me worth more than five hundred dollars?"

Whispering Leaf shrugged. "Someday maybe I tell you. But first you tell me why you kill Army major."

Jethro flushed. When he failed to respond, she asked, "You mama—she Indian?"

"Yes."

"But papa, no Indian?"

He shook his head.

"Moccasin made like Whispering Leaf no see before. What Indian, you mama?"

Jethro stared at the buttermilk bucket, then reached for a dipper. After taking two gulps, he said, "Blackfeet."

"You papa trader?"

"Trapper."

"Ah, trapper." She studied him thoughtfully. "Papa live wi' Indian?"

He nodded.

"But you more smart than Indian. You live wi' whites?"

He gazed blankly at her, then tipped up the dipper and drank the rest of the buttermilk. "I want some clothes," he said.

She took the dipper from his hand and said, "First, you come with Whispering Leaf."

"Where?"

She led him toward her bed, but halfway there, he tugged his hand free and went back to the window, leaning on the sill and staring out as if he was lost. Behind him, she said, "The Army major, he kill you mama. And maybe you papa, too, eh?"

"How could you know that?" he blurted, wheeling to face her.

She was pleased that her guess had struck home. "Whispering Leaf know much. No secrets from her. She medicine woman. All men 'fraid Whispering Leaf. But not you. You only say you 'fraid."

Once more her pupils dilated as she stared through him and the cabin wall at some unknown spot across the distant prairie. "I want Jimmy to be 'fraid of Whispering Leaf, too," she whispered.

His brow wrinkled and he shook his head and sighed.

"I like Jimmy," she said huskily. "You strong man. Maybe strong enough for Whispering Leaf."

"We'd better get a cloth over that crock," Jethro said, "and put it out to cool. Otherwise the butter could turn rancid."

Whispering Leaf's eyes cleared, returning to normal.

She gave her throaty chuckle and said, "You do. I fix supper."

———·—·———

Later that evening, Whispering Leaf pinched out the flame in the coal oil lantern as Jethro lay upon his pallet bed. Moments later, she slid in beside him. "You no come to bed of Whispering Leaf, Whispering Leaf come to Jimmy's bed."

He lay motionless, saying nothing until she rolled over on top of him. "You're a bitch," he said, voice taut as a fiddle string.

She chuckled. "Yes," she said. "I bitch and I in heat. You take bitch in heat, eh? You animal, eh? You take bitch in heat like you animal and Whispering Leaf make you 'fraid, too, eh?"

He reached for her squirming body.

Later, they lay exhausted, motionless beneath the robe, perspiration running in tiny rivulets between them. He was half-asleep; she stared holes into the darkness.

"What do you want of me?" he asked.

She chuckled into his ear. "I want Jimmy to kill for me."

CHAPTER THREE

Whispering Leaf shook him. "Jimmy, you wan' coffee?" Jethro opened his eyes and looked about the room. The woman knelt beside him. "You wan' coffee?"

His expression softened and he reached from beneath the buffalo robe to trail fingertips along the line of her jaw. Whispering Leaf bent closer and brushed her lips against his. She murmured, "I bring. You stay."

As she padded away, he saw she wore a print dress. He wondered why, after so many days of nakedness?

By the time she returned with two mugs of steaming coffee, he sat with his back propped against the wall. She handed him a cup, hiked her dress to her thighs and straddled him, kneeling. She lifted her cup in a toast and he followed suit. Their eyes met.

Her hair has the blue-black sheen of a raven's wing. And her eyes are as big and soft as a mule deer doe's.

"What you think, Jimmy?" she asked, lowering her cup.

"That you're beautiful."

A radiant smile lit her face. She set her cup on the floor, took his and placed it there, too. Then she took his head in her hands and brushed lips. He reached for her, but she leaned back and took up her coffee. Head lowered to cup, she asked, "Jimmy 'fraid of Whispering Leaf now?"

"God yes."

She handed him his cup, then arose, legs still straddling him, smiling. "Whispering Leaf put britches and shirt on bed. Today Jimmy leave cage for little while. But firs', you must cut off the whiskers, eh? Then you look like Cherokee—black hair, dark face, dark the skin." She continued to study him. "But not the eyes. No. The eyes, they not Cherokee."

He sipped his coffee. "Okay, I'll shave. And I won't look anybody in the eye. Anything else, madam?"

"Maybe you hair to cut."

"I'm sure that's true." He reached out and grasped her ankle, then slid a hand upward along her calf. She chuckled and pulled away.

After shaving and hacking at his hair, Jethro Spring slipped into the shirt and bib overalls. Whispering Leaf appraised the effect. "You need big black Cherokee hat with eagle feather. And you need the heavy boot. Then you look like Cherokee for sure."

"And that'll fool the army?" he asked.

"It will fool them, sure."

"But will it fool other Cherokees?"

"No. But when you kill Ocanee, it will not matter."

He laughed. "It sounded like you said 'kill' somebody."

"It is so."

"That's not funny, Whispering Leaf."

She changed before his eyes, chameleon-like once

again, suddenly years older. "You will do it. Only way you safe. Ocanee say to soldiers, 'Jethro Spring is here.'"

"Why hasn't Ocanee already turned me in?"

"He no know you here."

"Who is Ocanee?"

"You will see."

Jethro studied her until she shifted from one foot to another. At last he said, "You really mean it, don't you? You really want me to kill someone, don't you?"

Whispering Leaf's black eyes dilated, nostrils flaring. "You will do it. You will do it because Whispering Leaf say so." Then her eyes cleared and she smiled. Years fell away. "But you do it, too, for Jimmy. For if you do not, soldiers come an' take Jimmy away, eh?" She moved close to him, molded her print dress against his overalls and Jethro Spring could think no more.

————◆————

Several days later, Jethro trudged from the barn, a pail of milk in his hand. Whispering Leaf met him at the cabin door, took the milk and handed him a revolver; an old percussion cap, five-cylinder Colt. "Go play with you toy, Jimmy. Learn to use it well." She turned, leaving him standing at the threshold.

Carrying the big, unfamiliar revolver, Jethro shuffled back to the barn. He first leaned against the barn's weathered clapboards, then sank down to sit with his back against the rough surface, wrists and hands propped on his knees, holding the old Colt. He sighted down the barrel, pulled the hammer back, then eased it forward again, checking the gun's primers and loads. As he hefted the weapon from hand to hand, eyeing it from all angles, there came a rustling sound from the side. He twisted to look and the Colt twisted with him.

"A-i-i-i!" the old man cried. He whirled to run, but tripped sprawling in the barnyard.

"Wait!" Jethro shouted, leaping to his feet. Before the old man could rise, the younger one lifted him to his feet.

"Sorry. I didn't mean to scare you," Jethro mumbled as the old man looked at him in wide-eyed terror, staring from the gun to the younger man and back again.

"Yeah, well, I ain't never had a pistol before. Don't know much about 'em, you see. Never meant to point it your way. Sorry."

The old man nodded gravely.

Jethro shifted from one foot to the other, then blurted, "You sure got a real pretty daughter, sir."

Again, the old man nodded, still squinting up at Jethro.

Treading near what might be forbidden ground, Jethro said, "She may be a little funny sometimes, but she's smarter'n hell."

Taking courage at the old man's grave nod, he continued, "I just want you to know, though, that I had nothing to do with turning you out of your home, Mr. ..." Jethro realized he didn't know the old man's name, so ended lamely with, "You do know that, don't you?"

The man nodded.

Jethro thought the conversation one-side. "Mr.—uh, Papa—who is Ocanee?"

The old man nodded again and said, "Ocanee."

"Ocanee, yes. Who is he?"

"Ocanee." The Indian's head bobbed again.

"That's right. Ocanee. Who?"

Again the head bobbed.

"Do you speak English, Papa?"

The head bobbed several more times.

"English. You know. American. White man." Jethro brought his fingers to his mouth and made the universal sign to indicate speech.

"Ahh," the old man said, "Whi' man. No."

Jethro threw up his hands and whirled away. He turned immediately back, however, to clap the old man on the shoulder and say, "I'm sorry." Then he resumed his forlorn squatting against the building.

The old man squatted nearby, watching him in silence.

Whispering Leaf brought Jethro a pair of oversized lace-up farmer boots and a big black hat at least one size too small.

"Now you look jus' like Cherokee," she said, smiling at him after he donned the hat and boots. Then she said, "Where you gun?"

"I left it under the pillow."

"Fool!" she screamed, striking him across both cheeks with her open palms. Then she clenched her fists and beat him on the chest.

He caught her wrists and held her at arm's length until she subsided and the frown left her face. When he released her, she moved close and traced the red lines of her stinging slaps with an index finger. "Poor Jimmy," she said. "You mus' have always the gun. Someday Ocanee, he come, and you mus' use."

"Whispering Leaf, I don't want to kill anyone."

She melted against him. "I know, Jimmy. Whispering Leaf no want, too. But if you must, you will."

When he said nothing, she went on: "And, Jimmy, you must. Ocanee is bad. Ver' bad. He will say 'bout Jethro Spring to Army."

Jethro slipped both arms around her. He could feel her heat through the print dress.

"Come," she whispered. He allowed himself to be led to the bed. When they reached it, she dug under the pillow and brought out the old Colt, placing it firmly in his hand. Then she took his free hand in one of her own and melted against him.

Seated in the sunshine, leaning back against the barn's clapboards, Jethro studied his problem. He hefted the old Colt and gazed at it, then shifted to stare out over a field of half-grown corn. He pushed to his feet and strode to the cabin where he asked Whispering Leaf for an old rag—a long one.

"Why you want rag, Jimmy?"

"Why do you want Ocanee to die?"

She rummaged in a cupboard until she found a ragged towel. He held it up and said, "Not long enough."

She stood, hands on hips, looking thoughtful, then pulled out a worn cotton blanket. He took it, ripped off a narrow strip, unhooked his bib overalls and pulled up his gingham shirttail. He wrapped the blanket strip around his waist and tied it securely, dropped his shirttail and re-hooked his shoulder straps. Then he took the Colt, slid it through the side gap in his overalls, and tucked it into the sash. The loose overalls and shirt hid the bulky revolver.

Whispering Leaf clapped her hands and said, "Is good! Is ver' good!"

He shoved both fists into the overalls' side gaps just as he'd seen other men do. The revolver butt brushed his right hand. He snatched at the gun. Its front sight hung on the blanket sash. He went back to the barn for a file. With the front sight filed away, the gun glided easily in and out of its hiding place.

After supper, Jethro practiced firing the old Colt at a fence post. He felt awkward and slow with the unfamiliar weapon, but by limiting the distance to ten feet or less, he could hit the post every time. He reloaded the weapon and tucked it into the sash.

It was dark when he wandered back to the house and stepped inside. Whispering Leaf had not lit the lantern.

"Jimmy is ready for Ocanee now?" she asked.

He closed the door and leaned against it, head bowed with the weight of the coming deed. "I reckon," he said at last. "If I have to."

She padded to him in the darkness. "Is good, Jimmy. You are strong man, eh?" She patted the bulk of the heavy revolver and said, "Ocanee now can come. We will see who is more strong Cherokee—Ocanee or Whispering Leaf, eh?"

He held her, smothering his face in her rich, black hair. "Who is Ocanee, Whispering Leaf?"

"Ver' bad man."

"What makes him bad? What does he do to you?"

"You jus' kill him. If you do, you safe for always. Whispering Leaf will see. You will do, eh?"

"I guess, honey. God, I guess."

She snuggled closer, and whispered, "You so strong."

He held her at arms-length and asked, "When will Ocanee come?"

"Soon," she said, twisting with desire. "I will send for him soon."

Jethro became more tense with each passing day. A

mouse scampering across the floor startled him. He knew it was all wrong. Somehow he must get his nerves under control and do what he must for his woman. He tried not to think about Ocanee; tried not to imagine a face. Still, he could think of little else and, in order to end it, he found himself silently praying for Ocanee to come.

One day Jethro loitered along one side of a field to watch Whispering Leaf's brother as he crossed back and forth behind a mule, driving-reins tied together and wrapped behind his neck, hands on the wooden handles, cultivating the young corn. The idle man dug at the soft red dirt with his boot toe. So lost in thought was he that he hardly saw the rich soil—or noticed Papa running toward him. The old man's eyes were wide and frightened.

"Ocanee!" Papa cried, voice quaking.

Jethro jerked around to see a carriage pulled up before the house. He began to run.

He pounded up the steps and kicked open the door, gasping for breath. A small gray-haired man stood with his back to the door, waving a battered felt hat in one hand. He wore a dark pin-striped suit, moccasins peaked from beneath his trouser legs. As the man turned to face the door, Jethro saw his gray hair was neatly brushed and part-ed in the middle. The lines on his face made him look quite solemn and a little sad. A pair of steel-rimmed spectacles perched halfway on a nose far too undersized for an Indian. The man peered over the top of the spectacles. "Good afternoon, sir," he said in a musical voice. "You must be Mr. Spring. We've heard much of you. My name is John Ocanee, at your service." He ended with a bow.

Jethro switched widening eyes from Ocanee to Whispering Leaf. His right hand hooked into the gap of his overalls, his left gripped the doorjamb. "I ....I don't under-stand."

"He *Ocanee*, Jimmy," Whispering Leaf said from across the room. "He ver' bad."

Ocanee glanced at her, obviously annoyed, then returned to Jethro. "Won't you step inside, Mr. Spring? Surely you would be welcome."

"You see, Jimmy? Ocanee know who you are. He ver' bad. He tell soldairs."

Jethro fingered the revolver butt. However, the old man appeared innocent and disarming. Wild eyed, the youth again looked beyond Ocanee to Whispering Leaf.

"Jimmy," she cried, "you mus' do it! Ocanee is bad. He know you Jethro Spring!"

John Ocanee said, "What is it you are supposed to do, Mr. Spring? Are you to kill me? Is that it?"

"Jimmy, he come to say Whispering Leaf mus' leave her farm. Ocanee ver' bad." She began to cry. "He make us—papa and brother and Whispering Leaf—to leave. We mus' leave farm. He tell soldairs you kill major. You mus' do it, Jimmy."

Ocanee smiled wanly at Jethro. "Please come in," he said. "No doubt you have questions that deserve answers."

Jethro pulled the gun, eyes taking on an even wilder look.

"Shoot him, Jimmy," Whispering Leaf ordered. "Shoot him. Shoot! Shoot!"

The smile left Ocanee's face, to be replaced by a very different expression. His brow wrinkled and his eyes took on a piercing look over the steel-rimmed spectacles. "She's an evil woman, son," he said.

"Shoot him, I tell you!"

The gun exploded twice. Splinters flew from the puncheon floor in front of both Ocanee and Whispering Leaf.

"Shut up—the both of you!" Jethro snarled, gesturing with the gun. "Shut up and sit down at that table." Both stumbled to obey.

"All right, what is this? What the hell is going on here?"

"Ocanee, he take our home. He ..."

"It is not your home. It was never your home," Ocanee said.

"You lie! Jimmy, shoot!"

"Shut up, you bitch!" Jethro shouted.

"Okay, I shut up. And I bitch—in heat."

"All right, you tell your side, Ocanee. Who are you?"

"John Ocanee."

"No, goddamn it, why are you here?"

"To tell Whispering Leaf and her family they must leave this farm."

"You see, Jimmy? Shoot!"

Jethro ignored her. "By what authority, Ocanee?"

"Why, by the authority of the Cherokee Nation. Who else?"

"And who are you?"

"John Ocanee ..."

"Dammit! I'm not here to play games. Are you some sort of Cherokee sheriff, or what?"

"Oh, heavens no, Mr. Spring. I'm the Tribal Assembly President."

"You're *what?*"

John Ocanee peered over his glasses. "I'm the nominal leader of the Cherokee Nation."

"Oh God!"

Silence fell in the room. It was finally broken when Jethro softly asked, "Okay, tell me again why you are here?"

"These people must go, Mr. Spring. They've taken over another family's farm and have lived here for nearly two years in defiance of Cherokee law. I'm afraid the assembly is growing impatient. My purpose is, as she says, to evict them."

Jethro mulled over Ocanee's words. He glanced at Whispering Leaf and saw her eyes dilating. He leaned over and slapped her so hard her head whipped to the side. "That's one," he said as spite filled her face. "I still owe you a half-dozen, more or less."

Jethro turned back to Ocanee. "Is it standard for a president to serve eviction notices, Mr. Ocanee?"

The little man smiled. "Not normally. But you see, this is no ordinary case. This woman is a medicine woman—or my people think so. She wields enormous power among the less educated and most of my people are frightened of her. Frankly, none would serve such a notice to so formidable a woman. Unfortunately the task fell to me."

Jethro studied the floor at his feet. "If she's so powerful, how do you dare face up to her?"

"I hope through goodness, Mr. Spring. You must understand that she's an evil woman. Two centuries ago, our white countrymen would have burned her at the stake. You must realize, sir, that this woman, through use of sorcery and intimidation, forced another family from their home. For nearly two years, the assembly has been attempting to bring justice to this case. I'm afraid it came down to where I had to accept the responsibility of serving notice. As far as my method, there can be only one way to combat evil, Mr. Spring, and that is with goodness. Have I succeeded? Have I been able to blunt this woman's instrument of evil to some degree by appearing earnest and forthright?"

Jethro considered the question. He studied the gun and knew Ocanee singled him out as Whispering Leaf's "instrument of evil."

"Yes, sir. I think you have."

"Good."

"Now, what about me?"

John Ocanee looked puzzled. "You? I don't understand."

"You know who I am. You know my real name is Jethro Spring. No doubt you know I'm wanted for murder."

Ocanee nodded as Jethro finished. "Yes. But we also know some of the, ah, unfortunate circumstances surrounding your parents' death. After all, we are of the People, even though we belong to the so-called 'civilized' tribes. We've known of you, son, for some months now."

A flush stole across Jethro's face. He smiled and said, "And I'm safe here—is that it?"

The Cherokee leader glanced at Whispering Leaf and sighed. "Ordinarily I'd say yes, Mr. Spring. At least as far as the assembly is concerned, and probably for that overwhelming portion of our nation that believes in the fundamentals of honesty and decency. Here, however," he gestured at the woman, "we have another example. And frankly, if I were you, I'd tarry no longer in this vicinity than absolutely necessary."

Jethro met Whispering Leaf's withering glare, raising an eyebrow in question. "Shoot," she pleaded. "Jimmy mus' shoot." Tears welled into pools and trickled down her cheeks. "Shoot," she said. "Then you stay as long as you want. Have bitch in heat all time."

The young man turned to stare sightlessly out the open door as he considered his choices. Shuddering at how narrow had been his escape, he held out his hand to the Cherokee leader. "Well, Mr. Ocanee, I guess I owe you something. But I'll be running along now."

The little man jumped to his feet and pumped Jethro's hand. "Goodby, sir. The name James Storm-Walker is a good one. A pity that you must leave it in this place."

Jethro nodded and started for the door.

"I'll keep the woman here until you're well gone," Ocanee said to the younger man's back. "I'd guess you need not worry about pursuit until sometime tomorrow."

Chapter Four

Jethro Spring urged his little bald-faced sorrel, its sides heaving, to the high bank overlooking the Canadian River. It was but a short time until dusk. This portion of the Canadian meandered some twenty miles west of the isolated farm where he'd left Ocanee and Whispering Leaf.

After taking leave of the Cherokee leader and the medicine woman, he'd gone directly to the barn, saddled the only horse in the corral, and pounded away at a lope. Now, three hours later, Jethro nudged the horse into the river and let him drink sparingly before pointing him upstream.

He soon found what he sought—a high, deeply undercut clay bank, with tree roots and brush tangled within its recesses. Jethro rode the pony on upstream, leaving clear hoofprints in riverside sand and gravel. Then he reined the pony away from the river to head west across the prairie for a short distance until striking a low, rocky ridge.

Dismounting, he pulled up a small sagebrush and returned to the Canadian, using the sagebrush to brush out their return tracks. When he reached the river, Jethro mounted and pointed the small horse downstream, staying well out in the sluggish water until they reached the overhanging cutbank. There, he forced the little pony as far beneath the bank as he could, then tied the reins to a solid tangle of brush and roots.

"Sorry, little horse," he said, pulling the old percussion Colt from his overalls and jamming the muzzle against the horse's head.

The sorrel collapsed at the Colt's bark and the river's slow current caught its body. With the bridle reins snagged, the carcass swung farther under the overhanging table. Jethro tugged off his farmer boots and tossed them beside the dead animal. By the time he'd finished undermining the cutbank onto the tangle, darkness had fallen. Still the young man worked on until satisfied he'd hidden all evidence of the horse and equipment. Then he wiped out the last traces of human presence and started jogging east, back the way he'd come.

He reached the cornfield just as the night sky began to pale. Exhausted, he napped amid the rows.

Two hours after sun-up, a cavalry patrol rode into the farmyard, and Whispering Leaf was on hand to greet them. Jethro saw her gesture to the west and the patrol trotted off in that direction.

The fugitive again lay down to sleep, head pillowed on the freshly cultivated soil.

He was on the move again at dark, guided by the stars, feeling his way across several fields until he came out on a well-traveled road. Certain that any sign of his barefoot passage would be erased by morning traffic, he moved steadily eastward to an unknown destination. Daylight found him sheltering in a thick patch of briars along a fence row.

Traveling by night, sleeping by day, Jethro trotted barefoot across Indian Territory. He "stagged" the legs of his bulky overalls just below the knees, cut away the bib, and belted what was left with his cotton blanket-sash. He made an odd sight, had anyone observed: tousled dark hair, ragged clothes, unshaven, barefoot, old revolver thrust into the sash.

None saw, however, for Jethro Spring took great pains to avoid prying eyes. He trapped grouse and quail and rabbits, ate mid-summer berries, and helped himself to maturing field crops during the dead of many nights. Despite a powerful desire for a pair of shoes, a horse, powder and ball for his revolver, the fugitive avoided stealing traceable items.

In time, far to the east and drifting south, Jethro at last felt safe enough to chance moving by day. The region was isolated, supporting only an occasional farm and few small hamlets; he crossed the Kiamichi River and entered a hilly region of dense hardwood-scrub. He was gaunt once more—although this time his muscles were whipcords of iron, his feet tough and rock-hard. But he was tired; the long trek had begun to wear.

He followed a trail that was little more than a track winding through stubby white oak. Thirsty, he trotted downhill toward a creek. He heard the noise while some distance away and dove for sheltering scrub at one side of the trail. Then he heard it again—an unearthly bawling, and recognized it as a horse in distress. Then he heard a man curse.

Jethro crept nearer until he could see the tiny creek and a big black horse lying on its side in a quicksand bog. The animal lay half-sunken, almost covered with mud, some of which had caked and hardened. The horse was haltered and carried a high-backed, California-style saddle. A mud-encrusted bridle lay on the near bank. Across the creek, on the other bank, stood a packhorse—a big, well-shaped dun. The dun packed a couple of light panniers hanging from the forks of a sawbuck packsaddle.

The black's neck was stretched by his halter rope, one end tied to a nearby tree. A man wallowed waist-deep in the mud, holding to the taut halter rope and reaching for the saddle where a muddy lariat hung. The trapped horse bellowed again, thrashing with his forefeet, striking the man in the chest. Although the man had a firm grip on his rope, the kick sprawled him in the quicksand.

He cursed and, using the stretched halter rope, clawed himself back upright. Jethro could make out little of the man's features, but he could see a great shock of straw-colored hair and a wide handlebar moustache that dripped mud. The man appeared to be tall. He certainly was wide of shoulders; a powerful man.

The sun glinted on the polished butt of a holstered revolver that, cartridge belt and all, had been placed for safekeeping on the bank. A well-oiled Henry repeating rifle leaned against an oak tree. *Careful about his guns,* Jethro thought. He shifted for a better view.

The tall man reached again for his saddle lariat and freed it. Then he wallowed to the bank, wiping mud from the lariat. The man shook out a loop and deftly dropped it over the saddlehorn, backed to a small white oak and took a dally around the tree. Then he picked up a dead limb and pitched it at the trapped horse. When the animal bellowed and thrashed, the man reefed on the lariat for all he was worth. Gradually he pulled the horse upright, taking up slack around the white oak.

Jethro slid his Colt under some leaves, then said,

"You're goin' about it all wrong."

The man stiffened. "How'd you do it, friend?" he drawled in a melodious southern twang.

Jethro stayed hidden, but said, "You're propping him up. Hell, he'll only sink faster if he moves. He was better off on his side."

"Maybe so, maybe not, friend," the big man replied. "But just in case you don't know it, it ain't so much a lesson on which way that hoss is goin' to lay there and die as it is how he will get out and live. And the thought occurred to me, as it no doubt already did to you, that the two of us pullin' on this rope might be enough heft to do it."

"Not pulling there. Not from the horn. That'll push him down and won't give him any leverage. What he needs is to have that rope around his chest. Then when we pulled, we'd be jerkin' in the right place."

The big man turned casually and saw Jethro's outline through the brush. His eyes flicked to his holstered six-gun and the Henry leaning against the tree. Those eyes, blue and deep, swept back to Jethro, who pushed to his feet and walked to the creek bank.

"Hell," the big man said, "you are too skinny to be of much help, boy."

Jethro waded into the quicksand, following the lariat right to the trapped black. "Give me some slack," he said as he wallowed waist-deep along the horse's side. The black kicked violently as Jethro knelt to sink deeper into the slime and run the rope along the big gelding's side, trying to slide the lariat's end under him. Jethro spoke soothingly even when the animal's wild thrashing again rolled it back onto its side and brought Jethro in range of the striking hoofs. Still speaking softly, the young man moved inside, right up against the horse's belly. The animal gradually subsided. Again Jethro crouched in the slime to his armpits. "More slack," he gasped.

Moments later, Jethro said, "I need a straight limb."

Plunging down the rope, a limb in one hand, the stranger said, "You got more'n a little gumption, boy. Maybe more gumption than sense, howsomever."

Jethro took the limb. "Was I you, I'd be for pulling them panniers and getting that packhorse across the creek to help. He can surely pull more than both of us."

The big man's walrus moustache flared atop a huge grin. "Whatever you say, pard. Right now you are ramroddin' this outfit."

It took some time, but Jethro eventually pushed and prodded a lariat end under the big horse, scraping and pulling it from the other side until he had a loop around the animal. Then he tied a bowline—not too tight and not too loose—around the animal's chest. At last he flipped the rope's remainder between the horse's forefeet.

By that time the stranger had the packhorse off-loaded and across the creek. There, the big man took up the slack and lashed the lariat to the packsaddle's front "buck." He then tied the packhorse to a white oak far up the bank. As Jethro came wallowing from the creek, the man grinned. "You look worse'n me, boy. And that ain't sayin' much."

When Jethro walked to the trapped horse's halter rope, the stranger said, "I'm bigger. I'll pull on that'un. You take this switch and swat that packhorse."

Jethro took the supple limb and when the other grunted, "Ready!" lashed with all his might on the big dun's rump.

The dun leaped ahead. When the rope tightened around his chest, the trapped black lunged and kept lunging as the big man, corded muscles bulging, pulled for all he was worth.

Ever so slowly, the bogged horse gained ground.

Jethro redoubled his lashes on the dun, driving it forward again and again. The stranger yelled. At last the black had its feet and struggled wildly from the bog.

Sweat coursed through the caked mud on the stranger's face. Gasping for breath, he leaned against a scrub oak. "I owe you, boy," he said. "Don't rightly know if I could have got him out by myself."

The man bent to pick up his belted six-gun and slipped it from its holster. He cocked it, pointed it at the mud-covered lad and said, "You're Jethro Spring, ain't you, boy? You're wanted up no'th for killing a U.S. Army major, ain't you, boy?" He said it as he rubbed mud from his left shirt pocket, where a silver-plated circle with a star inside magically appeared.

Jethro looked about wildly.

"No use to think of your gun, boy," the peace officer said. "I found it awhile back and it ain't there no more."

"A hell of a lot of thanks I get," Jethro said bitterly.

The Texas Ranger moved cautiously to his quivering saddlehorse, covering Jethro all the way. He wiped mud from his saddlebags, then reached in one side and pulled out a pair of handcuffs. "Let's you and me mosey on down the creek, boy. There's a big pool there, and we can likely clean up a mite. You go first."

CHAPTER FIVE

The ranger sat wiping mud from his saddle while his prisoner stared balefully across the campfire. Horses stamped just outside the firelight, swishing tails at never-ceasing insects. "Name's Jeff Cole," the lawman said. "Ranger for northeast Texas, out of Greenville. Shore was lucky, comin' on to you like I did."

He paused to shake out his rag, then rambled on, oblivious to Jethro's baleful glare. "Aside from the fact you come in plumb handy helpin' me get Satan out of the quicksand, now I won't have to go back to Greenville empty-handed."

In the shadows, Jethro tested the handcuffs and the scrub oak sapling that held him.

"Embarrassin' it was," the officer said. "Plumb embarrassin' the way that Wilson bunch lost their trail up here in the scrub oak. Why, shoot, the Cap'n would have my ears if I come back with nothin'."

Ranger Cole paused and glanced across the fire. "Likely you ain't much, but you're the best I can come up with on short notice. You want coffee, boy? How 'bout some more of them venison chops? Fair to tell you I pride myself on my cookin'."

Jethro remained mute.

"Ain't much for talkin' are you boy? If you hadn't said a little something when you come on us in the mud, hell, I'd have thought a cat got your tongue." The big man returned to his chore. "Your bad luck, you're prob'ly thinkin'," he continued. "But hell, boy, a life of owlhootin' will get you nowhere." He laid down his rag, picked up his tin cup and sipped coffee. He stared across the fire. "Why'd you do it, boy?"

Malevolent gray eyes glared back.

Cole clambered to his feet, gathered up the plates and pans and carried them to the creek where he scrubbed and rinsed them. Alone, Jethro sawed furiously at the sapling with the handcuff chain. By the time the ranger returned, he'd worn through the bark and torn out some wood fibers. The big man stooped over the fire and Jethro lay still, watching furtively.

The man's bulk was deceptive, he decided. Lean-hipped, the ranger moved with a glide, yet was physically powerful. He appeared to be a master at conserving energy, seldom making an unnecessary move. Probably thirty, maybe forty, Jethro thought. He's seen and done a lot. No fool, for sure.

Cole poured another cup of coffee and said, "Shore you don't want none, boy? Hell, it's the kind that puts hair on an anvil's chest." When Jethro still said nothing the lawman left to check on his horses.

While he was gone, Jethro again sawed, wearing away more wood.

When the officer returned, he said, "Shucks, boy, I was lookin' forward to some comp'ny for the trip back to Greenville. But you're not worth much." Then he laid down, head on saddle, and pulled his sweat-stained Stetson over his eyes. After awhile, his breathing evened out and he slept.

Throughout the night, Jethro, kept watch on the exhausted officer and surreptitiously sawed on the sapling with the handcuffs' chain. Not once did Jeff Cole move. Shortly before dawn, Jethro had the sapling almost worn through. *Another ten minutes and I'll have it!*

Cole yawned, plunked his hat down at his side, clambered to his feet, and stretched hugely. He pulled out his Colt, cocked it and pointed it at Jethro. Then he dug in a pocket for the key and unlocked the cuff from the sapling. Motioning with the gun, he moved Jethro to a different tree. "Hell, boy, you keep that up every night, you'll be too tired to go to Greenville."

———◆———

The ranger was cautious. He allowed Jethro to ride the big packhorse, sitting on a bedroll, feet thrust into panniers. But Cole made sure both wrists were handcuffed and the chain passed through the forward packsaddle fork. Even so, in a vain attempt to escape, the youth had drummed his heels and shouted wildly to stampede the startled packhorse. After that, the officer tied Jethro's feet together beneath the packhorse's belly.

"Sorry, boy," the ranger said. "But you are the only thing I got to show for a month in the Nations. Hell, you are plumb *necessary*.

Jethro ground his teeth in frustration, but maintained his self-imposed silence. That night he tried to cut through another tree. Again, Cole switched saplings on him just before he freed himself.

The ranger and his prisoner crossed the Red River on the Ewing Camp ferry and headed into Texas. They traveled slowly, the big man in no hurry. Just past Ewing Camp, they paused for the night. Cole first handcuffed Jethro to a tree, then started away to picket their horses and set up camp. He turned back, his angular face blank. "You know, boy, if you'd give your word that you wouldn't chase away on me, I might let you help set up camp, and what not."

Jethro broke his silence: "Damn you! I'll promise nothing!"

Cole stared at him for several seconds. "Okay, boy. Whatever you say."

Two days later they passed through Paris, Texas, and the ranger stopped to buy food. Several urchins made faces at Jethro while he waited handcuffed atop the packhorse. Cole wandered out of the store in time to stop the children from throwing but four stones at his hapless prisoner.

Under way again, the lawman said conversationally, "Ain't easy leading an owlhoot life, is it, pard?"

"Goddammit, I'm no outlaw."

"Hell you say! This handbill I got in my saddlebags says different. How you account for that?"

They stopped for the night ten miles out of Paris. After supper, the ranger poured Jethro another cup of coffee and asked again, "Why'd you do it, boy?"

"I had my reasons," Jethro spat.

"Maybe so. What were they?"

Jethro sighed. He sipped the coffee, then said, "He

killed my ma and pa."

"That so? Tell me about it."

So Jethro did. He omitted nothing and it took a long while. He stopped as suddenly as he began and Jeff Cole measured him for a long time.

"What was the major's name again, boy?"

"Bates. Calumet Bates."

"Time we go to sleep, ain't it, boy?"

"Why don't you just go ahead and switch trees now?" Jethro said. "That way you won't have to get up in the middle of the night to do it."

Cole grinned, stretched out with his head to his saddle and placed his hat over his face.

They stopped at noon on the day following and Cole hobbled their horses to graze. Then he built a small fire, opened a tin of peaches and laid out some hardtack. But he seemed in no hurry to leave, and the two loitered, drinking cup after cup of strong coffee.

Cole carried his cup to the Sulphur River's bank and crouched on his heels, apparently enjoying the peace and serenity of the river and its surroundings. After awhile he pitched the grounds from his cup and walked back to Jethro. The ranger dug in his pocket for the key and unlocked the handcuffs.

"You step on down below the river bank if you need to go, boy. Best remember, though, that I'm right above you and I ain't about to lose you now."

Jethro eased over the bank and crouched in some cottonwood brush. He stood and glanced up at Jeff Cole towering on the bank above. The younger man said, "I don't guess you'd consider giving me back my gun so it'd be an even break?"

Cole grinned. "You think it'd be even then, boy? Hell!" The ranger pitched his cup toward the river. Like a striking snake, his hand dipped toward his hip and flame erupted twice from his fist. By the time the little tin cup hit the water it was unrecognizable. The ranger relaxed a moment, the smoking gun in his hand. Then he asked, "You think you'd get an even break if you had your gun, boy? Y'all figure you could beat that?"

Jethro's mouth hung agape. He'd heard of men who were quick and accurate with pistols, but he'd never seen one. He shook his head to clear it, then muttered, "If I had the chance, I'd sure as hell try."

"Would you now?" Jeff Cole pitched his own Colt down to the startled youth.

Jethro caught the flying revolver more in self-defense than through deftness of hand. Even then he bobbled it. After he held the revolver firmly in hand, Jethro stared up at the ranger in disbelief. Clumsy and slow, he eared back the hammer, raised the weapon in both hands and pointed it at the lawman.

Cole's face was expressionless as he leaned against a nearby live oak. The lawman hooked a thumb over his belt buckle and crossed his legs. "You goin' to shoot, boy, or ain't you?"

Tears sprang to Jethro's eyes and his hands shook. Then his mouth pinched into a determined line and his face hardened. The knuckles of both hands turned white. Finally he whirled and threw the Colt far out into the river.

A bee buzzed the ranger's nose before moving on. At last, Cole drawled, "Now that was a dumb thing to do, boy. That Colt cost a heap of money."

"You talk about dumb! Clods will thump your casket before many more moons go by."

The ranger straightened from his slouch, planted legs far apart, and casually opened his left fist so Jethro could see the four unfired .44 cartridges in his palm.

Jethro glared up at him. "Nothing to keep me from running."

"Yeah there is, boy." The big lawman reached behind and pulled Jethro's old percussion Colt from where he'd earlier thrust it beneath his belt.

"C'mon back up here, boy. You and me, we'd better have us a little council."

·—•·•—·

Jethro shuffled back to camp in time to see Jeff Cole drop the handcuffs into his saddlebags. The youth waited uncertainly by the fire. "How old are you, boy?"

"Twenty, I think."

The lawman offered him the coffee pot.

"No thanks. I've had plenty."

"Well, boy ..." The walrus-mustachioed ranger cleared his throat and seemed to weigh his next words: "Where was you goin' when I picked you up?"

"East."

"Why east?"

Jethro shrugged. "I don't know. Probably because I'd laid a trail west and they'd likely expect me to head there."

The big man sighed. "Sit down, boy. This may take a while."

Jethro sank to the ground, sitting cross-legged, Indian fashion.

Cole dragged over his saddle and squatted against it. "How was you figuring to live, boy? By stealing?"

"No, dammit. I just wanted to get far enough away so's I wouldn't have to run no more. Then I guess I figured to find work." He dropped his angry glare. "Look, Mr. Cole, if I was planning to make my way stealing, I could have picked up your gun when you was in the quicksand bog and shot you in the back a dozen times over. Then I could have had your gun and both your horses."

"Hell, I figured that out at the time."

Jethro was quiet again, staring at the tiny wisp of smoke rising from the campfire.

"Way you tell it, boy, your pa and ma wanted you to amount to something. That's why they sent you to school."

"Yes," Jethro said.

"You saw how that ferryman looked at you, didn't you? And how them kids chunked rocks at you? When you planned to kill that major, you just didn't think all them things'd enter into it, did you?"

Jethro hung his head.

"Ain't too much fun bein' chained to a tree at night and tied to a horse by day, is it?"

"No."

"How do you suppose it'd be, stuck behind bars for the rest of your life? Or standin' on a gallows with a rope danglin' around your neck?"

Jethro bit his lip and shook his head.

"I'm going to let you go, boy."

A sob broke from the youth.

"I give you a test awhile ago and you passed it. You ain't no killer."

"No, sir. I don't want to be," Jethro said.

"But you are a long way from bein' a credit to the republic."

"I … I can't argue with that."

"I turn you loose, what'll you do?"

The youth shrugged, raising direct gray eyes to meet the lawman's.

"You're still wanted, you know."

Jethro nodded.

"You'll still have to run. Ain't goin' to be easy, but you ain't got no choice." Both men stared at the wispy campfire smoke. Finally the ranger said, "So, only thing to do is make the best of it."

"If it can be done, Mr. Cole, I'll do it."

"You ain't goin' to make it, boy. Not the way you are now. Look at you. They don't come much raggedier. No shoes. No hat. No clothes worth callin' the same. You got to have a few necessities, boy. Man can't get along without 'em. Be nice if you left here mounted on a good horse, too. And you'll need a better gun than that old cap and ball."

Cole's voice reminded Jethro of his own pa's gentle advice when, as a boy, the youth had left home for the last time.

"Can you swim?" the lawman asked.

Jethro nodded.

"Underwater?"

"Some."

"Well, I can't. So you can get a decent gun by trottin' out in that river and divin' until you find one. It ain't mine no more. I done lost it. Howsomever, if you can fetch it up, that'll be a start. What do you say?"

"I'll try to get it, Mr. Cole. But if I do, I think you ought to have it back."

"Finder's keepers. That's the way it is, boy. Run along now and see what you get. You need a bath anyway. And while you look for your gun, I'm goin' to ride on in to Commerce. I'll be back in time for supper. You be here."

Some hours later, Jeff Cole rode into camp to find Jethro sitting cross-legged by the ashes of a cold campfire, wiping moisture from the Colt with his shirt. A neat pile of firewood was stacked nearby and a full bucket of water had been set in the shade of a nearby live oak.

"You'll need a little oil on that, boy. Need to take it apart to do a good job."

Jethro looked up uncertainly.

"Tell you what, let's cook supper first," Cole said. "Then I'll show you how to clean a gun the right way."

By the time the ranger tended to his horse, the youth had a fire dancing.

Cole brought a flour sack bundle that he tossed to Jethro. "Some duds in that sack, boy. See if they don't drape you better'n them ragged ones you got on now."

Jethro opened the sack as Cole continued: "Didn't get no boots. That's something a fella ought to fit himself. But there's a good pair of canvas pants and a heavy cotton shirt or two. They'll get you by for a few days."

Later, sitting side by side in the firelight, the big ranger took the revolver apart and he and his former prisoner wiped and oiled the weapon.

"A gun is no more, no less, than an implement, boy," Cole said. "Some people think on it different, maybe. But I don't. I think of a gun as a tool. It can be a good tool or a bad tool, depending on who holds it. In my line of work, I see enough guns used in bad hands until a man could grow sour thinkin' on it."

Jethro hung on the other's words while screwing the two walnut butt plates onto the handle.

"In good hands, a gun can bring in table meat and protect a cow herd from varmints. It can drive off renegades from a lonesome farm and even protect a whole nation from a shiftless king and his no-good nobles. It'd be a sorry world to live in, boy, was the good men not to have guns. If the heathens or varmints never stoled 'em blind or killed 'em first then the rotten apples 'mongst us would. The bad ones have no use for the weak and no unease about using a gun or a knife or a club to take anything that hits their fancy. And it's only guns in good hands that holds 'em at bay."

Cole paused, then nodded to himself. "Like as not, if there wasn't guns, somebody would have to come along and invent 'em just to even things out."

The ranger took the revolver from Jethro and studied it, turning it over and over in his hands. Then he handed it back, along with six cartridges. His voice was gruff. "That gun, boy, ain't never been used for no bad reason. But it ain't got no mind of its own, and it ain't got no conscience. That gun in bad hands would kill all the same as it would in good hands."

Jethro finished filling the Colt and snapped the loading plate into place. He leaned across the officer's knees and slid the revolver into its holster, flipping the safety thong over the hammer.

Cole picked up the holstered weapon and handed gun and belt to Jethro. "Where you're headed in life, boy, you might need a good tool or two. I want to see that you have at least one."

Jethro held the weapon in his lap, hanging on Jeff Cole's every word. The lawman continued: "I want you to use that gun only against varmints or in self-defense against varmints of your own kind. Hear?"

"I promise," Jethro mumbled.

"And you never, ever pull it unless you plan to use it. Hear?"

Jethro nodded.

"Now, it ain't no use to carry any kind of gun unless a

man knows how to use it. And you sure as hell showed me you don't know nothin' about usin' guns when I th'owed you that one and you bobbled it for an hour or two." Cole chuckled at the thought. "So tomorrow, you and me will set about some training."

The big man stood and pushed the campfire's coals together with the toe of his boot. "Right now, howsomever, we'd best turn in for the night. All that swimmin' must have tuckered you out."

That night Jethro Spring slept with his new Colt. It was low-slung on his hip—like the Texas Ranger had worn it.

———•◦•———

They spent the entire following day practicing with their new weapons: Jeff Cole with a brand-new Colt Peacemaker, Jethro Spring with the ranger's old gun. Jethro packed load after load of fist-sized rocks from the riverbank, stringing them along the top of a fallen log.

The mustachioed ranger took care to explain the whys and hows of the quick draw—a well-oiled, plain-leather holster, carried low and tied down; the fluid forward hand movement and the quick snap of a wrist as the muzzle cleared leather. Most of all, though, the big man emphasized the need to practice both drawing and shooting.

"There ain't no substitute, boy. Speed comes with training. A man has to practice reg'lar enough so's he can do it in his sleep, and do it without no mistakes. Let me tell you, boy, if you bobble that gun or hang it up while just practicing, it's bound to happen again when the chips are all on the table and you need it fast. Get to where you can pull it slick and clean every time. Even then, some men can go to pieces under pressure."

Cole glanced at Jethro to see if he was listening, then sighted along the barrel of his weapon and continued: "It's the same with shootin'. Ain't no good just to be able to get the damned thing in your hand if you don't know what to do with it after you get it there. Tell you the truth, boy, practice is even more important in shootin' than in pullin'. It ain't near so important who gets the first shot as who gets the last one. And many a gunfight ended with the last man to draw bein' the first man to hit what he shoots at. So practice, you hear?"

They blasted away at Jethro's rocks hour after hour, until blisters raised upon the youth's hand. Then Cole had him drill with his left hand. "I once took one in the right. It was over on the Red, and them hombres would a-got me sure, had I not got them first by usin' my left."

They kept at it until only small piles of splintered gravel remained of Jethro's rocks and Jeff Cole looked around in amazement. "I do believe we missed dinner, boy. And if we don't call it quits, we may even miss supper."

Jethro stumbled to their camp to build a fire.

———•••———

Revived by food, Jethro asked, "How much ammunition did you buy yesterday, Mr. Cole?"

"A case or two."

"There's five hundred rounds in a case, right? A thousand rounds in two cases?"

Cole nodded.

"That cost a passel of money. These clothes cost something, too. And you bought a new gun and belt."

"Mmm-hmm."

"You spent a lot of money on me. And that's not counting the grub you packed into me since you picked me up." Jethro swiped at a gnat. "How will I pay you back?"

Cole snorted. "You already have, boy. I paid two-fifty for that blooded black horse out there, and he might have died if you hadn't come along to help me get him out of that quicksand bog. And it may not look like it now, but I paid forty-nine dollars for this saddle I set."

"I owe you a lot, Mr. Cole. And I don't know how I can repay you."

The big man grinned beneath his moustache. "Only one way, boy. Someday you better amount to something. The biggest thing I'm giving you is a chance. Don't lose it or waste it."

"I won't, I promise. But I'll pay you back someday, too. I don't know how and when. But I will. You'll see."

The ranger shrugged.

"Now," Jethro asked, "why are you turning me loose?"

"You ain't all bad. I know that."

"You didn't know it up in the Nations. You dragged me a hundred and fifty miles down to damn near your headquarters before you figured it out. Why? What made you of a sudden believe in me?"

The big man poked at the fire with a stick. "Hell, I knew about you right off, boy. But the best way to get you plumb out of Indian Territory without trouble was in my custody. Worked, too. They was looking for you hot and heavy up there and if I hadn't picked you up, somebody else likely would have."

Jethro looked so dubious, that Jeff Cole went on. "Besides, I wasn't plumb sure about you. Way I figured, it wouldn't hurt a budding badman to find out what it's all about, the life he's headed for: wearing handcuffs, strapped to a horse against his will, the stares, kids throwing rocks. Did it hurt to find out?"

"No," the younger man said. "I sure as hell didn't like

it. And I might think you went a little far with the lesson. But hurt? No."

The ranger grinned and a companionable silence fell between them. Finally Jethro said, "I'm still not sure you've explained yourself. You don't make a practice of turning wanted outlaws loose."

"No."

Jethro waited in vain for an explanation. Finally he said, "Then why?"

"I knew your story, boy. Hell, any lawman worth his salt knows about the Musselshell thing. I wanted to hear it direct from you, though, to see was I readin' it right."

"And?"

"I was in the war, boy, with the Texas Red River Brigade. We was stationed in Tennessee."

It took a few moments for Jethro to realize the lawman had shifted subjects.

"I was taken at Lookout Mountain in '63. Maybe you don't know what that means, boy, but I was a prisoner for the duration. They turned us loose in May of '65 and we had to find our own way home. Well, things was all right around the home place when I got back, except for my brother, Ben.

"Ben, now, he was younger. He joined in '63. Wound up with Johnston in Georgia, then got sent on to the Army of No'thern Virginia 'cause he was a telegraph operator. He was assigned out on the Peninsula where some of the toughest, meanest fighting of the whole damned war took place. We didn't find out the truth for awhile, but Ben, he never came back."

"I'm sorry," Jethro murmured.

Cole went on as though he hadn't heard. "Ben was took by the blue-bellies late-on in '64. Like me, Ben was a prisoner. But he didn't spend his time at Nashville. Instead, he got sent to Fort Delaware."

Jethro propped his wrists on bent knees and leaned forward.

"Might be Delaware don't mean nothin' to you, boy, but it meant plenty to the Rebs spendin' time there. Delaware was a hell-hole on the face of the earth. And a passel of 'grays' cooped up there never come back. Ben was one of 'em."

"I'm sorry," Jethro said again.

"What may int'rest you more, boy, is knowin' who was in command at Fort Delaware." The ranger's voice dropped to a near-whisper. "His name was Bates, boy. They called him 'Butcher Bates'."

Jethro's eyes widened. "I ... I don't believe you."

Cole stared through the younger man. "Yeah," he drawled, "if I ever got the chance, I figured to blow a hole in the bastard—and I wanted it big enough to wave through! You done me a favor, boy. Me and ma and pa. Ain't rightly no way I could fo'get that, now is there?"

It took Jethro several seconds to find his voice. "Are you saying you was looking for me up in the Nations?"

A fleeting smile crossed Jeff Cole's face. "Now that would have been real luck, wouldn't it? No, let's just say that I headed that way lookin' for the Wilson bunch in the line o' duty. And say it was right after the last batch of telegrams come in saying they had a lead on you out in Cherokee country. Ain't no way I could have figured to come across you. But what the hell—it never hurts to weight the scales on the side of the lucky lady."

He looked at Jethro and grinned. "Hell, I knowed who you was the minute I laid eyes on you. Most near fell over from shock."

Jethro's heart was thumping. He swallowed.

"Fortune was on our side, boy—your's and mine. If

there's a next time, neither of us mightened be so lucky."

Jethro's brow crinkled. "But why here? Why bring me all the way here?"

The ranger chuckled. "Safest place I know, boy." He hooked a thumb over his shoulder. "Mine and Ben's home is just over yonder rise. This land we are camped on belongs to my daddy. Ain't nobody goin' to bother us here." The ranger came to his feet and stretched. "Pa's s'posed to have a pony shod for you tomorrow. In the mornin' we are goin' to ride over there and get it. Pa wants to shake your hand, too."

CHAPTER SIX

The harassed dock foreman, slate and chalk in hand, paused in front of the slender youth. "How about it, lad? You lookin' for work?"

"Yes, sir. I am."

"Name?"

"Snow. John Snow."

The older man scribbled, then said, "See Joaquin. He'll assign you." Then the dock foreman disappeared amid the sea of humanity boiling about the Natchez docks.

Jethro Spring, now John Snow, bewilderedly scanned the crowded dock. Barges and shallow-draft steamboats bumped against the wharves. It was the peak of harvest along the Mississippi River and this hot, humid, August day was no different from hectic harvests of past millenniums in any land; when crops ripened, men and women— black, red, brown, white—toiled against time and heat.

"Can you tell me where I'll find Joaquin?" Jethro

Spring asked a sweating laborer. The man ignored the question. "Joaquin? I'm looking for Joaquin." Finally a toothy black gestured with his chin and the youth stumbled on.

The press of workmen jostled Jethro, bumping him from side to side. "Joaquin? Where can I find Joaquin?"

Someone spun him around. The youth's hand darted toward his loose shirt front and the revolver it concealed.

"Easy," the huge mulatto drawled, features drawn in a knowing frown.

"What do you want?" Jethro asked.

"No, little man, it is what you want?"

"I'm looking for Joaquin. Do you know where I can find him?"

"You found him. Now you have, what you want him for?"

Jethro stared up at a man who towered at least a foot over his head. The man's muscles looked as though *they* had muscles. "Fella sent me to find you."

An ugly scar ran from nose to ear across one of the mulatto's cheeks. "Why would somebody do that?

"He hired me. Said to find Joaquin."

"You ain't big enough, little man. Not to be no Mississippi stevedore." Joaquin started away.

"Hey, wait a minute," Jethro cried. "He hired me."

"I'm firing you."

The youth hurried to catch the dock foreman's arm. "Why?"

Joaquin shook his bulging arm free. "You ain't big enough to tote a turd," he said. But he was smiling.

"I can do anything you can do."

The mulatto roared. "We loading a barge of lumber, little man. You can't keep up wi' nobody there, let alone Joaquin."

"Try me!"

Joaquin flashed a cavern packed with white teeth. "All right, little man. But you ain't got no bottom, I bounce you out on your punkin' head."

"A chance is all I ask."

Joaquin chuckled as he walked away, with Jethro dogging his steps. "All you want is a chance—is that what you say? Before this day is out, you gonna ask the good Lord to let you die."

Throughout the day, Joaquin grinned as the slender youth trudged back and forth, carrying an endless assortment of heavy planks to the barge. Before an hour had gone by, Jethro had reason to believe everything the mulatto had told him was true. At day's end, the young man sat on the dock, hands raw and bleeding, blood soaking through his linsey-wooley shirt from raw and bleeding shoulders, praying for God to save him from his misery.

At pay-off time, the shuffling line of stevedores carried Jethro forward. He saw some of the men ahead receive a slip of paper along with their day's pay. When his turn came, he held out his hand for the coins he'd earned. Joaquin put a paper in his hand, too. He stared at it, then looked up stupidly at the big man. Joaquin no longer smiled.

"You be here at daylight, little man. There's more work for you."

Jethro stumbled from the fast-emptying dock. He bumped into bales of cotton and trudged down the rows. Finally he slid down to rest his back against a bale and fell fast asleep.

In his dreams, Jethro rode from Texas in mid-summer.

He twisted in the saddle to wave goodby to a Texas Ranger, but the man was no longer there....

Jethro had traveled fast, camping in isolated groves, along sheltered watercourses. He practiced constantly, until the Colt seemed to appear in his hand almost by magic. He shot squirrels, rabbits, and snakes, popping heads from water moccasins at thirty feet.

He reached Natchez before the forty dollars Jeff Cole had given him ran out, a good bit of it going for ammunition. By then, he'd gained confidence and speed.

And not a little accuracy.

Jethro came awake to the sound of shuffling feet. He had enough presence of mind to keep his eyes closed.

"Hey, who dis?" someone said.

"Drunk," replied a guttural voice.

Jethro moaned and rolled onto his stomach.

"He hurt, maybe sick."

"Make no never mind. See if he got money."

Rough hands rolled him over. Shock was mirrored in the black man's face when he found himself staring down the barrel of a .44-caliber Colt.

Jethro cackled. The man was just another squirrel or rabbit or snake. Weary to exhaustion, angry with Joaquin, the Natchez docks, others who laughed at him, the youth eared back the revolver's hammer.

The black man held out his palms and eased away, taking as much care as if he'd turned over a milk pail and found a coiled rattlesnake. Behind him another shadowy figure backed away.

"Git!" snarled the youth. Both men wheeled and ran like frightened deer.

Jethro crawled wearily to his feet. Every bone in his body ached. He was standing at the dock when the big mulatto, Joaquin, began his day. "You a pretty big little man," Joaquin said. "Now we see if you got any stay in you."

"I'll stay," Jethro muttered.

———◆———

Two months passed. They were the most agonizing months of Jethro's short life. But gradually the young man suffered less and less from the tortures of his daylight-to-dark labors. His muscles strengthened, lengthened, and tightened. His shoulders broadened. He put on weight; most of the weight was rock-hard muscle. He became known around the Natchez docks as a tough and tireless workman and bosses sought him out. But he also earned a reputation as a touchy, sullen recluse who discouraged familiarity and seldom even talked with others. Only the towering mulatto, Joaquin, seemed to understand the quiet young man, inspiring his confidence.

One day, when Joaquin paid him off, the foreman said, "Little man, we 'bout done here. Maybe you find work, maybe not. You come back next year, huh?"

"If a man wanted to keep on as a dockhand," Jethro asked, "where would he go?"

"Maybe New Orleans, little man. But they got their pick of river people now, an' it might not be easy. They's ocean runners comin' in there, though. Maybe I could get the boss to write a letter fo' you."

———◆———

Rain pelted down, slanting in wind-blown gusts as the

muscular youth stepped inside the New Orleans grog shop. Stevedores, driven from work by the gale, crowded the room. Jethro Spring shivered and plucked his wet, clinging shirt from his body. He pulled the dripping cap from his head and shook water from it. Someone shoved in from outside and Jethro let himself be propelled forward by the crowd, squeezing between two burly men at the bar.

Jethro caught the eye of a bartender. "Beer," he said.

One of the men beside him, a swarthy, dark-complexioned Frenchman, glared at Jethro, then turned and mumbled to his companion.

"Aha!" Jethro heard the second man say as he shoved his companion aside to peer bleary-eyed into Jethro's face. "Well, well, if it ain't the Natchez wonder." The man's scarred face was splintered by a malicious smile.

Jethro's pulse quickened, but his own stare was steady as he reached for his beer. He took a sip, then another.

Scarface sneered, "I asked you a question, Natchez. What do you have to say?"

The question was convoluted, but Jethro understood it. Arriving in New Orleans a month before, he'd presented the glowing recommendation from his Natchez employer and been hired on the spot. The other stevedores resented the newcomer and lately, he'd seen their hostility grow as the young and inexperienced stranger, by dint of unflagging labor and reliability, worked his way into more responsible, better-paying jobs. "What do I have to say?" Jethro asked over the rim of his mug. "Nothing."

The man laughed, but there was no humor. "You hear that, Rafael? He has nothing to say." Scarface stopped laughing and, weaving from too much drink, stood away from the bar. "You come down here from upriver. You take our jobs. And you got nothing to say?"

Silence fell across the noisy room. Jethro took another

sip of beer, then set the mug on the bar. "What do you want me to say?" he asked in a low voice.

Scarface laughed again. "Say you'll go home. Back to Natchez. Now. Okay?" He grinned, showing a mouthful of broken, crooked teeth.

"No," the youth said.

"You hear that, Raphael? He says 'NO.' That means I'll have to talk him into it."

Jethro took a deep breath. "Yeah you will. You got another choice, though. You can forget whatever it is that's ranklin' you. We can both walk out of here and go our own ways."

"I eat Natchez half-breeds for breakfast."

Jethro thought of his gun; remembered the admonition of a Texas Ranger: *And you never, never pull it unless you plan to use it, hear?*

Jethro swept back his shirt front and pulled the Colt, saw Scarface's eyes widen. The surrounding crowd shrank back from the youth. *You ain't no killer.* He shrugged, glanced at the apprehensive bartender, slid the weapon across the bar and said, "Hold this for me, will you?"

Scarface laughed, his face venomous. "I teach you Natchez bastard not to pull a gun on nobody ever, you see?" The ugly man feinted a swing, then kicked at the younger man's crotch. Jethro swerved, taking the blow on the outside of his thigh. Scarface's clubbed fist exploded against his temple and he sagged against the bar. Another Scarface kick slammed into his stomach. Then Jethro lashed out with a wild right that connected more through luck than skill. A roundhouse left drove Scarface back.

Jethro stood panting, watching the dark Frenchman shake his head. Then the burly man renewed the attack, more cautious this time. Scarface threw a couple of measured blows, then ducked two of Jethro's wild swings.

Scarface backed off and took a beer held out by one of his friends. He glared malevolently at his opponent while Jethro merely stared in return, waiting. Scarface threw the mug at the younger man's face and waded to the attack.

Jethro ducked the mug, but doubled over in agony when Scarface finally landed a kick to the groin. Scarface pumped a series of rights and lefts into Jethro's head and neck while the slighter man bent over, gasping for breath, holding his crotch.

Scarface shuffled back and shook his head in disbelief. He'd landed enough telling blows to knock most men unconscious, but the kid from Natchez was still staggering on his feet.

The Frenchman rushed forward and aimed another kick. Gulping for air, Jethro dodged, then leaped to a furious attack of his own, lashing out wildly, again and again. His swinging fists drove the bigger opponent stumbling against chairs and tables.

The crowd made way as the heaving fighters careened into the center of the room. Then Jethro's crazed blows drove Scarface down, sliding halfway under a table, where he lay still.

Jethro, breath rasping and face twisted with madness, stood over the fallen Scarface, gathering his wits. Then a blow from the side staggered him and he jerked around to flail savagely at a new attacker. He saw a blur of angry faces. He caromed off a table, against a wall. He bounced from the wall, pumping wooden arms. One man went down, another surged forward. A third sprawled to the floor. A staggering blow struck him from the rear. Blood splashed from the young man's nose as another blow struck and he stumbled over an inert form at his feet. He caught his balance by grasping a stranger's shoulders, then flung the man aside. He had a maniacal fury about him now. He winced from a hammer blow to the kidneys and spun around, snarling, to swing in another direction.

Another assailant went down.

Battered and beaten from wall to table and back again, Jethro swung on, his energy and fury draining through wilder and weaker flailing until he could swing no more. With limp arms hanging at his sides, Jethro Spring still absorbed blows like some worn-out draft horse resigned to its fate. Stagger left. Stagger back.

"Enough ye fools," someone roared through the fog. "Don't you know a man when you see one? Blast him more if you will, but by the blessed saints, first you'll have it out wi' me."

"Back, Joe," came another voice. "We'll teach the bastard what."

"Get away, Barry, you Irish fool!" shouted another.

"And I'll do no such thing." The newcomer sounded indignant. "What's the matter with you? There's no ten of you who can take the lad from his feet. Don't you know a fightin' man when you see one? Don't you know a man wi' more guts than the lot o' you? Would you kill him, for the Holy Mother's sake?"

Jethro tried to focus on his savior, but the effort caused him to lose balance and he sprawled full length to the floor.

"Now look what you've done," moaned Joe Barry. "Mother o' God, you may well have ruined what could be as good a fightin' man ever to step into a prize ring. Not since Joe Barry stepped out, anyway." The red-haired man glared around him. "Somebody bring rags and a bucket o' warm water. Sure and none of us should just leave him lying there."

Nothing but a tiny slit of light filtered into Jethro Spring's right eye as he struggled back to consciousness. His entire body throbbed with pain. He tried to lift a hand to his face, but only moaned with the effort. After a moment, he closed his right hand, then the left. He moaned again and ran his tongue over swelled and split lips that hurt like hell. His chest ached and his nose was so blocked he breathed through his mouth.

He heard a throaty laugh and tilting his head in that direction, touched off more throbbing waves. "I reset your nose, laddie buck. Even if I do say so meself, it may look better than it did before."

"Who are you?" the battered man croaked. "I can't see."

The laugh came again. "No, bucko. Likely it'll be tomorrow before enough o' the swelling leaves the eyes for you to see again. Me name, though, 'tis Joe Barry."

Jethro only grunted.

"Perhaps you've not heard of Joe Barry, lad, but occasionally I'm for bein' a dockhand. Just now, though, I'm without work to fit me talents. Mostly," Barry continued, "I made me fame and fortune as a prizefighter. Now you've heard o' me?"

Jethro shook his head.

"Ah well, 'tis of no importance. What is important, laddie—I watched you fight at the Sealegs. You may yet make a fine fighter."

Jethro sighed and drifted back into a deep sleep.

The next day was better. Jethro could dimly see an outline of the Irishman. "Why are you doing this?" he croaked.

"Never a mind, time enough to talk come Lent." Joe Barry sat by the bed with a bowl in his hands. "Open up now, lad, and I'll spoon a little broth."

Jethro, despite the pain, was ravenous. He winced when the spoon bumped his teeth.

"I don't think you'll lose a tooth, laddie. Loose ones you've got, but they'll tighten with time."

Jethro again slept the sleep of the drugged.

A week passed before Jethro Spring could walk unassisted; two weeks before he shuffled to the New Orleans docks to seek work. His face was still puffed and discolored, and his body ached.

When he appeared on the levees, dockmen and wharfmen and stevedores avoided his approach. At the first shipping office, a clerk, wearing a knowing smile, hired him on the spot. Instead of their dark mutterings of the past, other workmen greeted him in silence as he went about his duties.

Days passed. Then one wharfman met Jethro's eye. Another ventured a smile and a roustabout murmured a shy greeting. Jethro Spring responded with stoic indifference, remaining aloof, ignoring all friendly advances, save one—Joe Barry's.

Barry's squalid ground-floor room, in an equally squalid hotel, fronted on Spanish Plaza, near the Bienville Street wharf. Down the block was the Sealegs Inn, where the Irishman first met the young man.

"Ah, there you are, laddie," Joe always said when his young friend returned to their room after work. "Tis a better place when you're here, you know." And Jethro always smiled at the welcome. Joe's ready humor and good natured banter brightened the dismal surroundings.

"Tis sorry I am, lad, that I cannot find work," the big Irishman said one mid-March day. "Dear God, one would think me not the man I once was, and nothing could be further from the truth."

Jethro shook rainwater from his cap. He laid the striped feed sack that held their bread and fish on the rough-plank table. "We're doing fine, Joe. I'm staying at your place. All's I'm kicking in is a little grub and grog."

"Still," the Irishman began, "I'd find it better if I, too, could make me own way. 'Tis always slow this time o' year, true, but ..."

"It's Lent, Joe," Jethro interrupted.

"Ah, laddie, you're right. And I've put no thought into what I should give up, have I?" The big man gazed toward the ceiling and muttered beneath his breath.

Jethro watched him, saying nothing. Barry shrugged, "What shall it be lad?" Then his face lighted. "I know, lad-die buck. I'll give up flounder. Truly I love 'em, you know."

"Yeah I know. That's why there's flounder in here, Joe." The younger man tapped the feed sack.

"Flounder is out then," the Irishman murmured. He brightened. "I know, lad. "I'll quaff no champagne for the rest o' Lent." Suspiciously, he added, "You've brought no champagne have you?"

Jethro grinned. "No, you're safe enough, Joe. There's a pint of applejack, though, should you feel a need."

"Best we have a touch, laddie. Not for me, of course. But likely you'll be needin' it to ward off the chilblains from your wettin'. And I'll not be heathen enough to leave you drink alone."

Later Joe sat on the edge of the room's single bed, sipping from a cracked cup. "Tell me somethin' of yourself, lad."

"No!" The response was blurted and Jethro wished he had it back as soon as he said it, but the damage was done.

The smile left Joe's face. "All right, lad," he said. "'Twas merely the prattlin' of an auld sod. Never again will I ask—nor listen to—any story of your past."

Jethro regarded the older man stonily, then said, "It's Lent."

"So you pointed out awhile ago. I gave up champagne."

"That's not what I meant."

The Irishman looked puzzled. "What, pray tell, laddie, do you mean?"

"Two months ago, you said we'd talk about why you took me in, nursed me back to health, maybe even saved my life. You said we'd talk about it during Lent."

Barry studied his applejack.

"It's Lent," Jethro prodded.

Joe turned his attention to the younger man. "How do you feel, lad?"

"Fine."

"The hands? The ribs? Any pain?"

"A little stiffness, maybe. But most of it's gone. Why?"

"You can breath deep? Through your nose?"

"Yes. Why?"

Joe's voice took on a stronger, more persuasive tone. "You're a born fighter, laddie. Never have these eyes beheld a man what took the drubbin' you did in the Sealegs." Joe's glance drifted past Jethro to the window beyond, then stayed there, attracted by the vision. "Holy Mother! A fight it was, laddie. Ye knocked down three, four, five—I know not how many. Three was out at the end. Others were bloodied. I saw it."

"Must have been a hell of a fight," Jethro said. "Wish I had seen it from a distance."

"And the pack o' dogs, they whaled on you wi' aught they had until you were a battered wreck. And never did they put you down."

Jethro shrugged.

"It was a hell of a fight, laddie! A hell of a fight. You've got a fine future, especially could you make the middle-weights."

"Maybe you'd better start over, Joe," the young man said. "I don't follow you. Or maybe you'd best give up applejack, too."

"Laddie, don't you see? You fought ten, fifteen hounds that night. And you put lots of 'em down, while they could not do the same to you. And you did that wi' no training. Holy Mother! What you could do if you'd learn to bob and weave and straighten out that roundhouse. You've got a jaw like granite."

"You mean you want me to be a prizefighter?"

"Yes, yes," Joe said, containing his excitement no longer. "Laddie, there's reason to believe you'd be one o' the best!"

"Just because I was in a brawl in a New Orleans grog shop?"

"No, no, no, laddie," Joe said. "Because you can punch like a mule and take a mule's punch wi'out blinkin'. You're quick on your feet, and you've got the strength o' two men. Like strikin' snakes are you wi' your hands. Boy, you're a natural!"

"No more applejack for you," Jethro said good-naturedly, refilling his friend's cup.

"'Tis the truth I speak, laddie. I know. I was once a boxing master meself. I know one when I see a man what can lick and take a lickin'."

Jethro said, "Don't seem to me like it'd be real important to be able to take a licking. I'd rather not get hit at all."

Joe Barry jumped from the bed to pace the room. "That's where I come in, lad. I can teach ye. As fast and quick as you are, you'll hardly be touched when you learn to parry and block."

"Well, I ..."

Joe cut him off. "But many's the good man what fell by the wayside because of a jaw of glass that shattered with a lucky punch. The best prizering fighters must be able to take a blow."

Jethro took another sip from his cup as Joe paused in front.

"And if ever fortune smiles and ye become as good as I think you will, you'll find others near the top o' the heap what's as good. The time will come, laddie, when you're fightin' for the big purses and the big glory. And you must get it clear right now that the best man wins." Barry began pacing again. "And the best man is always the one what's standing at the end."

Jethro sifted the big man's words. "Joe?" he said finally.

"Yes, laddie?" Barry paused at the window, his back turned to his companion.

"What if I say I don't want to be a prizefighter?"

Barry turned and his watery blue eyes fell on Jethro's gray ones. He shrugged.

"Where does that put us?" Jethro pressed. "Are we still friends? Are you sorry you took me in? Saved me from the mob?"

Joe Barry shoved both hands deep into his trousers pockets and began pacing again. A soft smile brushed his lips. "I loved the ring, lad. I loved the smell and sweat of it all. I loved to pit meself against another who was there to put me out o' it. I loved to take and give and spit and hate. I loved the blood pumpin' and the crowds roarin'. I loved workin' for a few minutes once each week or once in a month, and I loved the pay-offs at the end. I loved the money I made—more money than I'd make workin' the docks for a month. Holy Mother—I loved it!" His raspy breathing seemed to fill the room.

"I'm too old now, I know. I cannot do it meself. 'Tis admit, I should, that I would like to return. But I cannot do it except through another man's body." He paused, then continued, "But I swear to you, lad, I had no thought to go out and look for such, 'til I saw ye fight at the Sealegs. 'Twas only then that I says to meself, 'Joe Barry, yonder is champion timber. If that man knew half what ye know, with his speed and youth and body, you could both write your ticket out of these infernal docks'."

The big man's eyes watered still more, and he stopped pacing to throw off the last of his applejack. His eyes locked on Jethro's. "I'll admit it, lad. Admit it and more. I looked at you as a ticket out of here instead o' who ye are." He paused, took a deep breath. "But there's more. You sneak up on a man, laddie." The Irishman sighed, then smiled. "Whatever ye decide, we're friends—you and me. And that'll be the end of it." Joe turned and shuffled to the window.

"Yes," said Jethro.

"Yes what?" the Irishman growled.

"Yes. When do we start?"

Joe wheeled. "Ye mean it, lad?"

"When do we start?"

"I can think o' no better time than now." The big man rubbed his hands excitedly. "The first thing we'll need to work on, laddie, is the name. No matter how much punch you put into it, John Snow rings no bells."

Jethro laughed. "Don't make no difference to me, Irish. How about Barry? It's a proud name. Would that suit you? Maybe 'Lad Barry'."

Joe beamed. "'Tis indeed a proud name, me lad. And one I would gladly lend. But 'Lad'? No. Lad Barry just falls apart. Too flat. Kid Barry? That's something else. Don't you like that better?"

"Kid Barry it is, then. What the hell, one name is as good as another."

The prizefighter billed as Kid Barry squinted through shimmering heat waves at his opponent who leaned nonchalantly against the ring's far corner. Joe swabbed at sweat glistening on *The Kid's* shoulders.

"Not a thing to worry about, lad. He's a little over your weight, but after the Sealegs brawl, no dockman your size would touch ye."

Jethro's mouth was dry. He wished he had half as much confidence about his first fight as did his mentor.

They'd gone into training the very night of their decision, and it wasn't easy. Joe Barry proved to be a demanding taskmaster. It was run, punch the bag, footwork, punch the bag, run some more. Jethro could scarcely believe the combination of skills required to be an accomplished prizefighter and for a time he was discouraged.

Joe taught him the proper stance and how to hold his hands. At first, he concentrated on defense, learning to use his hands to block and parry; how to slip a blow. He learned to slide inside and outside, and like a dancer, how to bob and weave.

In the beginning, Joe could slap Jethro when he wished, feinting a left, following with a right. The first exchange left the younger man bewildered and gasping. "What did I do wrong?" he cried.

"Practice, laddie. Practice. You've only begun to learn your skills. Guard up!"

For weeks, Joe kept working at defense, until gradually Jethro began to see his own improvement. It's just like working with the gun, he thought. It's practice—like Jeff Cole taught me. Joe, always the aggressor, kept up the pressure until Jethro learned to block and parry and slip each of his punches automatically. After one particularly strenuous exercise, a panting Joe Barry said, "Faith and I just gave you me best, lad. Tomorrow we'll begin to teach ye more."

The next day, Jethro began learning to lead and feint. Then it was to punch from the shoulder and to jab and hook.

"The uppercut, laddie, is for infighting. So are the chop and the short hook. There are those you'll find who are better at it than you'll ever be. Them's the kind ye must stay away from. Use your speed and footwork and jab. And when they get you cornered, you must learn to tie up their hands wi' your arms. There's a skill to breaking free and clean wi'out taking a lick, too."

The daily roadwork continued, as did the everlasting sessions with the bag. Jethro Spring's job as a stevedore also continued, however, and his weight fell until he was skin and bones.

"You're down to one-forty-three, lad," Joe said as he straightened from reading the granary scales. "That's more lightweight than middleweight, but you'll put it back on soon as ye start bringing in purses and quit the docks."

Jethro smiled wistfully and waved at the big Irishman as he jogged off for his roadwork.

"He looks tough, Joe," Jethro said. "What did you say his name is?"

"Turk Wasserman. And he's not tough, lad. Just experienced. The only reason yonder lad fights is for the purse. He's been punched out by every serious prizefighter in southern Louisiana, including me ownself a few years back. But he's experienced and he's sly. If yon man sees he'll not stand and toe wi' ye, he'll fake a hurt and surprise you when you go for the kill."

"If he's so experienced and he outweighs me by forty pounds or more, how come most of the betting is going our way? Especially in my first fight?"

"Sealegs, laddie. The boys around here haven't forgot your Sealegs brawl. 'Tis likely we'll have to get away from here to get the odds. That'll come later; after ye win today. There's the referee."

Joe gave him a gentle push and Jethro Spring shuffled awkwardly to the ring's center to begin his prizefighting career. An expectant hush settled over the assembled crowd.

"A'right," the referee growled, glaring at both fighters. "This is a fight to the finish. London prize ring rules. Each round to end when a man goes down—even one knee counts. It's to be thirty seconds between rounds. When the bell rings, you got eight seconds to toe the center line. Any questions?"

Both fighters ignored the referee and returned to their corner. The bell rang.

Turk Wasserman moved to the scratch line. Oddly, Jethro could see only the two strips of tape wrapped around his opponent's hands—and the bare knuckles shining behind. Wasserman led with a cautious left, then threw an overhand right. Jethro instinctively brushed aside Wasserman's right with a flick of his wrist and whistled the same arm straight on in. He was surprised to feel how solidly the blow struck Wasserman's cheek. Wasserman backed off, then shuffled forward again.

No footwork, Jethro thought. A plodder. He moved ahead, jabbed, jabbed again, shifted suddenly to the side and crossed with his right. Again, the blow jarred along the length of his arm. Wasserman threw a right, then a wild left. Jethro Spring slipped inside both punches and rammed a left to the midsection and a swift right uppercut to Wasserman's jaw. He moved away again, just as Wasserman sat down with a stupid look on his face.

Jethro drifted to his corner. "A combination, laddie!" shouted Joe. "Ah, 'twas a beauty to see! But Holy Mother! Where did ye learn it? We've not worked on that before!"

Jethro grinned. "I've been takin' 'em from you for a couple of months." Then he was serious. "I don't know, Joe. It just seemed like the thing to do."

"Ye're a natural, laddie," Joe shouted above the crowd's pandemonium. He was laughing and slapping his fighter on the back. "A bloody damned natural!" He swabbed a towel across his fighter's shoulders and leaned forward to speak directly into his ear. "Watch him now for his trick."

The bell rang and Kid Barry moved toward ring center. Wasserman wobbled out to meet him and covered up at the first exchange. Jethro backed off, saw the man peeping at him through his bent-stance guard. Jethro glided left and pecked with his right as Wasserman edged away. Then Wasserman straightened and backed up. Jethro wheeled toward him, leading with his left. Again

Wasserman covered and the younger man stepped in, smashing a left uppercut through the man's hands, into his nose. Wasserman lashed out with both hands in short, swift blows, but Jethro blocked both with his elbows. A straight right slammed Wasserman full-length on the canvas. A bell rang. Jethro heard individuals shouting—lost almost at once in the crowd's belated roar!

"It's over, Kid," an awed Joe Barry said moments later. "Wasserman cannot answer the bell. I don't believe it. Holy Mother! I saw it and I still can't believe it!"

CHAPTER SEVEN

It was months later when Joe Barry crouched by Jethro Spring's cot, wringing his hands in despair. "Ah, laddie, laddie. I'm sorry. I pushed ye too fast, lad. 'Tis me ye should blame."

Jethro lifted a wet towel from his face and grinned, wincing at his cut and bleeding lips. "'Sall right, Joe. I just—ouch!—want to know who stopped it? Did I ..."

"No, laddie. I threw in the towel, I did. Ye'd suffered enough. Ye give it your best and it should've been enough. It would ha' been, too, if a decent referee, we'd had."

Jethro lowered his towel and groaned.

"'Tis me own fault, lad," Joe Barry continued. "I should've taught ye all them dirty tricks of the trade. 'Tis the only defense—to use them yourself."

Again, Jethro lifted his towel and glared at the flicker of the coal oil lantern. "He was good without the head butts and the groin busters, Joe. We might have lost, anyway."

"We'll never know, laddie buck. Valkyrie Johnson will want nothin' more to do wi' you, lad, no matter the purse. He took a drubbin', too."

"Works two ways." Jethro said it tiredly as he lowered the towel and smoothed it over his eyes.

Joe sighed. "You've done well, lad. You've made a name for yeself on the trip to your first loss. If you'd had a fair referee this time out, ye'd still not be beaten."

Lying on the grimy cot, head swathed in wet towels, Jethro reflected that it had indeed been a memorable trip. He'd fought a Bayou Lafourche Cajun who could take a drubbing almost as well as Jethro Spring, but couldn't dish it out nearly so well. After Robideaux, it'd been a Bogalusa logger, a Gramercy farmer and a hulking Ponchatoula plodder who was far over Jethro's weight class because no south Louisiana middleweight dared crawl into a ring with the rising young phenom. Then came the "ringer" English boxing master, brought in to take the half-breed down to size—and to rake off lucrative betting odds.

The Englishman was the first journeyman prizefighter Jethro had faced and for a time it seemed he might lose. But the oppressive Louisiana heat, Joe's training, and Jethro's ability to absorb and dish out punishment finally began to tell upon the over-confident older man.

After his big win over the Englishman, Jethro and Joe spent the fall and winter touring the Mississippi Delta and along the Gulf. First it had been Biloxi and Mobile, then Pensacola and Tallahasee and St. Petersburg. He'd fought in Galveston where the purse was impounded by Texas authorities bent on enforcing federal laws against prize-fighting. So they'd scratched Corpus Christi and returned to Lake Charles and the friendlier confines of Louisiana.

Joe arranged a tour up the Mississippi River through Baton Rouge to Natchez and Vicksburg, with a whirlwind

side trip to Alexandria and Shreveport. The name Kid
Barry came first on lists of lower Mississippi middleweight
prizefighters and Joe received offers for matches from far
and near. In March, they began their northward drift,
more like a triumphal procession: Memphis, Cairo, St.
Louis. Louisville, Cincinnati, Dayton, Toledo. Chicago,
Indianapolis, Milwaukee, Duluth. It'd been an unbroken
string of triumphs. Until St. Paul, that is. Until St. Paul
and a tough Norwegian known as Valkyrie Johnson who
knew every dirty, crooked trick in the book. Until St. Paul
and a local referee who wore blinders to the point that
even the hometown crowd yelled in outrage.

Jethro returned to the present when Joe said, "I can-
celed Davenport and Peoria, laddie. 'Tis no big thing, anyway. It'll give ye a chance to rest before we go east. You're
not lacking for fights now, lad. Yet 'tis the big prize we
want, remember? 'Tis Sailor Dan we want. I'm hopin' for
him in Cleveland or Pittsburg. If we get him, Tommy
Tucker might yet come to bay."

At mention of the champion, Jethro groaned. By now,
he knew he was still a comparatively untrained fighter.
During their tour across middle America he'd crossed
knuckles with many prizefighters who possessed his own
skills; some with even more. They may have been older or
slower or softer or weaker. Maybe they were cursed with a
glass jaw. But they were skilled. Oh yes, they were skilled.
Yet they were universally below the level of top-flite mid-
dleweights. Jethro assumed the likes of Tommy Tucker and
Sailor Dan Grimes had even greater skills. For certain, they
would be tough, have speed, stamina, and a hellish punch.
For now, however, there would be a respite. Jethro sighed
in relief.

The girl, seated behind her desk and surrounded by file cards, spotted Jethro Spring the moment he entered. *The poor man has been in an accident,* she thought. Jethro ambled to a row of books and moved along them, as if absorbing their titles. He pulled a volume from the shelf and thumbed through it.

The girl thought that interesting, wondering if he could really read, or if he was, as often happened in her library, merely a vagrant killing time. The man drifted her way, so she bent nearer her work. From the corner of an eye, she saw his idle gaze sweep past, then return. She said, "May I help you find something?"

"No thank you, ma'am. I'm just browsing." He moved on, stopping at the newspaper rack where he picked up a copy of the *Pioneer Press*. Something seemed to catch his eye as he turned pages and he moved to an overstuffed chair to continue reading.

Tucking loose auburn hair behind one ear, the lithe librarian shoved back her chair and walked to a bookshelf, her path taking her behind the mysterious stranger. She selected a volume and while returning, read the headline that so intrigued him: **Local Fans Embarrassed By Hometown Referee**. She took the second copy of the *Pioneer Press* from the newspaper rack to her desk and became absorbed.

"Not normal reading for a librarian, I'll bet."

She jumped, her cheeks flaming. "No, I ... you're the man in the article, aren't you? You're Kid Barry, the—ah—'Louisiana Bullet.'"

He gave a sweeping bow. "At your service ma'am. But you have me at a disadvantage. You see, I don't know your name."

She frowned at a familiarity she'd been taught to discourage. Nevertheless, she said, "Nora Andersen."

"I'd like to read about the Sioux uprising, ma'am. It's been ten years and I wondered if anything's been written."

"Oh yes. We have two excellent texts on the subject. May I help you find them?"

"If you please."

She found the man's manners intriguing; not at all the picture of the uncouth prizefighter she'd drawn from news stories and gossip. She sensed his nearness as he followed her down a musty aisle. Nora handed him the book by Dutton.

"Thank you, ma'am." He smiled through bruised lips. To her surprise, his teeth were even and white; again, unlike her concept of a prizefighter.

"There's another volume by Major Hatch, who commanded a unit of volunteers. But I think Dutton's book is the better. If you wish, I'll get Major Hatch's book."

"This will do for now, ma'am." She found his gray eyes unsettling.

Nora returned to her desk and finished reading the newspaper article. Then she retrieved the previous day's paper. The story she sought was front page: **Valkyrie Johnson Inflicts First Defeat On Louisiana Fighter In Slugging Match**.

She read it slowly, glancing from time to time at the young man who seemed totally absorbed in the book about Little Crow and the Santee Sioux uprising.

Nora and the man she knew as Kid Barry exchanged pleasantries when, on the next day, he returned to continue reading Dutton's text. By the time he'd completed the first book, she had Hatch's text ready.

"I believe there's a pamphlet by General Sibley, Mr.

Barry. If you'd wish to read that, too, I could try to find it."

"That would be nice," he murmured, gazing at her a shade longer than proper decorum permitted.

At closing time, he surrendered Hatch and asked, "Would I be too forward if I asked to walk you home?"

"Yes, you would be," she replied. "Nevertheless, I accept."

His laugh was warm and pleasant as he helped her into her coat.

"I do believe your swelling and discoloration have faded noticeably, Mr. Barry," she said as they strolled along the tree-lined street. "Since yesterday, I mean."

"I hope so, Miss—it is Miss, isn't it?"

She nodded and he continued, "… Miss Andersen. I don't care over much for the role of frightening children and pretty young maidens."

"You didn't frighten me, Mr. Barry." She said it without thinking, then her face flushed and she searched his face shyly. "Does that mean I'm not …"

"Oh, I believe I did frighten you," he cut in. "At any rate, you'd qualify as a pretty young maiden, and then some."

Nothing else was said between them until they'd covered the short distance to her home. For the first time, she wished she lived farther from the library. She stopped at her gate, a swinging barrier in a picket fence. Jethro looked at the white, shingled bungalow beyond and his face softened as he opened the gate.

"Good night, Miss Andersen. It's been a pleasure."

She paused. "Good night, sir. Will you return to the library?"

"Oh yes," he said. "I must finish Hatch. Then there's the Sibley pamphlet." He closed the gate and she listened to his footfalls retreat down the boardwalk.

———•◦•———

Jethro Spring arrived earlier than usual. Nora Andersen flashed her best smile and said, "I placed Hatch in your chair, Mr. Barry. And I shall begin looking for General Sibley's pamphlet soon."

"That would be fine, ma'am." He paused for a moment, then glided away.

He'd not finished Hatch when she passed him a note. It read:

> You cannot go 3 days without eating something between breakfast and supper. Mother insisted I put a slice of roast for you in my dinner pail.

Jethro grinned. "That's kind of you and your mother," he said. "I am hungry, sure enough. And I'd enjoy eating with you, but I'd not care to compromise your reputation."

She smiled. "My name is Nora, Mr. Barry. Miss Andersen, if you'd prefer. And I hardly think my reputation could be compromised in any way if you pulled your chair over by my desk for dinner."

"It's good," he said a few minutes later. "Lamb, isn't it?"

She was surprised. Most people couldn't readily identify lamb roast. "You are right, sir. We eat quite a bit of it since father died."

"I'm sorry," he said. "How did he die, may I ask?"

She focused on a spot beyond him. "He was a soldier. He died at Fort Ridgely. In the Sioux uprising."

Jethro's face went blank, eyes unfathomable. Then he took another bite of lamb. "Again, I'm sorry."

"It's all right. I was just a child then, and we've become quite used to his being gone. Mother owns a dress shop."

He shifted uncomfortably, with the same wariness as a lobo wolf that knows they're there, but can't see traps hidden around a bleating goat.

"Father was quite a bit older than mother." Nora paused then added. "She's adjusted well."

He decided to confront the problem. "My mother was Indian."

"I suspected as much. Is ... was she Sioux?"

"No."

She exhaled quickly. "I should have guessed not—your being from Louisiana and all."

He said nothing.

"Here are some cookies I baked," she said, extending a small tin. "Would you care to try one?"

"Thank you."

That evening, Nora again accepted Jethro's invitation to walk her home. As they left the library, she suggested they take a more leisurely route to the north, through a prosperous residential area. He smiled and his fingers lightly brushed her elbow, gently guiding her. Huge oaks and elms lined boardwalks leading to staid, richly-gilded homes. Jethro studied them with interest—such as he could spare from the attractive red-haired beauty at his side.

Nora was confused by this strong but contradictory man who seemed lonely and wanting for friendship, yet so guarded against familiarity. She stole a glance at him and saw he was engrossed by "gingerbread" work on a gabled two-storied home. "Aren't they beautiful?" she murmured.

For a moment she thought he'd not heard, then he nodded. "Nora," he said without looking at her, "more than anything in the world, I want something like that. A home." He faltered, then walked on, almost as if she wasn't there.

She waited for him to continue. When he didn't, she asked, "And?"

"I want a home like that, preferably. But I'll settle for less. A home I can return to every evening, with a wife and kids underfoot."

"This wife—?"

"Red-haired," he said quickly, smiling at her. She smiled also and his fingers again brushed her elbow. They walked on in companionable silence.

At her gate, she said, "I've told mother about you. She said to offer you a cup of tea. Or coffee."

He peered thoughtfully at her before murmuring, "Coffee sounds wonderful."

"Won't you please come in, then?"

Nora Andersen's mother was a tall, statuesque woman with streaks of gray in hair of an indeterminate dishwater color. Probably she had been a striking blond. The mother appeared quite formal, wearing the latest, stylishly bustled velvet dress. She also seemed stiff—and frosty.

"I've looked forward to meeting you, Mr. Barry, since Nora first spoke of you two days ago." Mrs. Andersen frowned at Nora, then returned her gaze to their visitor.

"It is my honor, ma'am," Jethro said, bowing politely. He felt she was dissecting him.

"She said you were mannerly—a feature not normally associated with those engaged in prizefighting."

"I suppose not," he murmured, "although I've had little contact with the breed, except for one close friend and, except for sometimes painful experiences in the ring."

There was only the faintest of smiles at his attempted levity. "I can see some evidence of one painful experience, Mr. Barry. I trust your wounds are healing satisfactorily."

"Fine, thank you."

"He prefers coffee, Mother."

Nora's mother nodded. "We weren't sure if Louisiana people even drank coffee," she said as she headed for the kitchen.

Later, as all were seated in the parlor, Mrs. Andersen asked, "Was coffee hard to obtain during the late war, Mr. Barry?"

Jethro's guard went up. "I was too young to drink coffee then, ma'am," he said, trying to sound congenial; wanting to overcome the barrier Nora's mother, for some reason, seemed bent on raising.

"How long will you be in St. Paul, Mr. Barry?" Nora asked. Jethro turned to the daughter, wondering if the girl was trying to offset the awkwardness created by her mother's apparent hostility. "I'm really not sure, Miss Andersen. Joe, my manager—and friend—says we'll stay here until I heal. A month, perhaps. Maybe less. Your Minnesota Norwegians are hard on outsiders.

Nora laughed.

"I gather from the papers, Mr. Barry," said Mrs. Andersen, "that you are dissatisfied with the way the referee handled your prizefight here." When he did not respond, she added, "I gather, in some way, you feel you were cheated."

"Mother!"

"May I ask where you gathered that from, ma'am?"

"The *Pioneer Press*, I believe."

"I think you may be mistaken, ma'am," he said, trying to smile pleasantly. "I've carefully read each St. Paul paper since the fight and have seen nothing that indicated either my manager or I was displeased with the refereeing. I have, however, noted several instances where folks from St. Paul who attended the fight decried the, ah, quality of the official's performance."

Mrs. Andersen waved her hand as if at trifles. "I stand corrected."

"Where will you go from here?" Nora asked, blushing at her mother's rudeness.

"I'm really not sure. Although I do know we'll go east. Joe sent a couple of telegrams and I suppose our destination depends on their replies."

"You do not sound to have a Louisiana accent, Mr. Barry," the older woman interrupted.

"No?"

"No. As a matter of fact, you hardly sound like a southerner at all."

Jethro Spring drained his cup before replying, "I never said I was, Mrs. Andersen." He set the cup and saucer on a nearby table and stood. "Miss Andersen—Nora—good night."

Nora walked him to the door. "I'm sorry, Mr. Barry," she said softly as they stepped onto the porch.

"Sorry for what? The coffee was a wonderful gesture on your part. Thank you, and good night again."

"Good night, Kid."

The young man's retreating footfalls sounded hollow on the boardwalk.

Jethro Spring stumbled into Joe Barry's room later that same evening, a little drunk and a lot more angry. "Did you cancel Davenport and Peoria?" he demanded.

"Huh? Is that you, laddie? Is something wrong?" Joe vaulted from bed, pawing sleep from his eyes.

"Davenport and Peoria. Did you cancel those fights?"

"Are ye daft, lad? Comin' in here in the middle of the

night ..."

"Dammit, Joe. Did you cancel Davenport and Peoria?"

"I sent telegrams canceling them two days ago. Why?"

"Well, send two more uncanceling the cancellations."

"Are ye mad? You're not ready. We'd bare get there in time."

"Do it anyway."

Joe Barry scratched a match to light the lamp. After it flared and he'd adjusted its flame, he studied Jethro. He leaned forward and sniffed, wrinkled his nose and twisted away. "Rotgut," he said in dismay. "Potato whiskey. From the time o' the famine, it smells as if. What's become o' ye, lad?"

"I wanta fight. And I wanta do it now."

Joe stared at his young protege. "Well, if it's fight now ye must, it looks like it'll be wi' me."

"I wanta fight the Dutchman in Davenport. Or is it Peoria?"

"What, may I ask, is the reason for the sudden change of heart?"

"I don't have to have a reason."

"You do wi' me, lad. I'm still ye manager."

"Then I'll fire you."

"You'll think different when ye sober up," Joe said.

"I'm not drunk."

"What is it then, lad?"

"I just want to get the hell out of St. Paul."

Joe studied the young fighter for a long time before nodding. "Faith and it's a woman, for naught else could twist a man so quick."

"Yeah," Jethro replied, his tone grim. "It's a woman. Two of 'em. And one of 'em hates Indians." He ran his hand over his face. "And if you don't wanta foul your barley breakfast, you'll get us both to Davenport."

Joe pulled the room's only chair away from a small table. "Here, laddie, sit down." When Jethro slumped into the seat, Joe stood before him, arms crossed. "Now, number one," he said, "you're far from proper healed from the Johnson fight. Two, you've done no training whatever for a week …"

"Four days."

"Three, the Dutchman is tough. The man knocked Sailor Dan down three times before the Sailor put him out for the count. But, come to think on it, you'd not meet the Dutchman until Peoria."

"I don't care, Joe. I want to get out of here. I'm okay. You'll see. I'll start my roadwork right now. Go hire a hack for yourself and follow. You'll see I'm okay."

Joe leaned toward his young friend. "Tell you what, laddie. Why don't we both go to bed just now? We'll talk about it in the mornin'. If the idea holds up under the bare light o' day and ye still want to do it, then we'll talk of it. All right?"

"Okay, Joe. But I'm warning you—I still want to get the hell out of here. And I want to fight. You're damned right I do."

CHAPTER EIGHT

The Dutchman must be older than when he fought Sailor Dan, Joe."

"No, lad," Joe Barry said, chalking a small cut on the Jethro's cheek. "'Tis not that the Dutchman is too old or too slow, but that Kid Barry is raving mad. The poor man in Davenport hardly had time to say hello; now this thrashin' to poor Dutch Mueller. Laddie, you've come possessed."

Jethro laughed.

Joe took his fighter's face between both big freckled hands. "But you're takin' chances. Do ye hear? And the Dutchman is the one who can make ye rue that day. Do ye hear?"

"I hear, Joe." Then he leaped to his feet, saying, "There's the bell."

Jethro headed for ring center, Joe's words following him: "Mind his left, laddie. He's a natural left one." Joe's words continued to follow: "Keep moving left. Stay away from the Dutchman's left!"

Perversely, he went right, into the Dutchman's strength, into a slugging match—his right against the other man's left. He and Joe helped carry the unconscious Dutchman from the ring shortly thereafter.

Columbus and Cleveland. Youngstown and Wheeling, Pittsburgh and Buffalo....

"Is Sailor Dan avoiding us, Joe?" Jethro asked as he watched a late November rain slant against their Norfolk hotel room window.

"Aye, lad. That he is. He still wants a rematch wi' Tommy Tucker. But the Tommy'll have naught to do wi' him wi'out he first comes through us."

"How about Davis, then?"

"Davis will come south if the price is right, lad. But so will Grimes. And I'd rather have the Sailor man, wouldn't you?"

"I just wanta fight, dammit. This rain is getting to me. How many more postponements will there be?"

"'Tis me fault, lad. With winter comin' on, I should never have scheduled a fight this far north." Joe shoved his hands into his trousers. His expression was morose as he joined Jethro by the window.

"Let's get out of here," Jethro said. "Let's head some-place where the sun shines and the local sheriff is a prize-fight fan."

"Offers we have, lad. I'll send some telegrams today. But 'tis for New Orleans we should be headin' way to. New Orleans, our home town. New Orleans and Sailor Dan Grimes. Or maybe Nabob Davis, if we can't get

Grimes. What do ye say?"

"I say whatever you say, Joe. You're the boss."

Savannah and Jacksonville, Atlanta and Birmingham, Chattanooga and Jackson....

———•◦•———

Nabob Davis frowned from across the ring, his surly scowl an obvious attempt to intimidate Jethro. Davis raised his right fist in salute at his introduction, but was met only with boos and catcalls from the partisan New Orleans crowd. Then it was "KID BARRY—THE BAYOU BUL-LET!" and all hell broke loose!

Jethro danced on his toes to the center of the ring, rais-ing both arms to whistles and screams and hats tossed high in the air. He smiled at Nabob Davis—it was a friendly, knowing smile. The Nabob's scowl deepened.

The two fighters toed scratch. One hour and forty-one savage minutes later, Nabob Davis sank to the canvas, oblivious to the surrounding bedlam. And Bourbon Street hosted a wild celebration that night.

Jethro missed the fete, spending the night wrapped in wet towels and holding ice bags against his throbbing head.

Joe wandered in at daybreak, much the worse for wear. He sat at the foot of Jethro's bed, feebly waving a telegram. "Sailor Dan," he croaked. "He'll fight."

"When?" Jethro asked, clutching an ice bag to his swelled right hand.

"He wants it in April, laddie. Likely you'll be healed by then."

"Where?"

"That I don't like. He says Fort Worth. He says the city fathers there have made us a princely offer. I'll try for

New Orleans, lad, but I know he'll not agree to ye home-town."

"Let me rest in peace, Joe. Do what you have to. But God, I don't want to think about fighting for a couple of days."

A weary Joe Barry stood. "Aye, lad. Ye talk good sense. 'Tis rest old Joe Barry needs, too. Sailor Dan Grimes can wait."

———•+•———

"He insists on Fort Worth, laddie," Joe said two days later. "He's thrown out every reason under the sun, all the way from his sainted mother watchin' the fight, clear up to them heathens opening up the Texas National Banks to guarantee our purses."

"I didn't know he was from Texas."

Joe snorted in disgust. "The man's from Bangor, Maine, laddie. But if you're gullible enough, Sailor Dan would have ye believe anything."

"What's the purse, Joe?"

"'Tis good, lad. Better even than this last New Orleans purse. And that was ye best yet."

"How about the split?"

"Not quite so good. He wants two-thirds, one-third. Winner-loser."

"Sailor Dan is figuring on winning this fight."

"No, lad, he isn't. Sailor Dan isn't even plannin' on the fight takin' place. That's the reason for Fort Worth. He's countin' on it bein' stopped. Sailor Dan still wants Tommy Tucker."

"I don't understand," Jethro said. "Why even go to the trouble then?"

"Because he cannot sidestep ye any longer, lad. When

ye laid out Nabob Davis, ye made yourself too big to push aside. Now he's for fearin' if he don't face you, Tommy'll bypass him and give you a title shot. So he ties ye up wi' a fight that'll never come off. And he makes it a big purse for the winner so it'll look like he's sure he'll win. No, laddie buck, I fear 'tis a slick plan. And who knows? It might yet work."

"What do we do?"

"Take it, lad," Joe said, spreading his hands in resignation. "What else can we do?"

"I don't understand. If you say there's not going to be a fight ..."

"We don't know that for certain. Nor can we prove it. If we try to duck the fight, though, Sailor Dan would surely go to Tucker and tell him we won't fight. Then Tucker'll give the title fight to the Sailor. No. We must accept."

"Perhaps we can by-pass him and get a title fight from Tucker ourselves?"

"I tried that," Joe growled. "Tucker says he'll fight neither man 'til we prove who's best between us."

"Then it's damned if we do and damned if we don't."

"Faith and it looks that way, laddie."

––––––––

It was clear from the placards and bunting spread about Fort Worth, that April 19, 1875, was to be a day closely akin to Independence Day or Sam Houston's birthday. Leaflets proclaiming the coming middleweight championship elimination bout were passed to boarders of the Texas & Pacific train at Texarkana, including Joe Barry and the rising fighter known as the Bayou Bullet. Kid Barry and his manager detrained at Fort Worth two days before the big day, to a blaring band and a chubby mayor and several of his councilmen. Pompous welcoming speeches followed.

"There's talk," Joe later said while accepting a glass of Puerto Rican rum, "that Texas will not let the fight go on."

"Rumor, sir. Mere rumor," the mayor said, tugging nervously at his lapels. "Fort Worth has gone to a lot of trouble promoting this, the greatest of all sporting events in Texas history."

"That I can see," Joe said. "Surely the governor, even, and all his underlings, know there's to be an illegal prizefight in Fort Worth. How could the man miss the date?"

"It's been a great promotional effort for a newly incorporated city," piped up a dark little haberdasher. "Already people have arrived from as far as Abilene and Waco."

"And I suppose Dan Grimes helped ye wi' all the hoopla?"

"Not Grimes himself, of course," the mayor said, "but Mr. Facing, Grimes's manager. He was most helpful."

Joe Barry's blue eyes caught Jethro's with an I-told-you-so look. "How long has Grimes and the man Facing been here?"

"Oh, three weeks at least," a tall, thin saloonkeeper replied.

"Grimes has attracted considerable attention with his workout," the mayor added. "We here in Fort Worth have been a little disappointed the Bayou Bullet did not arrive earlier. Good for the town, you know." The mayor winked at Jethro.

"Do ye have any guarantee the fight will come off?" Joe asked.

"I don't understand."

"How do ye know it'll come off? That it won't be stopped by Texas law?"

"Well, Mr. Grimes and Mr. Facing assured us …"

"We had our purse impounded in Galveston," Joe cut in. "How do we know that won't happen here?"

"Well," the mayor said, "some things have to be taken on faith, Mr. Barry."

"Aye," Joe growled, "'tis a lot I take on faith. But faith in Texas and Texas prizefighting is not one I share wi' you. When me man works out later today, I'll be down to your office to talk wi' ye about guarantees. Now if you gentlemen would be kind enough to excuse us, the Kid and me need to rest a bit. The train was terrible hot and dusty."

"Yes, yes," murmured the mayor and his minions. "Yes of course. Perhaps we should remind you of tonight's banquet."

"You'll see me before then, your honor," Joe said.

As Joe and Jethro walked into their sparsely furnished hotel room, the manager kicked a flimsy cane chair across the bare oak floor. "Just as we reckoned, lad. 'Tis a put-up deal by Grimes."

"How can that be, Joe? These people must be acting in good faith. They've put lots of time and money into publicity for the fight. Surely you're not suggesting they're planning to lose it on purpose."

"Bah!" Joe roared. "Think, man, think. What'll they lose? Ye heard them say that people are arriving already from the outlying districts—which is all they want. If there's no fight, those same ones who visit will spend just as much money as if there was a fight."

"The gate," Jethro said. "They lose the gate."

"But they'll pay no purse, damn the Holy Christ! Is that head only stuck on ye shoulders for a punching bag? Likely the gate would not meet the purse anyway."

When Jethro said nothing, Joe continued, "Sure and 'tis, Grimes and his oily manager pointed all that out to them city fathers. Sure and 'tis, he told them they cannot lose, fight or no fight. No doubt they bought it hook, line, and sinker. And probably gave him a guarantee to boot."

"We don't know there'll be no fight, Joe. It sure looks like it will come off now."

"And that's where they've got us, lad. We must go on just like there will be. And the city fathers o' Fort Worth will go on smilin' and rakin' in their money. And Sailor Dan and that slimy Perley Facing will go on smilin' and wavin' to the oglers like they're the finest heroes in all the land. But mark me word, lad, either the fight will be shut down, or Grimes will come to us beforehand and tell us the purses will be impounded. He'll want us to go together and refuse to fight unless we're guaranteed purses in another state's bank."

"And that, Fort Worth will never agree to do," Jethro said.

"And that they'll never do."

———•◦•———

"I'm afraid I have some horseshit news for all of us," Perley Facing said as he and Sailor Dan Grimes stepped into Joe Barry's hotel room. It was the evening before their big fight.

"Faith and what could that be?" Joe asked.

"Texas authorities intend to stop our fight."

Joe stared at Jethro for a moment, then turned to Grimes's manager. "No!" the Irishman said.

Facing nodded solemnly.

Jethro studied the squat bullet-headed Sailor Dan, who stood just inside the door. One of Grimes's ears was cauliflowered and the crooked hump on his nose testified to its having been broken at least once. Scar tissue was thick over both eyes. But those eyes were sharp and clear and at the moment engaged in appraising the man he knew as Kid Barry.

"Where, might I ask," Joe said to Facing, "could you possibly have heard such an ugly rumor?"

"A bird told us that McNelly—that's the Captain of the goddamned Texas Rangers—debarked from the train a few minutes ago. Same bird says there are others in town, too. Looks like the fight won't come off."

"A terrible thing. What will we do?"

"Well, it seems goddamned logical to the Sailor and me that we can't hold the fight under these conditions."

Sensing Joe's growing anger, Jethro interrupted, "It doesn't seem that way to me."

Perley Facing snarled, "There will be no fight, I told you."

"How do you know?

"Those rangers ..."

"... May be here to see the fight."

Facing rolled his eyes. "My, my, Joe has kept you sheltered, hasn't he?"

"What do you think we should do?" Joe asked.

"Cancel the fight," Facing said. "Cancel the goddamned thing and try to reschedule someplace else as soon as possible."

"And where might that be?" Joe asked. "Nor when?"

"We'd have to get together on the details, but they can be worked out. That's not nearly as important as the shit that's ahead of us here in Fort Worth."

"I'm not canceling," Jethro said. "And neither are you. As far as I'm concerned, the fight will go on."

"Mr. Barry," Perley Facing said to Joe, "your principal obviously can't understand the urgency of this matter."

"Aye. I can do little wi' the lad meself," Joe murmured.

"Then I suggest you and I repair to my room and work out the details of what it is we're going to do."

"Oh, I could not do that," Joe said, grinning at Facing's shocked surprise.

"Why, for God's sake?"

Joe waved his hand in Jethro's direction. "Faith and didn't ye hear the lad? He says he's going to fight. We can hardly cancel if yon lad stands ready to fight, now can we?"

"You're both crazy, for God's sake! Does your ears flap over? I said Texas Rangers will stop the goddamn fight."

"Not necessarily, Mr. Facing," Jethro said. "I fought in Galveston last year and all they did was impound the purse after the fight."

"Well, I ain't fightin' for nothin'," Sailor Dan blurted.

"I will, gentlemen," Jethro murmured. "And no matter what happens, I'll be next in line for Tommy Tucker. If you're there, I'll win in the ring. If you're not there, I'll win by default. No matter what happens, I get Tucker."

Sailor Dan straightened from his slouch. "Like hell you will!"

"I must inform you," Perley Facing said, interrupting the strained silence following Sailor Dan's outburst, "neither me nor my principal will be at the goddamned prize ring tomorrow."

"And I must inform you, Mr. Facing," Jethro replied, "that both Joe Barry and I will be in the ring at ten tomorrow morning. If Sailor Dan does not show up and authorities permit the fight to proceed, we'll charge you and Grimes with default." He turned his attention to Sailor Dan. "And I hope, mister, if you got any guts, that you're there, too."

Sailor Dan blanched. He took a step forward, then laughed. "I'll be there, sonny. Just make sure your getaway is clear."

Impulsively, Jethro Spring thrust out his hand. Sailor Dan reached for it hesitantly, then said, "May the best man win—sonny."

Jethro grinned. "I will," he said.

———•————

Joe Barry walked into the hotel room to find Jethro stripped to the waist, already in his fighting tights, a towel draped over his shoulders.

"Anything yet, Joe?"

"No, lad. It looks as though they may let the fight go on. That means the purse. Are ye sure ye want to fight this one for naught?"

Jethro bobbed his head. "For me, for you, for Sailor Dan. For the people outside. Otherwise, Facing will keep us on a string."

"'Tis not bad reasoning, lad." Joe pulled out his watch and made a show of peering at it. "Well, laddie buck—let's wander down. We'll soon know will they stop it."

On their way to the stockyard ring, Jethro asked, "If the Fort Worth fathers were behind this scheme, wouldn't the time to stop the fight come just as it gets under way? That way they'd have the gate, too, without having to pay any purses?"

"Well, lad, we'll soon know."

Striding into the stockyards, Jethro noted that the huge crowd was oddly quiet, as though apprehensive. He saw nothing but faces: a sunburned little man in a ten gallon hat, a Mexican smoothing a slender, pointed moustache. To Jethro's surprise, several bonnets were sprinkled among the predominantly low-crowned hats of what he supposed were cattlemen and farmers, railroaders and shopkeepers, freighters and bookkeepers.

A roar erupted and Jethro knew that Sailor Dan Grimes was wending his way through the crowd. From the reception, Dan the Sailor Man was the crowd's favorite.

Jethro shrugged and let his gaze wander around ringside. He saw the mayor and his entourage. The mayor stared at Jethro, a glint of amusement in his eyes.

Sailor Dan climbed into the ring, followed by his manager. Perley Facing exchanged winks with the mayor.

The crowd met the introduction of Sailor Dan Grimes' with a lusty roar. But applause almost as hearty greeted the name Kid Barry. The fighters and their seconds were called to the ring's center to hear an explanation of the revised London Prize Ring Rules. Just as the referee concluded, a murmur ran through the crowd.

Joe, staring beyond Jethro, muttered, "Holy Mother, that's it."

"What is it, Joe?"

"'Tis over, lad. Yonder comes a ranger, his star shinin' so bright it hurts me eye. Sure and we know what that means."

"Well, Indian," said Perley Facing, glaring at Jethro, "better luck next time on your aspirations to great whiteness."

Jethro felt the ring lurch as someone else climbed up. "All right, what's goin' on here?"

Jethro whirled at the sound of a voice he would never in a thousand years forget. Texas Ranger Jeff Cole stood spraddle-legged in the ring, a smile flirting at his mouth corners.

Before anyone else in the ring could speak, Perley Facing said, "Officer, we were about to hold an illegal prize fight, but you're obviously here to prevent it—and rightly so, I might add. Therefore, let me assure you that my principal and I have every intention of obeying your instructions to the letter." Facing's hand gestured toward Joe and Jethro. "I cannot, however, vouchsafe for the intentions of our would-be antagonists."

Cole stared at Facing until the manager's face flushed. Then he turned to the referee and asked, "What'd the mouthy one say?"

"He said if you stopped the fight, they'd go along with it."

"Stop the fight?" Jeff asked. "Why?"

"Isn't that why you're here?" Facing blurted.

"Hell no. Why should I stop it? I bet on it. What I want to know, is if this here is London Prize Ring Rules, or them sissified Marquis of Queensbury regulations?"

"You're joking!"

The ranger thumped Sailor Dan's manager in the chest with an index finger. "You had your chance awhile ago, fella," Jeff said. "You rattled on for so long I didn't snare the hang of half of it. Why don't you let somebody else at the trough?"

Perley Facing's mouth snapped shut and he turned to Sailor Dan's corner, his face crimson. He looked toward the mayor who'd half-risen from his seat. Facing pointed at the ranger, then shrugged his shoulders helplessly and did a little circle with his right index finger pointed skyward. The mayor dropped his face into his hands.

The Texas Ranger turned to grin at Jethro. The young man returned the smile and said, "London Prize Ring, sir, to answer your question."

"Thank you, boy. I'm shore Captain McNelly will be pleased with that. He calls them new rules kid stuff."

"I hope you enjoy the fight, sir," Jethro said.

"I'm sure I will, boy. I been a-lookin' forward to it ever since I saw you fight in Shreveport last year."

The crowd roared as people realized the big ranger was permitting the fight to proceed. Jethro led a dazed Joe Barry from ring center and the two fighters toed scratch.

Shortly after the fight began, Jethro knew Sailor Dan Grimes's reputation was not overrated. The stocky man moved with an erratic rhythm that indicated tirelessness. His short stature and bent stance made him a difficult target—except for his bullet head.

Jethro moved at long range, nimbly circling his opponent, slashing at him with left and right jabs. He felt Sailor Dan sizing him, measuring him. Five minutes into the fight, Sailor Dan drifted to the offense, ignoring Jethro's stinging jabs, moving to cut him off from his steady circling. Gradually the older man forced the younger one back to the ropes. There, Sailor Dan moved swiftly inside and hammered several punishing body blows to Jethro's midsection. Jethro tied up Sailor Dan and in the clench, the man's head hammered against Jethro's jaw. That's when the lesson learned in St. Paul from Valkyrie Johnson was put into practice as Jethro rabbit-punched Sailor Dan twice behind his neck, and the squat man broke the clinch, snarling.

The round wore on, give and take, one fighter on offense, then the other. Jethro realized his style was more open, more picturesque, and he sensed the subtle mood of the crowd changing to favor him. But he also knew Sailor Dan's style wasted no energy and, in the long run, would be less draining. Therefore he wasn't surprised when a series of Grimes' body punches took him to one knee thirty minutes into the fight.

Sailor Dan smiled wickedly down at him, then spun on his heel and stalked to his corner.

"Any advice, Joe?" Jethro asked as his manager worked over him.

"None I can think on, lad. He leads well wi' his face, but he's near unbeatable there."

"Now we know why his face looks like it's been run over by a four-horse hitch."

"Aye. He's in condition, too. He's hardly worked up a sweat."

"I noticed."

"I think ye give as good as ye got in the clinches, lad. You don't look none the worse for wear, neither. He hasn't hurt ye."

"No, but he's conserving himself better than I am."

"Just remember. He can be put down. Dutch Mueller done it three times."

The bell rang and Jethro moved toward the squat Sailor Dan Grimes....

The round lasted nearly forty minutes before Sailor Dan staggered from an elbow to his jaw in a clench and went to one knee. The referee shook his finger at Jethro in warning.

"He's wearing me down, Joe. How can he do that and me ten years younger?"

Joe shook his head, plainly worried.

Sailor Dan peeked from between his fists at the bell and moved to the attack. Jethro bounced two long-range lefts off the Sailor man's cauliflower ear. Nothing seemed to daunt the hunter's inexorable advance. He jolted Jethro with a left hook and took a straight right to his head, boring in. Two more hooks, then an earth-shaking uppercut from nowhere and Jethro's shoulders bounced on the canvas. The younger man sat up stupidly and saw Joe hurrying to help.

Jethro scrambled up, shaking his head to clear it, waving Joe back to the corner. "Sonofabitch, Joe. He perfects that one and we're in trouble!" The pounding in the young fighter's ears caused him to shout to hear himself.

"Run, lad. Ye'd best run til ye get your wits about ye. He'll be after ye for the kill."

Sailor Dan rushed to the attack amid a bedlam-roar from the crowd. Jethro used his utmost skills in flight. But this was a game Sailor Dan had played often and the man moved up on his toes, continually cutting off Jethro's gliding retreat. The Sailor Man bulled in each time he trapped his opponent near the ropes, oblivious to any punishment Jethro inflicted to his head and face, ramming close hooks and uppercuts to his younger quarry at will. Again Jethro went down, this time partially through the ring ropes. Grimes paused to stare at Jethro a moment, his ugly, scar-tissued face a mask. Then he was gone.

Joe was near tears as Jethro returned to his corner. "Don't worry, Joe," the battered fighter said. "I know now how we'll beat the bastard."

When the bell rang, Jethro stayed at long range, flicking jabs and using his footwork until Sailor Dan backed him against the ropes. Then he closed quickly when the Sailor Man charged to the attack, tying him up and wrestling around until the younger fighter had the ring at his back. After the break, he resumed his jab and weave, jab and weave. Now, however, the jabs didn't come straight from the shoulder with all his weight behind them, directed at nose or cheek or jaw. Instead, they were surgeon-like flicks with specialized targets: the Sailor Man's scarred eyebrows.

Seven minutes into round five, Sailor Dan punched Jethro down once more. Jethro lay like an exhausted pup, taking great gulps of air. But he was on his feet within twenty seconds and saw Perley Facing working furiously to close an ugly cut over Sailor Dan's right eye.

The older man charged to the attack, confident of victory. But the first blow of round six saw chalk and blood fly from the Sailor Man's right eyebrow. Cowboys and farmers and shopkeepers roared. Sailor Dan bored on and Jethro fled in nimble retreat, his fists beating a steady tatoo, now above the Sailor Man's left eye. Down went Jethro. But lying there, with Sailor Dan standing angrily above him and pawing blood from that right eye, Jethro actually smiled. There was a small cut beginning over the Sailor Man's left eye, too.

"You're gonna do it, laddie buck!" Joe Barry shouted in excitement. "If ye can take his punishment, you're gonna do it."

"Nothing to it, Joe," Jethro drawled through clenched teeth.

Sailor Dan brought a different approach to round seven. He advanced more upright, hands high, sheltering his fragile eyebrows. The men sparred at long range for awhile, until Jethro understood and slipped quickly inside to throw several body punches. Sailor Dan grunted and dropped his guard, bending to a crouch. Then it was back to long range and the flicking, damaging jabs. Within minutes, both eyebrows bled into the Sailor man's eyes and he pawed furiously to clear his vision. And there could be little doubt of the outcome.

Cautiously, Jethro began circling the squat Sailor Man, stalking him....

CHAPTER NINE

The bloody murderers!" Joe bellowed, bursting into the room. "The dirty, rotten, yellow-bellied, slimy, sons-of-a-mither snakes!"

Jethro wrenched up from his bed, groaning in pain. He winced when Joe slammed the door so hard it bounced open again. "Calm down, Joe. For God's sake, calm down."

"The double rotten whores of perdition. The back-stabbin', mother-cheatin', wee-child beating bastards of the wild isles."

"Joe, dammit …"

"The sanctimonious spoutin', finger grubbin', lip cheatin', sons-of-a-mither snakes!"

"You said that before." Jethro clapped both palms over his ears and groaned as he leaned forward to rest elbows on knees. "Who?"

"The tin-star totin' …"

"Rangers?"

The big Irishman subsided as suddenly as he'd begun, racking and skittering into a nearby chair. "Yes," he said, wiping a sleeve across his nose. "They impounded the gate."

"And that's the end of the world?"

"After the greatest comeback since Saint Patrick ridded snakes from the Emerald Isles, these slimy slitherers impounded our gate. How can you just sit there, lad, and watch your rightful-earned purse stoled by the thievingest bunch o' legal grafters with which the world was ever cursed?" The manager's voice was rising again!

"We knew it might happen, Joe. It's not the end of the world."

"Sure and no carpetbaggers crawled from Lincoln's tomb could match Texas Rangers for perfidy."

A voice floated in through the open doorway. "Yeah, this must be it." Jeff Cole filled the opening.

Jethro said, "Come in, Jeff. We were just talking about you."

"Somehow I got that idea."

Joe Barry leaped to his feet, still flushed with anger. Ranger Cole sauntered in, followed by a slight, stoop-shouldered, older man. "This here is Captain McNelly, boys. He wanted to meet y'all."

"If you've come to arrest us ..." Joe began, but Jethro cut him off. "I'm Kid Barry, Mr. McNelly." He reached out to shake hands, then waved at his manager. "This is Joe. Joe Barry. Joe, meet Texas Ranger Captain McNelly and an old friend of mine, Ranger Jeff Cole."

"Friend?" Joe said. "Uh, McNelly. Cole. Pleased it is I am to make your ..." He trailed off.

"Good to meet you, too, suh," Jeff said, an affable smile broadening his handlebar moustache. "Always a pleasure to meet a relative of young Kid Barry's."

Joe abruptly sat down on one of the room's two beds.

"A great fight, Kid," Captain McNelly said to Jethro.

"Thank you—although I must say there's not much pleasure in winning the way I did."

"No false modesty, son. It was a fine comeback."

"Sailor Dan Grimes is a good fighter," Jethro said. "Maybe even a great one. Forgive me, Jeff, won't you and the Captain have a chair?"

"A pleasure, boy." Jeff pulled out the two chairs and straddled his, resting both arms across the back.

Joe suddenly flared, "We are given to understand—the laddie and me—that you've impounded our purse!"

"Glad you brought that up, Mr. Barry," Captain McNelly said, smiling. "I have a bankdraft here for your winner's two-thirds tally, as per the agreement. Less, of course, a suitable fine for conducting business of an illegal nature in the sovereign state of Texas. McNelly handed the draft to Joe, who looked at it stupidly.

Jeff grinned. "We won on your fight, boy. I'm takin' home a hundred, and the cap'n here, I believe, bet a little more, as befits his higher pay scale."

McNelly nodded.

"And now, if y'all won't think it amiss, we brought a bottle of Texas' finest to toast the occasion." Jeff pulled a pint flask from beneath his shirt and waved it. Joe hastened to the cupboard for glasses and Jethro, his steps slow and painful, shuffled to the door and closed it.

Ranger Cole raised his glass high. "To the next middleweight champion of the whole world and Texas."

"I'll drink to that," said McNelly.

"Hear, hear," said Joe Barry, blanching and sputtering as he tossed off a big mouthful of "Texas' finest."

Jethro sipped his whiskey. "Why are you fellows doing

this?"

"Well," Jeff began.

"Let me," McNelly interrupted. "It stunk, that's why. First off, we get our initial report of an illegal prizefight from a man named Perley Facing."

Joe and Jethro exchanged glances.

"Then when we got here, we learned that Facing happened to be one of the men arranging the fight. Wouldn't you say that stunk?"

Joe nodded.

"We talked to some of the Fort Worth crowd and discovered that town fathers didn't seem to care whether the fight came off or not. So we figured out just who was liable to be hurt by what looked more and more like a swindle."

Joe ventured another sip. A coughing fit overtook him and McNelly pounded him on the back before continuing.

"Way we calculated, the folks comin' for the fight was the big losers, and most of 'em was already here. The other loser would have to be one of the fighters. Well now, since one fighter had already called in the dogs, we figured the loser had to be the other fighter—you.

"Then last night, we get an anonymous note under our door. The note said Grimes was willing to cooperate in observing the law of the land ..." The Captain paused to sip from his glass.

"Go on," Jethro prompted.

"Well, mister," McNelly said, eyes narrowing, "I don't like to be part of a swindle. I don't like to see a bunch of barefoot farmers or down-at-the-heels cowpokes beat out of the paltry savings they'd put aside for a big day like this."

Joe coughed again and looked into his empty glass.

"And I don't like to see someone cheat an honest fighter who's giving an honest effort to climb the ladder of success—be it nominally illegal. So what do we do? Well, Jeff and I kicked it around some and decided the best way we could throw a knot in their rope was to let the fight go on. We couldn't do that legally, though, unless we had the court's approval."

Jethro said, "There's a hell of lot to this."

"Luckily for all of us, Judge Gavin is a close personal friend—and a closet supporter of classical pugilism. The Judge and I worked out an equitable system of fines so me and the boys could let the fight go on."

"If I ever say a mean thing about ye, Major, I'll cut me tongue out," Joe said solemnly.

"You may be interested in knowing that Judge Gavin, in his infinite wisdom, saw fit to fine the fight's instigators somewhat more than he did you people, whom he considers innocent victims."

Joe cleared his throat. "Pure as the driven snow, General."

"The city fathers of Fort Worth, who Judge Gavin felt were most guilty of intent to swindle friends and neighbors, received the heaviest fine of all."

Jethro switched his gaze from the Captain to Ranger Cole. "I think I like Texas justice," he said.

"You look some diff'rent from the ragged scarecrow I first laid eyes to, up in the Nations." Jeff Cole dabbed at his moustache with a napkin and reached for his coffee cup.

Jethro Spring trailed a fork through his scrambled eggs. "I suppose I feel different, too. The day after a big fight is always the worst."

"You've filled out one hell of a lot. Look like a fella

that's walked around some in the world. Broad shoulders. More confidence. A little moustache might help."

Jethro nodded thoughtfully. He glanced around at the near-empty cafe. "You think they're still looking?"

"They'll never quit, boy. That was back in '72, but your name is still on Post Office walls and telegraph poles. Once a man is wanted, he's always wanted. Y'all best figure it that way."

Jethro sighed.

"Something you ought to know, boy—they tracked you to me. Army bloodhound named Bleeman, it was. Talked to the ferryman up at Ewing Camp, and to some townsfolk over to Paris. Said he knew I brought a half-breed kid down from the Nations and wanted to know what I done with him.

"I told him it wasn't you. Said the one I had was a Mex wanted fo' horse stealin' down to San Antone. Told him the Mex got away on me before we hit Commerce; that I followed him west afore I lost his tracks in a live oak thicket."

"Did he believe you?" Jethro asked, staring at his plate.

"Don't rightly think so. But wasn't a whole hell of a lot he could do about it with McNelly backing me. Leastways we ain't heard from him since. And you must not, neither, for you ain't a-hidin' much these days."

"What did he look like, Jeff?"

"Mean. Not tall, but square built. One side of his face was bad scarred—been burned. Pretty sharp hound, though. Asked all the right questions in all the right ways. But..." The ranger's voice trailed off.

"But what, Jeff?"

"He's been gone for near three years now. The search for you ain't active—been too long. But you can't figure like that. You could run face to face into a blue-belly you spent Army time with and the next day the hounds would be on your trail again."

"Not a bright picture, is it Jeff?"

The big man grinned. "It's a hell of a lot better than it was three years ago. You got a new name, good cover, enough money to spend. You got a good friend and a trade that's in demand. I'd say you made the best o' your chances, boy, and I'm feelin' real good about you."

"Thanks, Jeff. I still haven't forgotten that I owe you. I'd pay you back right now if I thought you'd take it."

"You already did, boy. Like I said, I won a hundred on the fight. And seein' you turn out all right is more than enough int'rest."

The waiter, a one-time cowboy who'd been crippled by an outlaw horse, brought more coffee. His hand shook, spilling dribbles from the pot across the table. "Anything else, gents?"

"No, this is fine," Jethro said.

"Shore thing, Mr. Barry," the man said. "Say, that was some lollapaloozer of a fight. Think you could do it again?"

"Not today, I couldn't. Today my warts have bruises on 'em." The cowboy moved away, cackling.

"Still got the gun?" Jeff asked.

"In a suitcase."

"Strange place for it, don't you think?"

"I haven't worn it in a couple of years. Actually I'm hoping I never have to wear it again. You see, I made up my mind never to use it about the time I near killed somebody over a barroom brawl."

Jeff's smile faded. "A fool's wish, boy. Come time you need it, likely you'll not have time to dig it out of no cardboard suitcase."

Jethro grinned. "That's one thing about being a prizefighter, Jeff. Nobody dares force me to a gun. Would you like it back? I could get it for you."

The ranger's gaze was unyielding. "You keep it, boy. Who knows, your luck might hold and you might get a chance to dig for it afore all hell breaks on you."

Jethro turned to stare out the window. A farm wagon pulled by a horse and a mule, lumbered up the street. The wagon carried several sacks of seed grain. "He's late for planting," Jethro murmured. A woman, features shadowed by her bonnet, sat beside the sunburned driver. Two young towheaded boys trailed bare feet from the tailgate. Jethro wondered how it'd be to have a farm. A home. A wife and children. Then he wondered about the oddity of a wagonload of seed grain rumbling by on a Sunday morning.

Jeff sipped his coffee quietly, as though aware of his friend's thoughts.

Shaking himself from his reverie, Jethro said, "So McNelly knows?"

"He's fair," Jeff said, as if no further explanation was needed.

"Anyone else, besides your folks?"

The officer stretched lazily and shook his head. Then he asked, "Where will you go from here?"

Jethro shrugged. "Joe says we stay here for a few days while I rest. He's busy with telegrams now. I guess we'll go where Tucker wants us to go. He's the champion."

The lawman pushed back his chair and came gracefully to his feet. Awkward with soreness, Jethro rose with his friend. Jeff held out his hand. "I gotta get back to business, boy."

Jethro grasped the outstretched hand and squeezed. "Take care, Jeff," he said, tears springing to his eyes.

"You'll do all right, boy," the big man said, still holding the hand. He smiled, then sobered. "Just don't bury your gun too far, hear?"

Jethro nodded, swallowing. Then the ranger was gone, boot heels thumping down the plank sidewalk. *I forgot to tell him I learned to use it,* Jethro thought.

"Anything else, Mr. Barry?" It was the lame cowpuncher, wiping his hands on a flour sack.

"No thanks," Jethro replied. "How much do I owe?"

"Comes to fifty cents for the both of you. Say, I hope I get to see you fight again."

Jethro tossed a silver dollar on the table. "Keep the change," he said, and headed for the door.

Outside, Jethro thrust hands into his pockets and ambled down Fort Worth's main street. He breathed deeply of the smells: lilacs, sweet and overpowering; bluebonnets, faint but distinct. There was the pungent smell of the stockyards, and the clean, hot, dusty smell of spring in the Texas hill country. Jethro decided he liked cowtowns better than factory towns or river towns. He watched a cowboy go by on a snorty bronc and smiled despite his melancholy. He walked on at peace in the Sunday morning of the sleepy Texas village. A leather-topped, two-seater cabriolet pulled by matching blood bays rolled past. The two couples it carried were dressed in their Sunday best. Lacking anything better to do, Jethro followed the carriage.

There were several buggies and wagons parked beneath the shade of huge cottonwoods. Saddlehorses and buggy horses and dray horses stood about, lazily switching tails at lethargic mid-morning flies. A stream of scrubbed and polished families trickled to a large whitewashed board-and-batten building. A sign proclaimed:

TARRANT COUNTY FIRST BAPTIST CHURCH WELCOME STRANGER!

Organ music wafted from within. Jethro stood in the shade, chewing on a matchstick, listening. At last he threw away his matchstick and followed the last straggler inside.

He found an empty spot on a back row bench. A rail of a man spoke from the front as parishioners thumbed through hymnals. Someone shoved an open hymnal at him, but he took the book and passed it to an ample lady on his right. She waved a hymnal she already held, but he insisted, so she took it and rested it beside her, staring oddly at him. Several chords were struck on the organ, then its music burst forth. So did the raucous voices of the congregation. Jethro tilted his head back, eyes on the ceiling, listening to the music.

It stopped. The rail thin man behind the pulpit intoned, "Brothers and sisters, shall we pray?" The congregation's heads bent as one and the minister's booming voice filled the chapel. Jethro used the time to try to locate the organ. He had the pipes right away, but no organ. The minister concluded with an "Amen," followed by, "Let's see—how about page two-fourteen?" Another hymnal was thrust upon Jethro and he again passed it on to the matron on his right. She looked confused.

"Shall we stand?" the minister said, holding out his hands. The congregation rose as a single body. Jethro remained seated. The organ began again and he was annoyed that parishioners now blocked his search for the instrument. So he stood. The matron to his right had an annoying hound-dog wail. He cast her a pained look and she sniffed and turned her ample posterior toward him. Then he had it—the organ must be behind a lattice at the rear of the pulpit. Yes, there was the suggestion of movement—it had to be.

With the song concluded, the people took their seats. A review of coming events followed. Another song. A solo by a screeching, skinny woman whose voice resembled the sound of a cat clawing at a schoolroom blackboard. Then another song, for which the congregation again stood. This time, Jethro chose to sit it out, slouched in his seat, hands in pockets, shutting out all but the organ's lovely chords.

Then came the fire and brimstone. The preacher worked himself into a proper lather and Jethro was drifting off when the man next to him jabbed him awake with an elbow. It was a prizefighter's reflex that caused him to give elbow for elbow, and judging from the man's gasp of surprised pain, Jethro figured he'd not be bothered again.

He awoke when the organ began playing. A beatific smile spread across his bruised face. The preacher was still speaking, but it was a heart-rending plea, delivered over softened music from the organ. Two folks stumbled forward and then it was all over. The congregation stood and the preacher was talking to them neighbor-to-neighbor, inviting them all back again.

"And a special invitation to the next middleweight prizefighting champion of the world, who saw fit to join us today. Won't you raise your hand, Brother Barry?"

All eyes turned to Kid Barry. The red-faced prizefighter waved feebly. Then the organ began again and the congregation filed out. Jethro dropped into his seat to let them go. Several paused to say something, but hurried on when they saw the aquiline-faced man had his eyes closed as he concentrated on the music.

When it stopped, Jethro rose and headed for the door. The preacher cut him off, grabbing his hand to pump it. He confided that he'd watched yesterday's prizefight and had received considerable inspiration from the Kid's stirring comeback. He invited Kid Barry to return. Then Jethro was free, walking down the tree-lined street.

"In church!" Joe Barry exclaimed that evening in the hotel dining room. "Can ye imagine the insolence? Dortmann's telegram says Tommy Tucker's in church and can't be reached 'til Tuesday. The insolent farthing!"

Jethro shrugged, finished his liver and onions, and walked out into the soft April evening. Shoving his hands into his denim trousers, he started down the street, whistling tonelessly through his teeth.

Music flowed from the church. Jethro eased around the building in the darkness until he found a place where the organ music was more resonant and the garbled singing least. There he stayed, chewing on a matchstick, until the church service concluded.

The following morning, the young prizefighter jogged slowly along a country road. He stopped to chunk rocks, splashing a lazy turtle sunning itself on a riverbank, then began jogging again, staring wistfully at each farmstead he passed. He thought of the eight thousand dollars he had in a New Orleans bank and realized he had no idea of its real value, nor what kind of farm it would buy.

He came to the wagon ford across the Trinity River's Clear Fork and turned back, taking a different road. He began to test himself and felt better with each pounding footstep, running on and on. When the sun was at its highest, he turned to retrace his steps, jogging steadily now, sweat streaking his shirt and the churning crotch of his trousers. Hours later, he jogged through Fort Worth, heading for his hotel, passing the Tarrant County First Baptist Church. He stopped abruptly when he heard the music.

He pushed open the door and stepped inside. A flat

note was struck and he knew the organist had seen him. He moved to a back row bench, perching on its edge, conscious of dust and sweat streaking his face and clothes. He assumed the organist was practicing, but he became entranced, almost believing the music was meant for him alone.

It stopped. He heard a chair or a bench scraping on the floor and he came to his feet, heading for the door.

"You are an inspiration, Mr. Barry," the girl said as she stepped from behind her lattice.

Jethro gasped at her loveliness. "It was beautiful," he murmured so low she could not have heard across the room. Then more loudly, "Please forgive the intrusion."

"You did not intrude, sir. Not in the least. Instead, you inspired."

He took a step toward her. "Do you play often?"

"Only occasionally. When I feel I must."

There was an awkward silence. Jethro broke it by asking, "I don't suppose there's any way one could know when you must?"

She smiled—a radiant flash of beauty in an already lovely face. She stood too far away for Jethro to tell the color of her eyes, but her face was oval and folds of rich straw-colored hair were pinned above her head. "Perhaps I must, soon," she said.

"Tomorrow?"

"Not tomorrow. But Wednesday, perhaps."

"Do you know what time you must?"

"Two o'clock, perhaps. After dinner."

Jethro considered that. "I believe I'll have an overpowering urge to listen to some of the most beautiful music in the world—say Wednesday, about two o'clock. May I?"

"Please do."

If Joe was surprised when his young prizefighter returned early from Wednesday's roadwork, bathed, and donned his best suit, the manager hid it well.

The church was gloomy when the Jethro entered at precisely two o'clock and took his back row seat. He felt keen disappointment that the girl was not already at practice. The young man contemplated his hands while waiting, opening and closing them, testing them, thinking they were ready to start on the bag. He felt rather than heard a door open somewhere behind the pulpit. The organ whooshed a few times, then there was music.

Jethro sat in rapture throughout. Finally the last hollow note died and he clapped for a full minute, until she appeared from behind the lattice to curtsy.

"You are very talented," he said, walking forward.

"And you are very kind," she replied, seeming to grow edgy at his approach.

"I would appreciate knowing when you feel you must play again."

"I'll wear out the ears of my greatest admirer."

"You may well be right on half of that statement, ma'am." He smiled at her obvious embarrassment. "Please?" Her eyes were hazel, her cheeks dimpled, and her lips the color of the wild rose. Those lips pursed as he studied them.

"Friday?" she asked.

"Friday it is."

They stood facing each other at three feet, both willing the other to end the uncomfortable silence that somehow had fallen between them. His hands were at his side, hers

twisting together at her waist. "I must go," she murmured.
"Yes. Well I ... thank you."

"Thank you, Mr. Barry." Her voice was melodious. She held out her hand and he took it, bowing ever so slightly. Then he turned and left the church.

———— • • ————

Jethro leaned against the hotel's registry desk. "Do you know the church organist? Down at the Baptist Church, I mean."

"Only organ in town," the bespectacled clerk said. "Only organist, too, far as I know."

"You know her?"

"Sure. Sadie Nell Tucker. Know everybody in Fort Worth."

"Isn't that a coincidence?" the prizefighter murmured, comparing the lady's surname with that of the middleweight champion he stalked.

The clerk was plainly puzzled. "I don't follow you," he said.

"Never mind. She married?"

"Naw. She's too high-falutin' for us cowboys."

"How old is she?"

"Old enough, I reckon." When the man saw Jethro frowning at him, he said, "Let's see, my boy Willie is the same age, and he's twenty-three. No, she's a year or two younger. Twenty-two maybe. That one's goin' to be an old maid, sure." Before Jethro could reply, the clerk shook his head and added, "A waste, too."

"She live in town?"

"Yeah. Over along the tracks. A block off the Breckenridge Road. Lives with her crippled maw. Takes care of her, I reckon."

"No father?"

"Not since he got killed in the feed mill blow, back in '68. That's when her maw got hurt, too. They was nice folks. First-class town boosters. Too bad it had to happen to 'em. One o' them things, I reckon. The girl, she went all to pieces then. Thought a bunch of her paw, she did. Why you ask?"

Jethro pushed from the registry desk. "I just like organ music, is all."

———•＋•———

When the organ's last notes died, Jethro rose and strode to the shrouding lattice. She stood and, as before, stepped out. "Once more, it was beautiful, Miss Tucker."

She jerked. "You know my name!"

"Seemed only fair. You know mine."

She pondered that a moment, then laughed. "True, Mr. Barry. Do you know also that my given name is Sadie Nell?"

"Yes."

"Now you have me at a disadvantage. I only know your given name as 'Kid'." When he did not immediately reply, she said, "Come now, there must be more than just 'Kid'. Fair is fair, you know."

Jethro? James? John? The names ran together. "John," he said at last.

"John Barry," she said slowly. "It's an honorable name. Would you rather be called 'Kid'?"

"Yes."

"Very well, Kid. I am still very much flattered by your appreciation of my music."

"Such appreciation as I have, Miss Tucker, is, I assure you, well deserved and every bit sincere."

"I believe you, sir."

There was a moment of awkwardness before he ventured, "It would be an honor to see you home. If you are going home."

"That would be kind of you. Yes, I shall accept."

She's no bigger than a minute, Jethro thought, gazing at the top of her piled straw-colored hair as they strolled down the street. "People say you'll be prizefighting soon for the championship, Mr. Barry. Is that right?"

"I guess I'm in line for a chance. Yes. Whether I get the chance depends on whether the man who holds the championship now will give me a go at it."

"Why wouldn't he?"

"I don't know. A variety of things, I suppose. Not enough money, fear of losing perhaps."

"Do you want this ... this championship a great deal?"

He considered. "I suppose so. The closer I get to it, the less important it becomes."

"What will it gain you? Being a champion, I mean."

"I guess I don't really know. Fame and fortune, I suppose."

"Can you eat fame?"

He grinned down at her. "No."

"But you can, fortune?"

"From it—yes."

"Is it an honorable way to make money?"

"What are you driving at, ma'am?"

"I just wondered if you feel that prizefighting is an honorable way for a man to make a livelihood."

They walked for several yards before he replied. "I think so," he said. "It's better than most. The hours are better, for one thing. I worked on the Mississippi docks before I started prizefighting. That was hell, I'll ... I'm sorry ma'am."

She seemed not to notice. "You are seldom home, are you not?"

"True," he murmured.

"Do you have a home?"

He stopped. So did she, turning to look up at him with big swallowing eyes. "No I don't," he said. "But I want one."

"That would seem difficult, Mr. Barry, as long as you continue to pursue a prizefighting career."

They began walking again. She stopped soon after. Her home was a small frame bungalow, painted white and set back from the street. Planted round about were lilacs and roses. A tiny garden grew in the rear. "I shall be there listening on Sunday, Miss Tucker," he said.

"My music will be inspired," she murmured.

———•·•———

"There ye are, laddie buck," Joe said when Jethro walked into the hotel. "Me mother would be proud o' the way ye look, all duded up in that fancy suit. And for the second time this week."

"You had supper, Joe?"

"Faith and 'tis only one-thirty, laddie. They're still serving dinner."

"Let's have dinner then."

"Hear anything from Tucker yet?" Jethro asked a few minutes later, toying at his potatoes.

"No, lad. 'Tis the run-around we'll be getting, I fear."

"What is there about us, Joe? Do we smell bad?"

"Think, lad. You've not one single weakness. You're fast, strong, and can take a lick. Ye jab well, ye block well, and ye roll wi' the punches. Your footwork is some of the best and ye can duck and weave wi' anyone. You've learned to fight dirty if you have to, and ye gave clear proof to Sailor Dan that you are a smart wallop. The only thing you've ever been guilty of is bein' green around the edges. And after two years, time has taken care o' that. By the Holy Mother! If I was Tommy Tucker and on top o' the world, I'd be for tryin' to duck ye, too."

Jethro stared through a wall, into the distance. "I want Tucker, Joe. And I want him the sooner, the better."

Chapter Ten

It was hell-fire and brim-stone at its finest and Jethro was on his best behavior. He dutifully stood when others did, listened attentively when the preacher gave the local quilting bee schedule, and when the service was over, waited for Sadie Nell Tucker.

"You played beautifully again, Miss Tucker," he said as she walked up to him.

"I'm afraid you're prejudiced, Mr. Barry."

"I'm sure I am. But that wouldn't make a bit of difference when it came to the truth."

"Would you care to walk me home?"

"I wouldn't be fit for a thing," he said, "this world or that, if you never allowed me to do so."

They strolled in companionable silence until she asked, "How long will you be in Fort Worth?"

"I'm not sure. As long as I can."

"That doesn't really tell me much."

"No, I suppose it don't. Two weeks. Three weeks. Perhaps a month."

"Will you then leave for this championship fight?"

His voice took on a more urgent note. "Miss Tucker, way I feel right now, I'll leave *only* for the championship fight."

"Am I becoming so important?" she murmured.

"Let's just say you are becoming very, very important."

She paused at the walkway to her bungalow. "Please come in and meet my mother, Mr. Barry. She would appreciate that."

"An honor."

"You know, of course, that she's an invalid?"

"Yes."

"Follow me, then."

The cabin was neat and clean inside, but felt stuffy and airless to Jethro. It contained three rooms: a parlor, a kitchen, and a bedroom; the last to which Sadie Nell Tucker led her visitor.

"Mother, we have a guest."

Sadie Nell's mother was propped up in the bed, thin white hair spreading on her pillow in disarray. Her voice cracked when she said "What? What did you say?"

"A visitor, mother. You have a visitor. A man. Do you remember the one I told you about? The one who liked my music?"

Curtains were drawn across the room's single window and the room was dim. "A man? Here?"

"Say hello to Mr. Barry, mother." Sadie Nell propelled Jethro forward by an arm. "Mr. Barry, this is Mrs. Tucker, my mother."

"How do you do, Mrs. Tucker. It is a pleasure indeed." He bowed at the waist.

The mother lay there staring at him, mouth open, eyes

strangely disconcerting. "Say hello to Mr. Barry, mother. He's come to wish you well."

"Hello," the white haired woman said, voice again cracking. "Not ... many ... do that ... these days."

Searching for something to say, Jethro blurted, "You have a beautiful daughter, Mrs. Tucker. And she's talented, too."

The old woman stared for the longest time. "Yes," she said at last. "I suppose she is." Then her eyes closed and Sadie Nell touched Jethro's arm, leading him from the room.

He didn't know what to say—didn't know what he was supposed to say. And his confusion must have been apparent because when they were again outside the home, Sadie Nell said, "Now you know why I cannot allow your interest in me to progress further, Mr. Barry."

"No, I don't," he said. "Why would my visit to your poor mother affect my interest in you?"

"Because there is no way I can leave Fort Worth, don't you see? My mother requires my constant presence. It would be tragic for me even to think of leaving her. Or even to move her unnecessarily."

He ran his fingers through his thick, black hair. "I guess my thinking hasn't progressed as far as yours, Miss Tucker. But I have a feeling nothing has changed as far as I'm concerned."

"Your trade hardly lends itself to stability, Mr. Barry."

"I'll not always be a prizefighter, Miss Tucker."

"Fort Worth is a dumpy little cowboy town with a railroad running through it," she said, staring up at him with those liquid hazel eyes. "I'm sure it hardly compares with New Orleans, or Chicago, or any of the great cities you've visited."

"You're right," he chuckled. "I like Fort Worth better."

They were quiet together. Then he asked, "About your mother—how bad is she?"

"Paralyzed from the neck down. I must even feed her."

"No hope?"

"None. She, too, has given up, I fear."

"Is there a facility? A place to keep and comfort ..."

She waved an arm in dismissal. "Certainly not. Not in Fort Worth, Mr. Barry." She sighed. "Perhaps elsewhere—I do not know. But that's really irrelevant for the expense alone. Besides, she is my mother."

He nodded. "It just seems so unfair. To you. To her. To us."

"Do you think these situations do not exist, Mr. Barry? Just because we would will it so?"

"No, of course not. I never implied ..."

"There are many other unfortunates in Fort Worth, sir. Would you care to know how many?" Tears welled.

Jethro placed his hands on her shoulders. "If you wish to tell me, go ahead."

"Or would you care to visit them with me? I do so twice each week, on Tuesdays and Thursdays."

Hers was a challenge, and she had trapped him neatly.

"Of course I'll go with you. What time do you usually begin your visits? I could swing by and we could walk together."

"I try to spend three hours in the morning and three in the afternoon. I usually leave around nine."

"I'll be here at nine on Tuesday."

"'Tis no go, lad," Joe Barry said during Monday's noon meal. "Schusberg in New York wires that the heathen bastards have scheduled a summer tour in England. 'Tis sure now and they duck ye."

Jethro toyed with his fork. "Why is it that's a relief?"

Joe appeared not to hear. "'Tis to California and the West Coast we should be heading now, lad. I didn't tell ye of the offers before. But from the figures, California must be the land o' milk and honey, for sure."

"Joe."

"I'll send the telegrams today and we can be away from here before the week ends."

"Joe,"

"We'll do ye up a proper tour that will rival anything Dortmann and Tucker can put together wi' the yellow-bellied lobster-backs and ..."

"Joe, dammit!"

"What, laddie?"

"Don't get in a hurry to set up California."

Joe leaned over to clap his back. "Aye, laddie buck. I was gettin' carried away. Ye're not healed yet from Sailor Dan are ye?"

"That's it."

"But maybe we could find a place where ye could heal better than at Fort Worth."

"I like Fort Worth."

"Have ye forgotten what the city fathers tried to do wi' ye?"

"Everybody else is nice."

Joe studied his fighter for a few moments, then frowned. "So ye' want to stay here a bit longer?"

Jethro nodded. "I can't see where it could hurt."

Old Mr. Henderson was a double amputee. He opened the door for them, a broad welcoming smile spreading across his face. Jethro, expecting anything but this, was stunned when he saw their host sitting upon the floor.

"I've brought a guest with me today, Mr. Henderson," Sadie Nell said. "This is Kid Barry."

"The prizefighter! Golly!" The man extended a long and powerful arm.

Jethro checked a natural urge to bend forward as he reached for the proffered hand, mumbling, "A pleasure, Mr. Henderson."

"Well, come in. Come in." Mr. Henderson spun and bounced ahead of them across the polished floor, propelling himself with hands and arms. "Would you like some coffee? I got a fresh pot made. If you do, just help yourself."

"I'll get it, Mr. Henderson," Sadie Nell said. "You go ahead and visit with Mr. Barry."

Both men watched her to the kitchen. "Sit down, Kid," said Mr. Henderson.

After Jethro seated himself in a straight-backed chair, the older man, still on the floor, said, "Boy, I sure woulda liked to see the fight, Kid. Folks say it was somethin'. Little hard for me to get around, though. My circles have been shortened since Shiloh."

Jethro was grateful that Sadie Nell reappeared carrying two big mugs of coffee. Later, as the men talked and sipped, the woman moved about the house tidying up. Then she murmured that it was time to go.

"I picked up your shopping list, Mr. Henderson. I'll see that Weaver's delivers it on Friday. If you need anything else, just tell me on my Thursday visit."

"Oh I will, Nell. I will. Did you take the money from the sugarbowl?"

"I didn't. Pastor Jenkins said the offering appears generous enough this week."

"Bless you, Nell." The man bounced with them to the door, chattering all the way. He waved and called, "Come back, Kid. You're always welcome—a hell of an honor."

The next stop was to see William Farrer and the next at the home of Guterrez Domingo—both mutilated Confederate Civil War veterans. The last stop before noon found them visiting an arthritic spinster named Millie Thompson. At each cottage or shack, Sadie Nell Tucker picked up grocery lists to be delivered Friday by Weaver Mercantile. At each home she refused pittance offers of financial assistance, with the words, "Pastor Jenkins said the offerings were generous enough this week."

"I don't know if I can take much more," Jethro said as they trudged back to the Tucker bungalow.

"Now you can see why I cannot leave," she murmured.

He said nothing. When they arrived at her home, she said, "I left a pot of beans on. Will you have a bowl? There's cornbread, too."

He shook his head. "But I'll be back at two. Please wait for me if I'm late."

When he returned, he was weighted down with two feed sacks of heavy canned goods of all kinds. "They are for you and your mother, Nell—is it okay if I call you Nell? Tomorrow we'll go shopping for the others."

She began crying. While she regained control, he emptied the sacks, stacking the cans on the counter. Finally she said, "We'd best go. Mother is sleeping and Mrs. Crowell will be disappointed if we're late."

The afternoon was more of the same. That evening, Jethro missed supper. Joe Barry found him lying on his bed, hands behind the head, gray eyes staring holes through the ceiling.

"Are ye all right, lad?" the manager asked.

"Yes, Joe. For the first time in my life, I'm all right.

You see, I'm in love with the most beautiful woman in all the world. And given enough time, I'm going to ask her to marry me."

Wednesday was shopping day and Thursday was visitation day. But Friday? Ahh, Friday was music day. He sat as before on the rear bench, believing as always that she played for him alone. Afterward, as they strolled to her home, his hand stole around hers. "Miss Tucker—Nell—there's something I want to say."

"I'm not sure I want to hear it ... Kid," she murmured.

"You are a very special person to me. And I've come to like Fort Worth. I think maybe this is the place I've always intended to be."

"No," she said. "You don't know what you're saying."

"Why?"

She stopped, turned to face him, removed her hand from his and fumbled at an imagined piece of dust at her bosom. "Mr. Barry—Kid—I do what I believe God called me to do. And I cannot do less. I cannot leave."

"I'm not asking that, Nell. I can see "

"And I think very highly of you. You are a fine man. A fine individual. But prizefighting is your life. Do you think I could bear to be the cause of your leaving it?"

"I think I want to leave it," he muttered.

"No you don't. It would be a festering sore between us forever. It would grow and grow and someday you would hate me because I prevented you from rising to the top of your profession."

"My goal is to have a little farm somewhere, a wife I love and who loves me, and snot-nosed little kids running around under foot. Would you deny me that?"

She whirled to run down the street, sobbing. He caught her after a few steps and turned her to face him. "Damn it, woman! I love you."

She buried her face in his shirt and clung to him, weeping. He gently lifted her away and said, "I know it's too early and too sudden to talk of marriage. And I know you'll have a thousand questions you'll want to ask. But all I'm saying right now is to give me a chance. Give me a chance to think things through and come up with the right answers. Don't say 'No' right now, no matter what. Give time a chance to work things out. Hear?"

Her eyes were closed and her face tear-streaked, but she nodded. "Mother?" she said, so low he almost missed it.

"We can work it out, Nell. You must believe that."

She nodded again and pulled away. They were at the walkway to her home. She plunged down the walk and her door slammed behind.

———·•·———

It was later that same evening, at their supper meal, when Jethro spotted the man watching him.

"As I was saying, Joe, I want to stay here. I don't think it's fair to tie you up any longer." He put a hand over one of his manager's freckled paws. "I feel rotten about this for your sake, Joe. And I appreciate ..."

Joe slipped his hand away and there was a catch in his throat as he said, "Think nothing o' me, laddie buck. 'Twas an honor to be part o' your life for as long as I have. And don't be for worryin' about old Joe Barry—your winning ways set me up wi' more nest egg than I'll need for the rest o' me life."

The heavy-set man still stared their way.

"When will ye be married, lad? I'll not want to miss it."

"I don't know. It'll be awhile. Too long for you not to put time into figuring your next move. If you go, let me know where, and I'll wire you as soon as we set the date."

"I don't like leavin' ye in the lurch, laddie. Maybe I'd best stick around for a few more days."

"You're a fine friend, Joe. And I'd love to have you … By the way, who's that guy in the corner? You ever see him before?"

Joe turned and the chunky man eating alone at the corner table looked away. "No. Can't say as I have. Why, laddie?"

"He's been staring our way most of the meal. Stranger to me, too. I suppose I'm just jumpy."

Some inner sense was triggered in Jethro, however, and when the stranger left the hotel minutes later, the inner sense told him to follow. The man went directly to the Post Office, where Jethro watched through a window as the stranger browsed along a wall full of WANTED posters.

He trailed the stranger to the sheriff's office and eavesdropped outside until the man left a few minutes later, mumbling an apology. "Probably a mistake, sheriff. But I'da swore he rings a bell."

Jethro took a seat on a livery stable water trough while he pondered his options. Finally he dropped his head into his hands and whispered, "How can I put her through this?"

Five minutes later he pushed into Joe Barry's hotel room. "Schedule us out on the first train west tomorrow morning."

"Are ye daft? Not more than an hour ago ye was saying …"

"Joe, listen. We are friends who trust each other. Are we not?"

"Yes, of course."

"Then I'm going to ask you to trust me more'n I've ever asked anyone to trust me before. I'm asking you to

pack our bags—yours and mine. And I'm asking you to
schedule the 6:02 to California. I'm asking you to check all
the baggage through and have my tickets. I'll board at the
last minute."

Joe's booming voice lowered. "What's wrong, laddie?"

"Never mind. Will you do it?"

"Of course."

"See you in the morning."

———•••———

Pastor Jenkins answered Jethro's first knock. "Mr.
Barry! This is a surprise. Won't you come in?"

"Haven't much time," Jethro said, stepping inside.
"But it's absolutely necessary that I talk to you."

"Of course. How may I help? Have a chair, please."

"No time."

The pastor raised his eyebrows.

"Who is your banker?"

"My banker?"

"Fort Worth's banker."

"Well, we have two banks."

"Which banker is most honorable?"

"Is this some joke, Mr. Barry?" Pastor Jenkins
demanded.

"I assure you it is not."

"Both are honorable."

"To which one would you entrust your money? 'Cause
that's what I'm talking about—a hell of a lot of money.
First Baptist Church money."

Pastor Jenkins frowned, peered more closely at the
man he knew as Kid Barry, leaned close to sniff, and finally said, "Barnaby. First Bank of Texas."

"Where does he live?"

"Just down the street. See here, Barry ..."

"Fine. Let's go see him."

"Certainly not. Not without I know what this is all about."

"I want to set up a trust for your church, preacher. And I want to do it now. Tonight. It'll require Mr. Barnaby's assistance. Let's go."

Jenkins hesitated, then said, "I'll get my coat."

The banker, Merrill Barnaby, was even more confused by his evening's interruption than was Pastor Mordecai Jenkins. But when Jethro dropped the hint of several thousands in deposits in the First Bank of Texas, he smiled engagingly and asked, "What can I do to help?"

"You can get your coat, Mr. Barnaby," replied Jethro, "and join Pastor Jenkins and me in a midnight stroll over to Judge Gavin's."

Judge Henry Gavin, an orderly man who resisted any break in his well-fixed routine, was indignant at the intrusion, even though the time was, in reality, far short of midnight. But he was, as Captain McNelly had disclosed, a closet supporter of prizefighting. Just now, Kid Barry was one of his heroes. And when he saw the Kid amongst his uninvited guests, he grudgingly agreed to a kitchen discussion of a matter of 'grave importance'.

"I want to start a trust—I suppose that's what you'd call it," the man the others knew as Kid Barry, said minutes later. "What I want to do is found a hospital. Well, not exactly a hospital, but some sort of nursing home, or something like it. I want it to be for the poor crippled unfortunates presently in Sadie Nell Tucker's care. And those like them, to come later. I want the trust to be under the guiding hand of the First Baptist Church, headed by Pastor Jenkins. I want to stick money in a trust fund set up for that purpose, in Mr. Barnaby's bank. I think the trust fund will initially begin with about eight thousand dollars."

Jenkins gasped and Barnaby blinked. Gavin still wiped sleep from his eyes.

"The details are to be worked out by you gentlemen over time. You know my wishes. I'd like very much for you three to serve as a governing board, guiding the church and the town in this project. I ask only two things in return."

He saw the banker frown and the judge's face go blank. "I want the nursing home or hospital to be under the direct management of Sadie Nell Tucker, and I want an organ installed as soon as a permanent home can be located and purchased."

"A wonderful thing you're doing, Mr. Barry," murmured the Reverend Mordecai Jenkins.

"Indeed it is," said banker Barnaby.

"Then may I suggest we get to work," Jethro said. "My train will be leaving early in the morning. At the very least, I'll need to work out the necessary drafts with Mr. Barnaby, to draw my money to his bank."

"I'll make coffee," said Judge Gavin.

———————

Jethro found Joe Barry seated midway in the third car, reading a newspaper. The train had just begun to move when the younger man sat down. "You can send some telegrams from Abilene," he said.

"Why?" Joe asked, lowering his paper.

"To see if you can arrange a California tour."

"I sent them earlier this morning, laddie buck," Joe said flipping his paper back up to read.

CHAPTER ELEVEN

Bakersfield and Modesto. Sacramento, Grass Valley, and Angel's Camp. Merced, Monterey, and Walnut Creek. San Francisco, Placerville, and Virginia City. Fresno, San Jose, and Marysville. Jethro Spring fought the best middleweight fighting men in gold camps or trading towns on a weekly basis. Some were merely clumsy toughs, but others demonstrated reasonable skill. Still, Jethro chafed under the strain of inferior competition.

"Dammit, Joe, my edge is going. I can't fight tie-hackers or pick-slingers all the time and hope to keep an edge. That guy over in Nevada, he's the only real fighter I've faced since we came west. And hell, he's Welsh."

Joe shook his head and buttered another biscuit. "And pray tell, the man in Fresno—what of him? He must have had some talent, he knocked ye down twice."

Dishes and utensils rattled as Jethro slammed a fist on the table. "Why do we stay here?"

"Holy mother, lad. Must ye ask? Money. Why else? Never have ye made so much as you've made this past few weeks. These poor souls are starved to see one wi' your skills. And they pay well for it."

"I don't care about the money, Joe. I just want to fight people who can fight back. I want to go east."

"No, lad. We cannot go back 'til Tucker comes home from England. We must show the man we won't mope around and pick up his leavin's. Besides, ye surely cannot turn away from this kind of Heaven's manna."

Jethro shrugged. "You're the manager. You're the one who knows about these kinds of things. Where do we go from here?"

"They say there's a fair middle up in Seattle."

"Where's that?"

"Come, lad, 'tis in Washington Territory, near a great harbor. Some say there's a fortune to be made there."

"When do we go?"

"The packet leaves at nine Thursday morning. We loaded our share of boats in our time, lad. Now let's see can ye ride one."

"Ride a boat?" Jethro said. "Why couldn't I?"

"Ye ever been on one, lad? Out to sea, I mean."

"Just in the gulf is all. You remember Galveston, don't you? But that was only a coaster."

"Like as not, you'll see what I mean, laddie."

———•◆•———

The sluggish steamer heeled to port in the erratic October seas. Jethro Spring grabbed the bunk to steady himself as he called, "Hey, Joe, they're serving supper in the salon."

Jethro caught himself again and picked his way to the

shadowy hulk lying in one of the tiny stateroom's bunks. "Joe, what's wrong?"

"'Tis naught," Joe Barry whispered. "A touch of the upsets. I'll be all right. Go on wi'out me."

"Can I bring you anything?"

"No."

Jethro grinned as he closed the door. "Thought I'd get seasick, did you?" He whistled tonelessly through his teeth as he entered the dining salon.

———✦———

"It's a lot calmer now, Joe. It's smoothed down since we turned the point at Cape Flattery. They say this Juan de Fuca Strait is calm most times." Jethro frowned at Joe's sickly pallor. "Three days is too long to go without something in the stomach. Don't you want to try to eat something?"

Joe's eyes fluttered open and he wagged his head.

"We're supposed to be there by mid-morning tomorrow. Right on time, I guess. Sure I can't bring you something?"

"Fresh milk if they have it," Joe whispered. "But a wee bit o' canned, if they don't."

Jethro returned in a few minutes with a glass of thick, dark-colored, canned milk. He lifted Joe's head and helped the big man drink a couple of swallows. No sooner did the milk hit Joe's stomach than it spewed back.

"You want me to bring the doc?" Jethro asked, sponging Joe's shirtfront.

"No," the sick man whispered, shaking his head. "Seasick. Just seasick is all. Never happened before. Don't know why now."

"We'll be there soon, Joe. It always gets better when a

man sets his feet on solid ground. Leastways that's what the captain says."

Joe nodded and Jethro slipped out. He sauntered to the mail packet's starboard rail. Night shadows stole across timbered slopes of the Olympic Peninsula and he thrilled to a haunting alpenglow on snow-covered mountains beyond. When full darkness claimed the scene, Jethro Spring entered the dining salon where he put away a huge steak, fried potatoes, corn on the cob, and two slices of pumpkin pie.

—·•·—

The black-bearded man turned as Jethro Spring asked, "Captain McGwynn?"

"What is it, matey?"

"My friend is still too sick to get up. I'm worried about him."

"Think nae thing of it, lad. We've only just tied up. He'll get better by and by. There's nae hurry. Leave the mon be for a time. He'll be doin' the hopscotch before you know it."

"I'm worried about him."

"Don't. He'll be all right. Take my word on it."

But after McGwynn's cargo was unloaded, the captain's concern took quantum leaps. "How is he, lad?"

"Not good, captain. He vomited a little blood a few minutes ago. I don't think it's just seasickness."

"Tell you what we'll do. I'll get a husky seaman or two to help get his two feet on the ground. He'll be better then, I'll wager."

"I want your ship's surgeon to look at him before we move him," Jethro murmured.

"No need, lad. He's just seasick. I've seen lots of

cases."

Jethro's face turned prizefighter ugly, gray eyes going flat and cold. "Captain, I don't give a good goddamn if he's got the measles. I want a doctor to see him before he's moved. And by God, a doctor he'll get."

The captain returned in a few moments with a seedy-looking man Jethro had barely noticed during the voyage. All three trooped to Joe Barry's bedside. After a brief examination, the surgeon said, "I do not know what is wrong with this man, Mr. Barry. But I do not believe him to be merely seasick."

"What should we do for him?"

"The best course would be to take him to the hospital. I can arrange ambulance transport, but it will be expensive. So will the hospital. And such doctors as required to treat him. The least expensive course would be to carry him to a hack and take shelter in a hotel until ..."

"Get an ambulance," Jethro cut in. "Take him to the hospital. The best hospital if there's more than one."

"Yes, of course."

"And hurry!"

———•—•———

Three Seattle doctors examined Joe Barry and offered three differing diagnoses.

"Pleurisy," said one.

"Consumption," said a second.

"Okay, doctors. What does that mean?" Jethro asked.

"Pleurisy," said the first doctor, "is thought to be a mild form of consumption. It's easily cured, normally responding to rest, plenty of sleep, proper diet, and the like. Consumption is, of course, more serious."

"How serious?"

"Difficult to cure. Takes a long time, if and when successful. Normally, though, the patient grows progressively worse over a long period of time."

"How does he grow worse, doctor?"

"Develops a dry, hacking cough that eventually progresses to bloody sputum. The patient's body weight withers. He's easily afflicted with other maladies. Bodily functions fail to respond properly. Normally, death from consumption is a long, lingering one."

"But a cure is possible?" Jethro asked.

"Some success has been had, so I've heard, by moving a patient to a warm, arid climate; preferably to higher elevation. Apparently a low-elevation, moist climate is not especially beneficial to unfortunates afflicted with the disease."

But the third doctor's opinion confirmed Jethro Spring's worst fears:

"Hmm. Showed up for the first time only four, five days ago? Began vomiting blood yesterday? Has your friend complained of stomach cramps or excess gas, Mr. Barry? Before this particular illness, I mean."

"No," Jethro replied. "No, he's always been as healthy as a horse."

"How about spirituous liquors? Does the man imbibe?"

"Yeah, sure. Joe'd have a drink now and then. Not to excess, though. Not often, anyway."

"And what would you call 'to excess'?"

Jethro looked puzzled. "I don't know. I s'pose Joe might average two fingers a day. I never paid any attention. Why?"

"Uh hmm. Can't be anything else. Your friend is in grave peril."

"What's wrong with Joe?"

"All the signs indicate it, I'm sorry to say." The doctor placed his fingertips together under his chin, staring intently at Jethro. "Your friend has a rapidly spreading form of cancerate blight."

A cold chill gripped Jethro. "A cure? What do we have to do for a cure?"

"There is none."

"None? No! There has to be!"

"Mr. Barry," the doctor said, sighing, "if I am right in my diagnosis and Joe Barry has cancerate blight, there is no known cure."

"Then you're wrong."

The doctor sighed again. "Let us hope so."

Jethro made no move to leave. The doctor folded his hands across an ample stomach and waited for the question he knew was on its way: "But if you're right," the younger man said, "how long does Joe have?"

"There is no way of knowing. If the disease struck as fast as you described, I would guess it to be spreading rapidly."

"Meaning?" Jethro persisted.

"Meaning your friend may have but a few days. Perhaps merely a few hours."

Jethro Spring slumped in his chair. "You're wrong, doctor. You've got to be wrong."

"Joe. Can you hear me, Joe?"

The long, claw-like fingers feebly squeezed Jethro Spring's hand. But Joe's sunken eyelids remained closed; not even a flutter. Nor did his cracked lips move.

"We can win this one, Joe," Jethro whispered. "We can still win. That damned doctor was wrong. He said you only had a few hours, maybe a few days. That was two months ago. Hell, Seventy-six will be a better year than Seventy-five. You'll see. A hundred years of independence. Be a big blow-out come the Fourth of July. You'll be there beside me."

The withered claws squeezed again, but Joe's breathing took on a more labored note. Jethro stared around the hospital room, at the tiny Christmas tree on a corner table, and the decorations he'd hung. "Hell of a Christmas it was, too," he muttered.

Joe wheezed, then moaned. He opened glittering eyes to Jethro's anxious face. "Hurts," he said, lapsing into unconsciousness.

New Year's Eve, Jethro thought. Be plenty of dancers out tonight, but Joe and me, we won't be among 'em. Precious little to celebrate. He stared down at his friend's withered body and wasted face. "Why did this happen, Joe. We had the world by the tail. Why?"

The claw clutched again while Joe's frail body writhed in pain and Jethro writhed with him. A low rumbling moan came from the unconscious man.

"Soon as you get on your feet, Joe, we'll head south and east. Get out of this damned rain and back to New Orleans and our friends. Tucker'll be ready to fight by then. We'll win and be on top of the world. How's that?"

This time there was no return squeeze.

———·•·———

Joe Barry died January 16, 1876. He died desperately clasping Jethro's hands as his pain pulsated, screaming in agony from the fires that tormented him. Suddenly, the withered body wracked in one great convulsion and fell back, forever stilled.

Jethro laid his forehead on the rumpled sheet beside the body of his friend. Great tears welled, coursing down his cheeks. Then he pushed to his feet, crossed Joe's limp arms on the still chest, closed the eyelids and went to inform the medical staff that Joe Barry was no more.

Jethro arranged for Joe's funeral in Seattle's imposing new cathedral, a ceremony he knew would make the Irishman beam with pride. Jethro tried to remember the church's name as he sat stone-faced in his pew while the old priest, clad in ceremonial robes, droned an incoherent language. At last, Jethro glanced around the empty auditorium and shook his head. Hell of a way for Joe to be buried, he thought. He deserved better than this— deserved a big wake and a host of friends to see him off.

Joe's casket squatted to one side of the priest. Two altar boys stood nearby while six hired casket-bearers knelt in the front pew. The undertaker waited near the open casket, his long head bowed, his horse-face professionally solemn.

Jethro thought about how dismayed the man was when he refused to sit in a front row. The priest stopped droning and Jethro looked up. The undertaker beckoned discreetly for him to walk by the casket. *See Joe in death after remembering how full of life he really was? Hell no!* And he stalked angrily from the building, through the cathedral's huge double doors. Outside he glared up at a lowering sky and muttered curses to God.

A drenching rain began just as they lowered Joe's casket into the muddy earth. Jethro stayed until the last shovel of dirt was thrown over the grave.

⇒ CHAPTER TWELVE ⇐

T-I-M-B-E-R-R-R!"

Jethro Spring watched in awe as the gigantic Douglas fir shivered and swayed before beginning its arc to the ground. Branches snapped as the behemoth brushed against an ancient, lifeless-but-still-standing spire. Broken limbs—some twenty feet long and as large at their bases as a man's thigh—cascaded downward as the monster tree gathered in the smaller spire. Jethro remembered the lumberjacks calling these falling limbs *Widowmakers*.

"Sometimes," one garrulous sawyer said, "they'll hang up there and drop days later, when nobody expects 'em. They'll fall without so much as a whisper and drive the top of a man's skull to his bootlaces."

Rain—the ever-present, never-ending, godawful deluge—pounded down.

Jethro felt rather than heard, the muted popping of the dead spire's roots as the irresistible weight of the falling giant leaned upon it. Suddenly the spire snapped free and both it and the giant fir whooshed groundward, locked in a final embrace. Mud and rocks and forest debris hurtled skyward at the multi-ton impact.

Jethro broke from his entranced stare. He hefted his heavy double-bit axe and clambered atop the fallen tree to methodically cut away its remaining limbs, then measure and mark proper log lengths along the trunk for the following team's work. In the distance could be heard the roar of the sawmill's steam engines, even the whine of the big circular saw. Two men followed Jethro with a long, wide-blade "bucking" saw and soon began swaying to the rhythm of their work.

Jethro pulled his soggy wool coat more tightly around his neck, wiping impatiently at water droplets streaking down his cheeks and from the end of his nose. He hated the incessant pelting rain, hated his work, hated Oregon and Oregon City.

The waitress shoved a cup of steaming black coffee across the counter. "And what'll it be today?"

"Whatever's on special, I guess," Jethro Spring replied. "Any papers left?"

The blonde girl reached under the counter and handed him an Oregonian. "A man down from Portland left it here this morning."

Jethro took the newspaper and sorted through it until he had the pages in sequence, then began to read.

"Tough week?" she asked, breaking into his concentration.

"Huh? Oh, yeah. Guess I don't like my job overmuch."

"Why do it then?"

"Man's got to make a living somehow."

Jethro returned to his paper. The girl brought a big plate of corned beef and cabbage. "More coffee?"

"Please," he replied, folding the paper.

"You haven't always been a logger have you?"

"No, not always. Matter of fact, just for the past couple of months."

"What did you do before that?"

Before Jethro could answer, the door opened and a couple of lumberjacks sauntered in. "Excuse me," the girl said.

Later, she leaned on the counter near him. "Well?" she said.

"Well what?"

"What did you do before you began working in the woods?"

"This and that. I was a stevedore for a while."

"Did you like that?"

"Not especially."

"Have you ever liked anything you've done?" she persisted.

Jethro considered. He thought of the army, his dockwork, the prize ring. "No," he said at last.

"But you're still looking?"

"I suppose you could say that."

"Have you any idea what you'd like to do?"

Jethro's eyes fixed on a cupboard hinge beyond the girl's head. "I ... I think so." He was silent for twenty full seconds while the girl waited. "I think I'd like to own a little place, like a farm, off by itself, away from folks. I'd like a ..." He broke off, embarrassed.

She smiled at him and cleared away his empty dishes. He laid out the newspaper again, mind occupied now by the past. He dwelled there for some time, then thoughts returned to the dream. *Let's see, the house should be a tight little bungalow, probably built out of logs, with a fireplace at one end and a sleeping room or two—depending on kids—off to one side. Be nice if there was a cool sweetwater spring just up the hill, where water could be run gravity-feed into the house.*

His thoughts turned to a wife, and the children he hoped would be theirs. *Would they have dark hair like his or straw-colored hair like a certain Texas cowtown organ player?* He shook his head to make the thoughts angle off in another direction.

How much would a small farm cost? And where should it be? Oregon? No, God no. Too much rain. California? No to that, too. Run-amuck gold fever there. Too many people coming and going from all over. Risky with his past. Louisiana? Too much heat and water and sweat. Texas, then? Maybe a small cow ranch. No, too close to Indian Territory where he was wanted. Montana? God, I'd love Montana. Then he remembered his reason for fleeing Montana in the beginning.

"More coffee?"

Jethro slid his cup across the counter.

"You read slow," she said, filling the cup.

"Why do you say that?"

"You've been staring at one spot on that page for the longest time."

"I guess I was just thinking."

The blond girl studied him. "My name is Sally. Sally Rayburn. What's yours?"

He hesitated a moment. "Kid Barry."

"That's a funny name. Is 'Kid' a nickname?"

"Yes, but it's the name most people call me."

"Someday, as you grow older, you'll have to change it."

"Maybe. If I grow older. I'll worry about it then."

The two lumberjacks paid for their dinner and left, and the girl moved off down the counter to clean their places. Jethro looked back at the paper and his eye caught a headline:

Portland Fighter Takes On All Comers

Portland prize-fight promoters Al Nicholson and A.T. Solomon are looking for qualified prize-fighters to box-fight their sensational oriental middle-weight, Ling San Ho. Nicholson said they are offering purses of up to $2,000 depending on the opponent's experience and qualifications. Winner-take-all bouts will be held at the new Multnomah County Fairgrounds location. Anyone interested should contact Al Nicholson or A.T. Solomon at....

Al Nicholson and A.T. Solomon were anxious to sign a fighter of Kid Barry's reputation, establishing the purse at the maximum two thousand dollars. The winner-take-all provision bothered Jethro—it was Joe's cautious suspicion ringing in his ears.

"Why should it bother you, for Christ's sake?" Nicholson said. "Hell, you're the best fighter in the world. If I was you, I'd pick every winner-take-all fight I could get. That's for damn sure."

———

Jethro Spring crawled between the ropes. To his surprise, the Oriental, shorter than Jethro, but tall for a Chinese, appeared twice Jethro's age.

The referee called the two fighters to the ring center. "Okay, now," the official said, "this here fight is held under

International East Asia Rules and the way ..."

"What? What's that?" Jethro demanded.

"I said this is International East Asia Rules. Anything wrong?"

"Yeah, you're damned right there is," Jethro snarled. "What the hell is International East Asia Rules?"

"Just like the other rules," the referee said. "Asia rules maybe allows a little more than London Prize Ring, but ..."

"The fight's off," Jethro said. "Nobody told me about any change in rules and I'm not going along with it."

"You can't call the fight off now."

"Watch me."

Nicholson crawled through the ropes. "What's the matter?"

"Kid Barry here says he'll not fight Asian rules," the referee replied.

"That's what you agreed to, Barry," the promoter said.

"In a bull's ass!"

"Didn't you read your contract? The one you signed? It specifically called for International East Asia Rules to govern this fight."

"If this is some kind of trick, it won't work. I don't give a damn what I signed, I'm not going into a fight without London Prize Ring Rules. Or at least Marquis of Queensbury."

Unruly fight fans booed the delay. "Listen to that crowd," Nicholson warned. "You can't quit now."

Jethro started for his corner, shaking his head. Nicholson grabbed his arm. "If you quit, you'll lose the thousand you bet on the fight."

Jethro whirled. "You sonofabitch!"

Nicholson thrust his nose close to Jethro's face. "The contract calls for Asian rules and if you don't fight because

of that, you forfeit the fight." The man shouted to be
heard above the hooting, baying mob. "Besides that, I'll
sue."

Jethro hesitated and in a wheedling voice, the promoter pressed his point, "Hell, look at that old Chink. He's
twice your age. Everybody knows Chinks can't fight as well
as a bonafide American prizefighter. A winner-take-all
purse means two thousand, and you bet a grand. Hell,
Barry, you'll come out of this fight with three thousand
dollars. Are you crazy enough to walk away from that
'cause of a petty difference over what country's fight rules
we use?"

Jethro's senses cried, *NO!* But he thought of the three
thousand he stood to win, of the farm he'd buy. And he
thought also of the thousand he stood to lose—all the
money he had in the world after he'd paid Joe's hospital
and funeral expenses. "What's the difference between East
Asia and London Rules?" he asked at last.

"Very little," Nicholson said. "Mostly just feet. He's
barefoot. That can't hurt, even if he landed one of them
wild kicks. And hell, you can use your feet, too."

Jethro glared at the Oriental. Throughout the argument, the older fighter waited impassively, his black eyes
shifting from Jethro to Nicholson and back again. Still
Jethro shook his head while the fight mob howled even
louder.

"How can you lose against somebody like that?" the
promoter shouted in Jethro's ear, motioning toward the
Oriental.

"Okay," Jethro muttered. "All right. But I don't feel
good about this."

No bell rang. The referee merely waved the two fighters together. Jethro approached cautiously, amused as his
opponent turned sideways with a wide-spread, bent-kneed

stance, his open hands vertical before him. Jethro circled, thinking of Joe, missing the big Irishman's solid presence in his corner.

As Jethro circled, the Chinese glided, kept pace, still in his peculiar bent-knee stance. Jethro threw a long, straight jab, more of a feint than an intended blow. The Oriental leaned back, easily avoiding it.

Suddenly Jethro darted forward on his toes, stabbing a hard straight left and an overhand right. He blinked as the old man vanished, reappearing three feet to one side, still gliding in his peculiar stance. Again Jethro moved to the attack. Again his whistling blows flailed the air. This time, though, a brown palm flicked the base of his neck. He backed off with respect.

The crowd roared approval.

Careful. He's not as old as he looks, and he's quicker'n greased lightning.

Moving more methodically, the younger man circled while the older one floated before him. Jethro darted forward, tossing rights and lefts—at nothing! He took two more wisping blows to his neck from those flashing brown hands and his eyes watered. Through a haze he saw the old fighter retreat, his back turned. Now! And Jethro rushed forward, throwing a hard overhand right. But before the blow landed, a foot lashed from nowhere, crashing into Jethro's pivot knee, and he smashed down on all fours.

Dazed, he waited for the bell. Then another foot exploded against his temple, knocking him six feet to the side, and through the ropes.

The crowd roared as Jethro grasped a ring rope in confusion. "C'mon," the referee snarled. "You can't fight out there."

Jethro shook his head to clear it, stubbornly holding to his rope while pulling up to stand on the apron. "The bell.

I didn't hear the bell."

"You won't neither. No bell in International East Asia Rules. You fight until one of you can't fight no more."

"You sonsabitches," Jethro said as he crawled back through the ropes. The Oriental floated toward his opponent. The audience roared so loudly Jethro could scarcely think. As his mind cleared, however, his gorge rose. He saw an opening and jumped into it, eyes wide, watching for the darting, retreating slap.

But the Chinese did not retreat this time. Instead, he flowed forward and smacked one of Jethro's ears with an elbow and buried the braced, extended fingers of his right hand below the brisket, into Jethro's rock-hard stomach.

Jethro flailed in reflex. The elbow punch had dazed him again and he wheezed from the mid-section blow. But he laughed when a wild right plopped against the old man's nose. Until Jethro's wild right, the Chinese had ducked and weaved and glided and floated away from the best of the younger man's blows. Jethro's lucky punch must have angered the Oriental because he began delivering a series of telling, carefully directed strikes.

The younger man grudgingly admired the older one and his arsenal of weapons: fingertips, sides of hands, elbows, feet. It seemed he used every extremity as a weapon. Jethro sensed real danger. He switched to the defensive, hoping to lead the older man on, hoping youth and stamina would win in the end.

But the Oriental proved tireless, too, flowing and shifting in a series of poetic moves, baffling the younger fighter with his grace, appearing first on one side, then the other. Jethro would have him pinpointed in one spot when suddenly an elbow smacked from the other side. The Oriental would be in front, then he'd disappear. A heel lashed out, catching one of Jethro's hips, knocking him into a spin. As he spun, fingertips struck his armpit a numbing blow and the edge of a hand smashed against his temple with a blinding flash of pain.

Dazed and battered, Jethro continued his dogged retreat. He knew his opponent had hurt him, but superb conditioning and three years of Joe Barry's intensive tutelage served him well. He fled, sometimes escaping by instinct alone, other times surviving by sheer force of will and wild anger at how he'd been tricked.

In lucid moments, when he'd been successful in buying sufficient time for his brain to clear, Jethro admired the floating, stinging, fighting man before him. And in his misery, he thought those impassive black eyes held a certain measure of puzzlement. Or was it respect?

The fight went on forever. And ever. Suddenly there came another spear-point finger to his abdomen and a shattering blow to the back of his neck. Jethro Spring sank slowly to the canvas. Battered though he was in body, his mind shouted, *Watch the feet!* Rolling as he hit, he landed under the ring ropes.

"Chickenshit, ain'tcha," the referee taunted as Jethro crawled wearily back into the ring.

"Time?" he croaked.

"You been at it a little over an hour," the referee replied. "I'll give you that much. You made it longer'n anybody else ever did with this Chink."

Jethro endured more of the same. Down the younger man went again and again. It dawned on Jethro that his opponent had stopped attacking while he was down. He rolled over to peer up at the Chinese. The older man waited, arms folded across his chest, shaking his head while Jethro staggered to his feet. The young man thought now that he read sorrow and pity in those supposedly inscrutable Chinese eyes.

Jethro went down again. And again. And again. The end came two hours and fourteen minutes into the fight. Pandemonium reigned as the hometown standard-bearer vanquished his nationally ranked opponent. Jethro Spring neither heard nor saw the hubbub. Instead, he was carried to a nearby office and unceremoniously dumped upon a cot.

When Jethro's eyes fluttered open, a graying, tousled-haired man with a two-day beard stood beside the cot. The stranger wore a dirty white shirt open at the collar. Wide red suspenders held up his trousers. "Hey Al!" the man called. "Your punk's awake."

"Be there in a minute."

Jethro twisted his head in a shower of pain. Nicholson was seated at a desk, counting money. The promoter pushed back his chair and walked over to Jethro. "Well, Kid, you put up a good, strong fight. I was scared for awhile I was gonna lose my two grand."

Jethro stared blankly up at him.

"No hard feelin's, huh, Kid?"

Jethro shook his head to another shower of pain.

"We're gonna let him go, ain't we Doc? No reason to keep him if he's awake is there?"

"Don't see no reason why we should," the unkempt man answered. "He might need a little help gettin' into his clothes, though."

"C'mon, Kid," the promoter said. "See if you can sit up. Doc and me'll help you get into your pants."

Jethro swung his feet from the cot and struggled upright. Fireworks popped in his head and he almost fell. Later, he remembered only their helping him to the door.

"You're a good prizefighter, Barry," Nicholson said, opening the door. "Stick to your class and you might amount to something someday."

The door slammed behind him and Jethro peered around in the dark shadows of an alley. Down the cluttered way, lamplight flickered along a street and Jethro lurched toward it. A dim figure detached itself from the alley's deeper shadows to block his path beneath the streetlamp's fluttering light. Jethro peered at the newcomer, saw the slanting black eyes and flattened nose of an Oriental.

Puzzled, Jethro reached for the lamppost to brace himself and leaned nearer the other's face, staring. Then it came to him! The gliding, wispy figure. The pain. The bland face and impassive eyes. The puzzlement. The admiration. The pity. The pain.

The Oriental held out a hand. "Please to come with me," Ling San Ho said.

≫ CHAPTER THIRTEEN ≪

Jethro Spring thought time spent within the serene household of Ling San Ho as the most pleasant of his life. The Chinese family lived in a wretched hut along the north riverfront, Portland's Chinatown. Despite being an amalgam of discarded material—old split shakes and half-rotted lumber, slabs from sawn logs (bark still clinging), even a piece of rusted ship's boiler plate—the home, though tiny and cramped, was neat and clean. Instead of nails, whittled wooden pegs held the shack together. Rotted canvas had been stuffed into air holes. The place was little more than a hovel. Yet that home was more peaceful and restful and relaxing than anything Jethro had known since the buffalo hide tipi of his childhood days.

His new friend's home presented a strange new world to Jethro. Conversation was limited and conducted in a soft melodious sing-song Jethro soon learned to associate with the Cantonese dialect. An ethereal serenity prevailed;

a strange peace and tranquility Jethro had never known before.

He identified that tranquility with Che'n Wei, Ling San's wife. Jethro marveled at the calm tone and quiet effort Che'n Wei put into making her home peaceful for Tse Deng, the nine-year-old daughter, her husband, and Che'n Wei's aged father. Tea was always hot and ready, meals always delicious and timely, seating mats always properly arranged.

A grateful Jethro lay quietly on a small pallet, with little to do except wonder where the chances of fate would next lead. He thanked Che'n Wei and her daughter for ministering to his needs—the pleasing sensation of soothing oil deftly rubbed into his aching joints, the healing balm applied to his bruises. He thanked them for bowls of fish gruel and boiled rice with bits of meats and vegetables. He appreciated the spoon given him by the dark-eyed daughter, but envied her dexterity with the strange eating sticks of her native land.

After but a few days, he spied Ling San dressed in fighting tights, wearing the long, flowing, silk robe he'd worn when he escorted Jethro to his quiet home. Jethro paid more attention when Ling San crept home hours later to receive the ministrations of oil and balm to his own aches and bruises.

"Another fight?" Jethro asked. "So soon?"

"Yes, fight," Ling San said.

"Why? Too soon."

Ling San's tense face broke into a smile. "Not soon. Make hundred dolla this time."

"A hundred dollars? That's poor pay, isn't it? Compared to last time, I mean."

Ling San shook his head. "Not understand. Say again."

Jethro fished for simpler words. "A hundred dollars—

not much." He thrust his thumb against his own chest, "Fight me, you make two thousand dollars."

Ling San looked puzzled. "Two thousand dolla," he said at last. "Is much?"

"Very much," Jethro said. He flashed his hands twice at his friend, ten fingers held up. "This many times one hundred dollars."

"Ayiii. Is not so much dolla in world."

"Well, how in God's name much money did you make when you pounded me out?"

"Not understand. Bar-ry speak so fast. So sorry I poor English."

"How much money," Jethro said slowly, "you make when fight me?"

"Oh yes. You. Fifty dolla."

"Fifty dollars!"

Ling San nodded.

"That was winner-take-all for two thousand."

"Not understand."

Jethro's anger mounted. "If I beat you, I get two thousand."

"Much money," Ling San said. "You great fighter."

"But you won. You should have received two thousand. That's what I was told."

"Two thousand," Ling San said in wonder. "Chinese live long time this many one hundred dolla." He stared morosely at the spread fingers of one hand as he held them for Jethro to count.

Jethro's eyes narrowed. "That sonofabitch. He held out on you." He lay back on his pallet with a sigh. "I think we'll see about this little scheme as soon as I get back to full steam."

"Not understand, Bar-ry. Say again, please."

"Never mind," Jethro muttered. "It's not important

right now." Then he popped up. "Who in hell did you fight that was worth a hundred, if I was worth only fifty?"

"So sorry."

"A hundred dollars to fight. Who you fight?"

"Two men." Ling San held up two fingers. "You better fighter than both."

"My God!" Jethro exploded.

"Soon, fight three. Make one hundred dolla and fifty dolla."

"No," Jethro said under his breath. Then louder: "No. You must not."

"Oh yes, Bar-ry. Soon we have many dolla. Then we go away to work rail-road. Then I fight no more."

Jethro sank back upon his pallet with a sigh.

The next day, Jethro Spring asked Ling San Ho, "Where will you go to work on the railroad, my friend?"

"Colo-rado. Other Chinese there."

"Ling San, it doesn't cost much to go to Colorado. Not many dollars. You fight me, fifty dollars. You fight two men, one hundred dollars. Other men you fight. Why don't you go to Colorado now?"

Ling San concentrated on Jethro's long question. At the end, he nodded and started to say something, then stopped, considered, and said, "Need more dolla."

Just then, Tse Deng brought her father and Jethro bowls of fragrant stew and the men lapsed into silence. After they finished eating, Jethro said, "You must not fight three men, Ling San."

"Why, Bar-ry?"

"Too many. You can't win."

"Yes, I must."

Jethro shook his head. "Will you get one hundred fifty dollars if you lose?"

"No."

"Tell me, Ling San, can you win against three men?"

"It is so. If one is not Bar-ry."

The next day, Jethro pushed painfully from his pallet and shuffled to the Portland waterfront. He located a tramp steamer loading lumber for California and told the dock foreman that he was an experienced stevedore. At the end of the day, he bought a newspaper with one of the coins he'd earned. He was disappointed that none of the stories mentioned Ling San Ho's upcoming battle with three opponents. With the rest of his money he bought food for Ling San's household.

Jethro continued to work at the Portland docks during the day, returning at night to Ling San's home, bringing food to help pay his way. A week later, he found the newspaper story for which he'd been watching:

Battle Royal On Tap With Oriental

Portland prize-fight promoters Al Nicholson and A.T. Solomon announced this week a new extravaganza for their sensational Chinese fighting master, Ling San Ho.

Ho will defend his all-comers claim to the northwest championship against three—that's 3—area prize-fighters this coming Saturday, April 27, in yet another $2,000 winner-take-all purse.

Ho, the Oriental master, is undefeated in a long string of Portland victories dating back to his appearance on American shores nearly two years ago. Included in that victorious string is a recent win over one of America's best middleweight prize-fighters, Kid Barry.

Promoters Nicholson and Solomon claim Ho to be the world's greatest fighting machine and say his upcoming bout against three chosen fighters will prove their claim, once and for all.

All prize-fighting fans are invited to watch this latest Nicholson and Solomon promotional fete at the
usual Multnomah County Fairground location, for
the same 25-cent fee.

Jethro crumpled the newspaper, his face set in grim
lines. Later that evening, he asked Ling San, "Did you sign
a contract with Nicholson and Solomon?"

Ling San's face screwed in concentration. "Con-tract?
I not understand what is mean by word."

"A piece of paper for fight. You sign?"

"Like chop? No. I not think so."

"Then how do you know you will get one hundred and
fifty dollars to fight three men?"

Ling San nodded. "Nicholson, he say so."

"But you put no mark on paper? Did Nicholson?"

"No. No mark on paper. Why Bar-ry ask?"

"It's a swindle, Ling San. Nicholson and Solomon are
cheating you. They've cheated a lot of other fighters, too.
This winner-take-all ploy they've got gives nothing to the
losers, and they cheat you out of your purse, too. That
means they pay neither fighter. No purse. It's a leadpipe
cinch they rake in two thousand bucks on each fight, over
and above their normal profit. They've got a neat swindle
going and no one to know."

Ling San shook his head. "You speak so fast. So sorry
I not understand."

Jethro pulled the newspaper from beneath his shirt and
opened it to the article about the fight. "It says right there,
in black and white, that the winner of your next fight will
receive two thousand dollars."

"Two thousand dolla. So much? Nicholson, he say one
hundred dolla and fifty dolla."

"They are cheating you, Ling San. And somehow, we
must stop them."

Ling San shifted on his cushion. "No cheat. Pay Ling San good for fight."

"Not nearly as much as it's worth, my friend. Tomorrow we'll go see a lawyer."

"Not understand. What is law-yer?"

"He will stop Nicholson and Solomon from cheating you. Go to police. Maybe take it to court."

Ling San emphatically wagged his head. "No police. No law-yer. We are Chinese. Bar-ry not understand we Chinese. A hundred dolla and fifty dolla much money for Chinese. Please Bar-ry. Do not go to law-yer or police."

"But, Ling San, they're cheating you."

"They pay Ling San what they say. It is enough. No trouble. They want fight again, they come see Ling San. Ling San make more money. It is good for Chinese. No trouble."

"But, Ling San ..."

"You go law-yer or police, Chinese have trouble. It is always so, Bar-ry. You will not do this thing. So sorry. No."

Jethro Spring settled further into his hiding place, beneath broken planks and discarded packing crates. The debris was piled just down the alley from Nicholson's and Solomon's office. Faint roars came to him from the distant stadium where Ling San Ho fought three opponents to the bitter finish for a hundred and fifty dollars—if he won. After the fight was over and the shouting died, Nicholson and his partner carried several canvas sacks of money to their alley office.

A short time later, Ling San Ho limped to the door and knocked.

"Did it again, huh, Chink?" Nicholson asked, his bulky

frame filling the doorway. "Looks like we ever find an American can whip you, he's gotta carry a gun."

"So sorry," Ling San said. "Not understand."

"Hey, Abie. Our Chink's here and wants his hundred. Bring it for him, will you?"

Jethro couldn't catch the muffled reply.

"So sorry," said Ling San. "Is one hundred dolla and fifty dolla."

"So sorry yourself, Chink. Is one hundred dolla. You can't cheat me."

"Ling San fight three men." The Oriental held up three fingers.

"And not a damned one of 'em could kick their way out of a schoolroom," Nicholson growled, unbuttoning his coat, exposing the butt of a revolver tucked into the waistband of his trousers.

Ling San subsided.

The round, florid face of the stunted Solomon appeared. Solomon handed Ling San several bills. The Chinese hesitated a moment, then took them, bowing. "Thank you."

"We'll be in touch," Nicholson said, "soon as we figure out your next fight."

Ling San backed away. As he did, Jethro got a clear look at his friend's battered face.

The door slammed shut and Jethro, mouth tightening into a grim line, settled deeper into his hiding place.

Solomon left the office after dark. Jethro clearly heard the door's lock click behind the departing man. Then he heard a heavy bolt thrown across the door. Al Nicholson slept with their cash receipts.

It began to rain, slanting into the pile of debris where Jethro Spring lay hidden. He turned up his coat collar and tucked his hands, Chinese style, into the sleeves.

Rain still fell in torrents at daylight. A wispy, swirling fog drifted from lowering gray clouds pressing from above. Some time later, Jethro, shivering from the cold, tensed as a buggy swung down the alley. He swiped a hand across his face and flexed fingers and muscles, every fiber coming alert.

The driver reined the light one-horse buggy to a stop in front of Nicholson's door. He was a burly man who carried a six-gun strapped over a yellow, knee-length raincoat. A double-barreled, heavy-gauge shotgun leaned against the buggy seat. The man wore a floppy wide-brimmed hat pulled low over his eyes. Rainwater dripped from the brim and coursed down the raincoat.

Nicholson unbarred his office door, peered suspiciously around, then waved the other in. The driver wrapped the reins around the buggy's brake handle and disappeared inside.

Jethro hadn't counted on the armed guard. He had only a moment to consider, but spent it thinking of his battered friend coming to collect his earnings from Nicholson, only to be swindled out of much of that. It was enough. Jethro yanked his wool stocking cap low over his eyes and tied a big, blue neckerchief over his nose. He crawled from his hiding place carrying a broken chunk of planking and sprinted past the buggy to flatten against the wall near the door. The horse shifted nervously and blew through its nostrils, cocking ears to the sound. However, blinders on the driving bridle kept the animal from actually seeing the man, and the tied-off reins kept him from turning his head. The horse settled down just as the door swung open.

"God, that chink's tough, ain't he, Al?" said the burly driver-guard as he stepped through the doorway, carrying a heavy sack in each hand. "What'll it take to beat him, anyway?"

"I dunno," the promoter said, following the guard with yet another money bag. "It'll happen pretty quick, though. Folks are starting to ..."

Jethro brought his club down on Nicholson's head. The guard whirled at the sound, dropping the two bags and clawing for his gun. Jethro leaped on him, thrusting the club deep into the man's belly.

The guard doubled over with the blow and Jethro brought the club down in a short, wicked arc to the base of the man's neck. The guard sprawled to the ground, unconscious. Jethro spun back to the promoter. Nicholson was on his hands and knees, shaking his head. Jethro whacked his club against the man's temple, then dropped the makeshift weapon, scooped up the three money bags and sprinted down the alley.

Traffic's too heavy on the main street. He veered and disappeared within the sprawling Multnomah County Fairgrounds.

CHAPTER FOURTEEN

The door banged open and a blue-uniformed policeman held a shotgun at the ready. Jethro stared up, face blank, then frightened. "This—this here toilet is closed fer cleanin' officer. You're supposed t'use the one at t'other end of the runway." He dumped another shovel full of excrement into a half-filled wheelbarrow.

The officer sniffed in distaste, but pushed on in. "I'm not here to take a shit," he said. "I'm looking for a killer and a thief." Lumber removed from the toilet seats lay scattered about and the policeman tiptoed through the exposed nails to stand over Jethro who stood to his knees in a long trough.

"A killer!" Jethro exclaimed. "Here? God, who'd he kill?"

"Nobody yet. But the bastard bloodied up a couple of men and stole the cash from yesterday's prize fight."

"You don't say." Jethro scooped up another shovel of

human manure and tossed it at the wheelbarrow.

"Seen anybody?" the policeman asked.

"I ain't seen nobody," Jethro grumbled. "I'm jist a toilet sweep what's s'posed to be good only fer shovelin' shit. What's he look like, anyway?"

"Nobody knows. That's the trouble. I guess neither of the two guys he tried to kill got a good look at him. We follered his tracks into the fairground, though. And from them, we know he's wearin' some kind of Injun moccasins."

"Do tell," Jethro said, bending again to his work. "If I see any Injuns, I'll holler. Don't know how I'll do that, though, bein' stuck in the shithouse all the time."

The officer backed away, wrinkling his nose, stepping carefully through the planks. Then he was gone, the door slamming shut behind. Jethro sighed, mushed a couple of steps through the vile goo, and scratched a buried money bag with the tip of his shovel. A frown crossed his face when he noticed the tip of a blue handkerchief protruding farther down the trough. He waded down and pushed it deeper into the muck, all the while pondering how he'd thus far avoided capture—and how he might yet escape....

———•·•———

Jethro, gasping for breath after his dash into the fairgrounds, jerked open first one door, then another, until he stumbled upon the toolroom. He quickly peeled off his own clothing and donned worn coveralls and a pair of rubber boots found there. Then he threw the money bags into a wheelbarrow, tossed his old clothes on top, and grabbed a shovel and a hammer. He wheeled the barrow to the nearest toilet, buried the money and his old clothes under some of the muck, and set about ripping the seatboards from the long public toilet trench. He spotted a partial sack of slaked lime used to temper the toilet's offensive odor and rubbed portions of the lime into the skin of his face. Within moments, he felt the caustic burning. Then he took a Barlow knife from his pocket and hacked at his hair until he'd trimmed it back to a rough inch-long. The policeman who pushed into the toilet an hour later quickly dismissed the filthy, ugly workman as beyond suspicion. Other lawmen who checked the toilet later that day did the same.

Night fell. Jethro Spring uncovered the money and his clothes, piled them into the wheelbarrow and shoveled excrement on top. Before leaving, he restored the building to the order in which he'd found it.

No one noticed as the grimy workman pushed the wheelbarrow through the deserted fairgrounds and on to the river. Hiding the wheelbarrow, he left in search of a boat. Returning minutes later, Jethro loaded money bags, clothes, wheelbarrow, and tools into the stolen rowboat and rowed far out into the flood-swollen Willamette River, where he tossed tools and wheelbarrow overboard. Letting the boat drift, he scrubbed the muck from his clothing, then bathed in the muddy river, shivering uncontrollably as he clambered back to the boat. He donned his hand-rung clothing, then threw the coveralls and his moccasins overboard. He tugged on the rubber boots and, setting his back to the oars, rowed for all he was worth downstream, warming at last to his work.

Shortly after midnight, Jethro felt his little rowboat slip into a surging eddy of the mighty Columbia, also swollen with late-April rains and spring's snow melt fron the far-off Rocky Mountains. Jethro began the long row across the huge river. It was daylight and ten miles downstream from the old Hudson Bay Post at Vancouver when Jethro beached the rowboat in Washington Territory. After making sure no prying eyes were about, he unloaded the money sacks and, with a rock, beat a hole in the boat before pushing it out to sink into the river. At last he picked up the money bags and walked inland.

A week later, outfitted in new clothes, seven-day's beard poorly covering the lime-burned sores, and a wool cap hiding his raggedly cropped hair, Jethro arrived at Oregon City, via stagecoach from Vancouver. In Oregon City, he collected a cardboard suitcase filled with his belongings and took the next stage back to Portland.

Tse Deng opened the door, a smile lighting her round, dark-eyed features. She spoke in Cantonese, calling Ling San, Che'n Wei, and grandfather. They all filled the doorway, bowing and chattering.

Jethro presented a flour sack full of groceries to Che'n Wei and set his suitcase on the floor. Removing his cap and coat, he sat upon the inevitably proffered cushion. Ling San sat across from him. The two men waited in silence until Tse Deng brought cups of syrupy-sweet, steaming black tea. Politely, Jethro waited for Ling San to speak.

"We have missed you, Bar-ry," Ling San said at last. "Our hearts are happy you have returned."

Jethro dipped his head at the compliment. "I am happy to be back in the household of Ling San. I, too, have missed you and Che'n Wei and Tse deng and Che'n Wei's honored father." As he mentioned each member of the household, Jethro nodded deferentially in their direction. "But I had urgent business that could be delayed no longer."

"We understand, Bar-ry, that you must some time go. We pray to our Gods and burn incense to their spirits that you will return safely to us."

"Your Gods are strong, Ling San. They watched over

me during my journey. Thank you, my friend, for your concern."

The two men sipped their tea while Che'n Wei spoke in sing-song to her husband. "My worthy wife," Ling San said, "asks if the places on your face hurt? She asks if it would be all right, Bar-ry, if she bathed and spread an ointment upon them?"

"Please tell your worthy wife she is welcome to do so. I have been bathing them, and they are much better now. But if she has an ointment that will cure them sooner, all the better."

Ling San nodded to Che'n Wei and she knelt before Jethro, gently bathing and anointing the slaked lime burns. When finished, she murmured again to Ling San, who asked Jethro, "My worthy wife asks if it would be all right, Bar-ry, to cut your hair. By cutting it same all over, my worthy wife believes you will look better."

Jethro smiled and nodded. "Tell Che'n Wei it is all right if she cuts my hair."

As Che'n Wei worked, Jethro said, "It makes me sad to see Ling San hurt from fighting so often to live. I say this, for I no longer care to fight for other's pleasure. I think Ling San would not do so if he did not have to do it." Jethro paused politely for his host's comments. When it was obvious Ling San wanted him to finish, he continued:

"I know it is your wish to go where you may work on the railroad."

Ling San's black eyes narrowed to slits.

"So I have purchased steamship tickets for you and your family to San Francisco. From there, I will buy railroad tickets to Wyoming, where you can transfer to a new rail line to Colorado."

Ling San meditated, sipping his tea. "I am not know all Bar-ry says, but I think I understand. It is kind thing Barry does for Ling San and his worthy family. But I can not do this thing."

"Why?"

"It may be that it is hard for Bar-ry to see, but is many other Chinese here who wish to go to rail-road. That is why I fight. To help others. Until Ling San has passage for all, I can not leave them."

"Cannot, my friend? Or will not?"

There flashed a faint smile. "As you wish, Bar-ry."

Che'n Wei finished trimming his hair and moved away. Jethro sipped his tea thoughtfully. At last, he asked, "And you figure to get the money you need by fighting all odds on Nicholson's demand?"

"Slower, please, Bar-ry. I not understand."

"You will pay passage for all Chinese by fight?"

Ling San shrugged. "Is only way."

"Even when they cheat you, Ling San?"

Again, Ling San shrugged.

"How much did you make—how many dollars for last fight?"

Ling San's face became a mask. He said, "One hundred dolla, Bar-ry. Is much money."

Jethro plunged on, fearing he'd committed a breach of etiquette, "What happened to the one hundred, fifty the bastard promised?"

"Not understand bas-tard."

"What about the one hundred, fifty Nicholson promised?"

"Ah yes. Ling San wrong. Nicholson promise one hundred dolla. Is much money."

"Goddammit, Ling San, you were supposed to get two thousand for winning that fight. You only got one hundred."

"One hundred dolla much money. Some day we all go

to rail-road."

"Railroad, my ass! By the time you shake loose from Nicholson's bondage, the goddamn railroad will already be built ten times over."

"So sorry, Bar-ry. Not understand."

Jethro muttered something unintelligible and lapsed into an angry silence.

Che'n Wei and Tse Deng brought steaming bowls of gruel, laced with bits of meat. The two men ate in silence. Later, relaxing on their cushions, Jethro said to Ling San, "How many Chinese are here in Portland? How many of your people are you helping to earn tickets?"

Ling San held up both palms twice, plus three fingers. "This many, I think."

"Twenty-three. That's not so many."

"Then family. Many times that number."

"Oh God!"

"All Cantonese Chinese save money for rail-road. Maybe half go now. But all wait until all can go."

Jethro considered for several minutes, then said, "Ling San?"

"Yes, Bar-ry?"

"I want to understand exactly how many Chinese, their ages and everything. Their money, too. When I know, I will go to the steamship office and buy tickets to San Francisco for everyone. And in San Francisco I will buy railroad tickets to Colorado for everyone. Okay?"

"No," said Ling San.

"No! For God's sake, why not?"

"Because, Bar-ry, you should not go out where is people. Police look for man with sores on face and hair that is short and poor-cut. I am not know how you were not caught by police before you come to our humble home. If tickets are bought for Chinese, better that a Chinese buy them."

Stunned, Jethro stared at Ling San. At last, with eyebrows lifted, he asked, "What more can Ling San tell me?"

"Only that police come looking for American who stay here. But he no longer here."

"But I'm here now."

"No, Bar-ry. No American here. Only Chinese. I tell other Chinese. No American. Only Chinese. When we count tickets, we buy five for household of Ling San Ho. You will go to rail-road with us."

Jethro leaned back on the cushion, his hands behind his head. Directly he said, "You seem to know more about this than a fellow would think. How about the two bastards I popped?"

"So sorry. Not understand."

"Oh hell. What about Nicholson? And the other one?"

"Yes. They mad. They go to police every day. Police bad for Chinese."

"Ling San, you're really somebody."

"Bar-ry, he somebody, too."

———•·•———

Wearing a silk robe with a dragon embroidered on it, and a lampshade-style coolie hat, Jethro Spring blended with the hundred and sixteen Chinese boarding the tramp steamer, *Northwest Coast,* bound for San Francisco. Crammed in steerage amid the packed Chinese, Jethro found peace with these shy people.

Sitting jammed against a bulkhead, with the dark-eyed, laughing Tse Deng balanced on his knees, Jethro said to Ling San, "Your people make me nervous, my friend. They treat me as a revered father, making extra room and offering me portions of their food. Why do they do this thing?"

Ling San smiled. "You are good, Bar-ry. Not all your people are so good to Chinese. And you are smart. Chinese not so smart. And you do thing that is kind for all my people. No one has done such thing for them. Not even Chinese do so much. Is no wonder they honor you. I honor you. Che'n Wei honors you. Tse Deng honors you. Honored father honors you."

The tiny girl shyly put her arms around Jethro's neck and hugged him saying, "Tse Deng love Bar-ry."

"I didn't know she could speak English!" Jethro exclaimed.

"She can not," Ling San replied. "But she asked for English word love."

"Why now? How could she understand what we were saying?"

"Children are wiser than we think, Bar-ry." Ling San gestured around him. "These people are like children. And like children, perhaps they are more wise than we think."

"I did for them no more than many others would do," Jethro said.

"There are not many like you, Bar-ry. Perhaps there are others among the Americans. Who would know? But there can never be another who would see our need and help in your way. Or place one's own head in the dragon's mouth, as you."

Tse Deng squeezed his neck again and Jethro Spring hugged her in turn.

At San Francisco, Jethro and his group took the ferry across the bay to Oakland and the Central Pacific depot. He purchased one hundred and sixteen tickets to the rail line's Utah transfer point with the Union Pacific, then on to Wyoming and another transfer.

"Okay, Ling San. Here are tickets for you and your people. These will take you the many miles to Wyoming. There you must change railroads to go to Colorado. And here is money to buy tickets to ..."

Ling San interrupted. "Why does Bar-ry give these tickets to Ling San?"

"Who should have them, if not Ling San?"

"Why does not Bar-ry keep them?"

"What good would that do? You and your people need them," Jethro said patiently.

"Will not Bar-ry be with Chinese?"

"No, my friend. You do not need me any longer."

"What will Bar-ry do?"

Jethro shrugged. "I don't know. Find a job. Wander some. I really don't know."

"Then Bar-ry could come with Chinese?"

The younger man chuckled and repeated, "But you don't need me."

"If Chinese need Bar-ry, he would come with Chinese?"

"I could, yes. But you do not ..."

"Good. Ling San buy Bar-ry ticket. He go with Chinese."

"Wait a minute, dammit. Why do you need me?"

Ling San looked puzzled. "Why we not need Bar-ry?"

"What good would I do? You speak English much better now."

"Where does Bar-ry go? He does not know. Where will he find work? He does not know. Go rail-road. Work with Chinese."

"Oh no you don't, you crafty Oriental. You told me why I can go with you. You didn't say why I should go. There's a difference between can and should, you know."

"Because Chinese need you, Bar-ry," Ling San slowly replied. "You are our eyes and ears. You are good to us. You help us, no matter we are Chinese. Bar-ry is fair. Bar-ry does not like others to trick or cheat us. Bar-ry tells us when that happens and stops those who do. There are no others to help Chinese. Most of Bar-ry's people fear us or will not care about us; or will not help us. We only wish to live quietly with our families and earn our rice. You must go with us. If you do, you will be honored by Chinese. You will be one of us, protected as one of us. Please, Bar-ry, say you will come."

Jethro studied Ling San Ho. *I never noticed the mole over his eyebrow before.* "I'll get my ticket."

It was at Donner Summit where fifteen Chinese were ordered from their seats to make room for a squad of U.S. Cavalry returning to Fort Humboldt. The soldiers had been on a futile search for renegade Modoc Indians still at large after their short "Lava Bed" war of two years before.

Despite his fear of Army blue, Jethro started toward them as soon as he heard the commotion. Ling San stopped him. "No, Bar-ry. They will give us seats in another car."

"Yeah, an empty cattle car! Let the soldiers ride there."

"No, Bar-ry. Chinese will ride in cattle car. Is all right. We do not wish trouble. I will pick strongest of the Chinese. You will stay with others."

"No, by God. If one damned Chinaman goes to a cattle car, I go."

"As Bar-ry wishes."

The car was hot, dusty and smelly despite the train's stopping long enough to load the soldiers' horses, and for the Chinese to clean their new accommodations as best they could. Jethro seethed as the train lurched and rattled down to the Nevada desert. He squatted against a wooden stanchion, arms folded across his knees, head buried in them.

"Bar-ry," Ling San said, "do you know of one called John Snow?"

Jethro's head snapped up at mention of his long-ago alias. "What? What did you say?"

"Do you know of one called John Snow?"

Jethro's face turned to stone—as inscrutable as his friend's own mask. At last, Ling San said, "A man came with Nicholson and police who looked for man with burns on face. Ling San heard this one ask of John Snow."

Jethro sighed. "What can Ling San tell me of the man who asked of John Snow?"

"That he frightened Tse Deng and Che'n Wei and even Ling San. Even the police and Nicholson seemed to fear him."

"Did he say why he looked for John Snow?"

"This he did not."

"And what did this man look like?"

"Very wide at shoulders. You say husky? He wore a black suit with tie."

Jethro digested Ling San's information silently. At last he sighed and asked, "Why did he frighten Ling San?"

"This man, he look bad. One side of his face was long ago in fire."

Jethro sighed again. "I must leave you, Ling San. When the train stops again for water or coal, I must leave."

When Ling San said nothing, Jethro continued, "This man follows me for something that happened many years ago. I have no choice but to flee from him."

Still, Ling San said nothing. "Perhaps I am a danger to

your people," Jethro said. "If it is known you shelter me...."

Ling San smiled broadly. "Ah, but it is not known that Bar-ry is one of us. How would any know?"

"How did he follow me to Portland? How did he know I had been at the house of Ling San Ho? There are many of your countrymen who know, and the knowing could be a danger to all of you."

Ling San shook his head. "Not so, my friend. There are none but Chinese with the Chinese here. And none but Chinese have been at the house of Ling San Ho. So the police and this man have been told. So have all Chinese been told."

Dusk crept across the desert and Jethro could barely make out Ling San's features in the fading light. "He knows of Barry, though," Jethro said quietly. "When he hears that Barry is with your people, he will come again."

Ling San nodded. "That is so. That is why from this moment forward, there will be no Bar-ry. I have told my people of this and all await your new name...."

CHAPTER FIFTEEN

Summers! Hey, Summers!"

Jethro Spring looked around. The gray gelding he led nuzzled his shoulder. "Yeah?" he said as a thin, pallid railway clerk hurried to him amid the confusion of men and equipment.

"Mr. Dickerson was hoping we could catch you before you got away. He wants to see you as soon as possible."

Jethro turned back to the rope corral and tied the gray. He paused to let two heavy tie wagons lumber past, then strode to the trackboss's car. George Dickerson sat at his desk, sleeves rolled to his elbows, cotton shirt open wide at the throat, exposing a tangle of curly black hair. The desk wobbled under an enormous pile of papers, books, and ledgers. A film of dust and soot coated everything.

The work train's engine gave two short blasts on its steam whistle and inched forward as Jethro stepped up to the rolling car. Dickerson didn't appear to notice him. He studied the trackboss as the man gestured animatedly to another of his foremen. The car came to a stop amid crashing couplings as the engine braked at head of track.

Dickerson, in his fifties, was tall and stoop shouldered, a blustering man, totally committed to building railroads. He wore no hat, and his few long strands of hair raked randomly across his head did little to shroud a shiny dome. The trackboss dismissed the other foreman and turned beetling brows to a surveyor who waited with charts under one arm. Dickerson glanced at the other men in the car and his eyes fell on Jethro. "Just a minute, Heinke," Dickerson said. "I want to talk to Summers."

Jethro moved forward.

The trackboss leaned back in his chair and rubbed his neck. "Summers, dammit, we're falling behind schedule."

"Why tell me, Dick? My crews are ahead of theirs."

"I know," Dickerson said, sighing. "Your chink grading crews are running away from the tracklayers and the trestlemen. I want you to think about cutting your grading crews in half and bringing the excess back here to start a second track crew."

"There's not enough daylight, Dick," Jethro protested. "It's late in the season and daylight's shorter than it was even a month ago. Laying track at night is dangerous. You know that."

"Not impossible, though," the trackboss growled. "Besides, we're going to cut the reg'lar layin' crews back to shorter days and split up the daylight."

"Oh my God! Does that mean cutting their pay, too? If it does and you put a Chinese crew on, they'll think the Chinese had something to do with it."

"Come on now, Summers. You don't expect us to pay tracklayers for work they're not doing. Of course their pay will be cut. It's not the D&RG's fault they're behind schedule."

"Then why don't the D&RG give full pay to men who're ahead of theirs?" Jethro demanded. "Why don't you pay my Chinese what they're worth? Or at least pay 'em what a white is getting for doing a poorer job?"

"Summers, I didn't set the standard," Dickerson growled. "Central Pacific did that eight, ten years ago when they first hired the chinks. You and I know the chinks were damned glad to get a job then, and they still are. They make a damn sight more workin' on a railroad—even for less money than we pay whites—than they would takin' in washing or putting out meals in some damned slop shop. And let me tell you something else. I, for one, am getting damned tired of hearing you bring up the pay differential every time I see you."

Jethro subsided into a stiff silence.

"Now," Dickerson continued, "I want you to split up your chinks and form a short track crew. You work out the roster over the next couple of days and get it back to me by Thursday. I'll want the second shift to start on the job next Monday."

"How long do you expect this second shift to continue?" Jethro asked.

"Until we get back to schedule. That depends on the chinks."

"And the whites," Jethro shot back, glaring around at others in the car.

"Clear?" Dickerson demanded.

"It's clear," Jethro said. "But I don't like it. There's trouble brewing and you know it, Dick. What you're doing is throwing the two races together so they'll be in direct competition. The way we've got it now, with the Chinese out on the grading crews, we've been able to hold that kind of trouble to a minimum. But if you're going to give the tracklayers shorter days and cut their pay ..."

"Goddammit, Summers! Will you do as you're told?!"

"All right. But I want an extra ironman for each rail."

Dickerson had turned to papers on his desk, but his head popped back up. "What did you say?"

"The Chinese are small. A seven hundred-pound rail is too much for five of 'em to handle. Make it six."

"No, by God!" Dickerson said, his voice rising with each word. "Why in hell should we?"

"Then pay them the same as you do the whites!"

Dickerson sputtered, then leaned forward and stabbed a finger at Jethro. "You just do what you are told, young man. Or find yourself another place to work. I want job rosters back by Thursday. And I want that shift to begin Monday. Do I make myself clear?"

"Yes you do, Dick. Just one more question. Who runs that second Chinese crew?"

"I'll leave that up to you."

"They won't work for just anybody."

"I know that, dammit," Dickerson said. "So far they haven't worked for anybody but you. Even the chinks we had on the line before you showed up won't work for nobody else now. That's the only goddamn reason you're still around." Then the trackboss's voice moderated to a more soothing note. "If they won't work for nobody else, you'll have to run both crews, both shifts. You can do it. You can start the grading crew in the morning, then come back to start the tracklayers at night. I know it'll be more work, but you'll be paid accordingly. My God, man, haven't we always bent over backwards to pay you well?"

Jethro glared down at the trackboss. "Maybe that's the problem," he said as he spun on his heel and dropped from the car.

The steam engine tooted twice and inched the work-train forward again. "He's a surly bastard, ain't he?" said one of the group by Dickerson's cluttered desk.

The trackboss stared at the empty doorway. Rubbing his aching neck, he quit his reverie and said, "That he is, that he is. But goddamn him, he gets things done. And there's almost a hundred chinks workin' this road who won't work without him."

———

It hadn't been easy, Jethro reflected as he swung a leg over the gray's back and put the big horse into a lope, heading for his grading crews twelve miles distant. *I must have sold my soul to the devil a dozen times, trying to level-up between the Chinese and the whites.*

Whites made up the majority of the Denver and Rio Grande's construction gangs. Nearly to a man, they looked upon the Chinese as a threat to their jobs—*unless they've worked directly among them,* Jethro reflected. *Then they find 'em okay.*

Jethro had arrived at the Pueblo construction headquarters of D&RG's central Colorado track on July 1, 1876, three days before the Nation reached its Centennial and a mere month before Colorado became the twenty-fifth state. He had in tow twenty-four able-bodied Chinese workmen and their ninety-two dependents. Jethro and the two-dozen Chinese were hired on the spot and herded to end-of-track near the great Arkansas River canyon. Their wives, children, and parents remained in hovels near Pueblo.

Woes beset D&RG construction. Schedules were so far in arrears that the company tried to make it up by hiring more men. They liked the Chinese who traditionally worked for less money than their Caucasian counterparts. However, animosity over the Chinese roiled just beneath the surface. The arrival of Jethro's group brought it to boiling. As a result, construction suffered even more until Jethro proposed segregating the gangs into Chinese grading crews and white tracklayers. Most of the white laborers accepted the idea because the grading crews were inching into the narrow, rugged canyon known as the Royal Gorge, and roadbed construction there was perilous work. Grudgingly, George Dickerson, D&RG construction boss, agreed to experiment with Jethro's proposition. Dickerson also sensed Jethro's influence over the Chinese and gave the man more and more responsibility.

The Chinese responded with zeal. They rushed about their work, started early, stayed late, and the roadbed crept steadily forward despite physical obstacles. The man Dickerson knew as Jed Summers, soared in the eyes of the trackboss and he placed the young man in charge of all D&RG's Arkansas River Chinese crews. The Orientals celebrated that day, then went at their work with even more enthusiasm.

———·•·———

"Things do not go well at end-of-track, Sum-mer?" Ling San asked as Jethro reined in the big gray.

"Is it that obvious, Ling San?"

The Oriental nodded. Sweat streaked his dusty face; the man's blue cotton blouse and trousers were begrimed. Jethro knew his chief assistant had been shoveling or wheelbarrowing or drilling somewhere among the toiling workmen. He stared around at the milling men. An inexperienced observer might think chaos ruled as every Chinese seemed to rush helter-skelter in every direction, without objective. But closer scrutiny unerringly proved that each man worked with a purpose accomplished through monotonous repetition: wheelbarrows were dumped, filled, and dumped again; picks swung; shovels sank; banks disappeared and reappeared in another spot. The roadbed advanced before one's very eyes.

"We'd better talk, Ling San. We got a heluva problem."

Ling San led the way toward a small headquarters tent tucked against a nearby hill. Jethro dismounted and followed, leading the gray. Inside the tent, Ling San lit a small fire and set a teapot on the stove. The two regarded each other for several minutes before Jethro explained Dickerson's orders. Ling San pondered a long time before speaking.

"It is as you say, Sum-mer. Not good to split Chinese. But is good for the rail-road, and rail-road must come first."

"That's how Dickerson feels."

"Their crews lay track slowly, and the Chinese grading crews are two, perhaps three weeks ahead."

"Three is more like it, Ling San."

"Work here is easier now that we have left devil canyon."

"That is true. Roadbed construction should go faster now."

"Winter is near. Two months? Perhaps three months?"

"Hard to say. Probably as much as three months."

"With easier roadbed to build, even half Chinese should build as fast as all Chinese in devil canyon."

"Maybe."

"Then," Ling San continued, "if you were bossman Dickerson, would you not do as he does? Would you not move half of Chinese grading crew to lay track, knowing they will not catch the half grading crew before winter?"

Jethro nodded. "I couldn't argue with it, Ling San. I

tried, but there really wasn't any way. But it sure as hell gravels me to see your people getting paid less for doing more."

Ling San smiled. "Sum-mer is too much ideal. Dickerson is right when he say China-man make more dolla on rail-road than as washy-washy. Chinese do not complain."

"But that still don't solve the problem of tension between Chinese and whites."

"But Chinese have lived in America for long time. Have tension long time."

"Can do?" Jethro asked.

"Can do," Ling San replied.

"What about a bossman?"

"You must do it, Sum-mer."

"Yes, Ling San. I know. But they should work for another, too. By rights, it should be you."

"Chinese can not make foreman, Sum-mer."

"I know, friend. It's not permitted. Just like your people aren't permitted to be teamsters. But I still can't be in both places."

"Here is not problem, Sum-mer. Chinese need only you come once, maybe, each day. No more. All will still work—all will be well. At track is where you must spend time. There, Sum-mer will be needed."

Jethro nodded deep in thought. "And with each passing day, with Chinese working on the track, the distance between the crews will shorten."

"That is true."

"That only leaves the hard part. Today and tomorrow, Ling San, we must select which men will return to lay track. They must be young and strong. They should be fearless, too. And it would help if they are also a little dumb."

"I will go as one of them," Ling San said.

"It'll be a tough assignment, my friend."

"Not understand. Assign—what?"

"Assignment. Duty. Job. You know, tough job."

"Yes. But with Sum-mer as friend, it will go swiftly."

"Who else do we choose?"

"There are many. Let us see...."

"Well, well, Summers, I see your chinks laid over six hundred rails again yesterday." George Dickerson leaned back in his chair. He was smiling. "Keep that up and we'll be back on schedule in a couple of weeks."

"They'll keep it up," Jethro growled, "if their backs hold out."

"You did a smart thing, when you made 'em rotate around from tie-setters to ballasters to spikers, then to the rails. That way they all take a whack at the iron."

"Ideas sometimes come when they are forced."

"Can't argue that," the trackboss said. "And you've had more than your share of ideas, boy. You work hard, too, what with keepin' the two crews goin' ten miles apart." Dickerson rubbed the back of his neck, staring at Jethro. "Are we treating you well enough?"

"Me? You're treating me fine. But it's my men you're crapping ..."

"It's you I'm asking about," Dickerson interrupted.

Jethro continued as though he hadn't heard. "Dammit, Dick, I know the figures. I can count. We're layin' half as much again as the other crew. And with fewer men. We took over the grading when work was coming to a halt in Royal Gorge."

"That's about enough, Summers!"

"We come back to bail out tracklaying schedules and we're doing it. Yet my crew gets ten bucks a month less. What the hell is wrong with you, Dick?"

"I said that's enough!"

"Where is your God-given sense of decency and fair play?"

Both men glared at each other. Then Dickerson said, "Summers, there'd be a hell of a future for you in this game if you weren't such a goddamn chink lover. You work 'em, but it's clouding your common sense. You better get it through your thick head that you're workin' for the Denver and Rio Grande."

"So are you, Dick. And maybe you oughta get it through Denver and Rio Grande's thick head that if it wasn't for those little yellow runts with pigtails and funny hats running around on your shittin' job, you'd be so damned far behind you'd never see the light of day."

The trackboss sighed and rolled his neck around as if it was on a swivel. "Why don't you just go ahead?" he murmured. "Why don't you get it out of your system once and for all? Spill your guts, Summers. Let it all spew out so's you and me can get on with our jobs and I don't have to listen to your infernal carping."

Taken aback at his boss's abrupt reversal, Jethro stammered. "Well, I ... you think I've got some sort of hold over the Chinese, don't you?"

Dickerson merely sighed and stared up at Jethro.

"Well, I don't. All I do to get the best out of 'em is to treat 'em just like I would anybody else. I do the best I can for them and they know it. In turn, they do the best they can for me."

The steam engine came to life, tooting twice; the worktrain inched forward.

"Dick, there's no telling what they could do if D&RG

treated them like they treat whites. Why don't you try it?"

Dickerson glared at Jethro for a few moments before asking, "Are you through?"

"Oh, hell. I guess. Will you try it?"

"No," Dickerson said, his voice firm. "But dammit, Summers, I listened. And now I want that to be the end of it. Will it?"

Jethro shrugged. "I doubt it. But thanks anyway."

"Think nothing of it, boy." Dickerson slapped his desk, happy to have defused the subject. "Anything else?"

"Yes, sir. But it's old hat, too. I think it's serious, though. I don't like the tension building in this camp between the two races."

The train stopped. "Don't you think that's just a natural part of life?" Dickerson asked.

"God, I hope not. If it is, the whole world is in big trouble. But even if it is, it's getting worse. Somebody poured kerosene in our tea cans yesterday."

"Just a prank," Dickerson said.

"Sure. Just like the iron truck left for our shift was overloaded and overbalanced. That little joke could have cost a life or two."

"What'd the chinks say?"

"Nothing," Jethro replied. "They accepted it just as they accept everything else, including the short pay. They just mark everything up to bad luck and go about their business."

"Why don't you do the same?"

"Because I don't believe in luck, Dick. I think good luck is something that happens to a man when he has the chance and he's prepared for it. Likewise, bad luck happens when he's not prepared for it and somebody deals him into a game he don't know how to play."

"What do you think we should do? Arm the chinks?"

"Of course not. That would only step up the problem. The best solution is to have 'em split into two different bunches, graders and tracklayers."

"We've been over that."

"We'll be back on schedule in a week or two, Dick. Maybe we can ride things out that long. Promise me, though, that when we've caught up, you'll send our Chinese tracklayers back to the grading crews."

Dickerson rubbed his neck furiously.

"Well?" Jethro persisted.

"Okay. I'll see what we can do."

"Good. I hope we can make it that long."

"We will," Dickerson said. "I got faith in Manifest Destiny."

CHAPTER SIXTEEN

J ethro Spring walked along the long row of toiling workmen, searching for construction flaws. He found none. He stopped to watch a coolie move the chair spacer from one crosstie to another, then help others shift the unset tie into place. The coolie then moved the chair for the crew to set another tie.

Jethro strode on to stand beside a watchful engineer as the man ordered finishing touches to the roadbed ahead and surveyed the placement of guide ties.

"Tireless, Summers," the engineer said. "Absolutely tireless. I don't know where the little slant-eyes get their energy, do you?"

"No, Peter. Maybe it's because they drink tea like we drink water. Though it's probably pride, more than anything. They're a proud and industrious people."

"I've sure changed my mind about them since I got assigned to this job. They're a pleasure to be around, although I think they're still suspicious of me. They act like I'll beat them if they look crossways at me."

"I'll put out the word, Peter. I'll tell them you're an all right fellow who just happens to have been born round-eyed and it's something you've been trying to live down ever since."

The engineer guffawed. When at last he subsided, Peter said, "I envy you the way you get along with them, Summers. How did they come to trust you?"

"I never gave them reason not to."

Jethro sauntered back the way he'd come. He passed the tie-setters, avoided a wagonload of crossties, watched the sweating ironmen set rails for awhile, then moved on to the head spikers. They checked rail-width, setting the three spikes with a minimum of blows from their heavy hammers. As he turned from the spikers, Jethro almost collided with a hurrying spike peddler. He excused himself by smiling and waving the workman through. And he received a bow and a dazzling smile in return.

A horse passed, straining to pull an iron truck loaded with rails. He heard a crash and whirled. An empty iron truck had been tipped from the track to make way for the loaded one. Farther up the track, back spikers finished spiking rails, while other coolies screwed on the fishplates that joined rail ends.

The engine tooted twice and inched forward. Jethro glanced nervously at a knot of white men standing a few feet from flatcars loaded with rails. Many in the little group had been there since his shift began. Jethro recognized some as ironmen from the first shift. The young foreman suspected them of having a bottle of whiskey, a violation of company regulations prohibiting drinking at end-of-track. The crowd of men had grown larger.

The worktrain stopped and Jethro walked toward the

flatcars. He passed ballast men and fillers bedding crossties with gravel brought up in wheelbarrows from occasional piles placed along the road bed.

Several coolies began loading an empty iron truck from the first flatcar. Jethro saw Ling San. It was like the man to be near trouble spots.

Jethro approached the cluster of whites. "Taking a little sun, boys?" he asked. His mouth may have smiled but there was no glint of humor in his gray eyes.

"What's it to you, chink-lover?" one man asked.

"I asked my question first," Jethro replied, still pleasant.

"But I gets mine answered first, chink-lover," the other man said.

"Yeah, we're just out here takin' the sun," another said. "Why?"

"Well," Jethro said, "I happen to know the sun's shining at the other end of this train, too. Why don't you boys trot on back there to take yours?"

"It's a free country, chink-lover," the first man said. "I likes to take my sun here. You can like it or not."

Jethro sighed as the man took a threatening step toward him. "How about the rest of you? How many do I have to fight to get you out of here?"

The audacity of it took them by surprise and they milled self-consciously.

"Go on, boys," Jethro said softly. "Beat it. The show's over for the day."

A big Irishman stepped forward and said, "Count me in, mister. I don't like chink-lovers any better than I like chinks."

The Irishman reminded Jethro of Joe Barry and it saddened him. Jethro wheeled sideways and his right hand shot out in a sudden short arc. Its edge connected with the temple of the man who'd begun the argument, dropping him like a stone. Jethro continued his spin, his left boot lashing back at the Irishman's knee, kicking that leg from beneath him. The man staggered off balance as Jethro whirled on around and smashed a hand-edge against the man's ear, his other hand against the base of his neck.

The first man lay still. The Irishman moaned and rolled to his back.

"Anybody else, boys?" Jethro asked. "No? Okay, get 'em out of here and get out of here yourselves. Like I said, the party is over."

Several men picked up their fallen comrades and the group shuffled away.

Jethro returned to the Orientals who loaded the iron truck, motioning for Ling San.

"You were poetry in action, Sum-mer," Ling San said. "I may have taught you so well the pupil can now teach the teacher."

"No, my friend. You are the tree. I am but a limb."

Ling San dipped his head at the compliment. "Even so, Sum-mer, I would not now wish to fight you for fifty dolla."

"How much would it take?" Jethro asked, grinning.

"Maybe seventy-five dolla. But even then, Ling San could not be sure of win."

Jethro's expression sobered. "Ling San, I fear for you and your people."

"Do not fear, Sum-mer. Chinese have always lived under the watchful eyes of the Gods."

"Those men fear your people. For that reason, they are dangerous."

"What the Gods wish, that will be done," Ling San replied.

"Bullshit, Ling San. You're in danger, and not from the

Gods. Won't you see?"

"I have eyes to see, Sum-mer."

"If it gets any worse, your people will suffer."

Ling San shook his head, but said nothing.

"It is time to do as we discussed," Jethro said. "It is time for the Chinese to strike. It will soon be November. Already the nights grow cold. Snow has fallen twice. Surely the work will end soon. If we are sent home now, very little work will be lost. Very little money will be lost. I fear for my friends."

"We are in the hands of the Gods, Sum-mer. We do not like being cheated, but it is as Dickerson says. For Chinese, the dolla is good. For us to stop working for a fairer pay would not punish those who cheat us as much as it would punish the Chinese. No, we must work as long as weather permits."

"It is dangerous. Chinese have been beaten and killed by jealous white workers many times before."

"Perhaps those Chinese brought their troubles to themselves."

"Perhaps they didn't," Jethro shot back.

"Then it was the will of the Gods."

The younger man threw up his hands, started to turn away, then turned back. "Let us leave this place, Ling San, before there is trouble."

"No, Sum-mer. The Gods will protect us. This I know. Why else would they send Sum-mer to watch over and protect us?"

"Next time, Ling San, it may be a lot more whites, and they might be armed with clubs and stones. If that pack of dogs wanted, they could have torn me apart."

Ling San smiled, his expression one of timeless patience. "The Chinese would not have permitted that, Sum-mer. We do not wish to fight. But we will do so if we must."

"But there were only a few here today, Ling San. What if others—lots of others—joined them? They are more than the Chinese. Even if the grading crew was here, you'd never have a chance."

"Then it is the will of the Gods."

"What of Che'n Wei? And Tse Deng?"

"The Gods watch over all people, Sum-mer. Che'n Wei and Tse Deng, as well as Ling San and all Chinese. What will be, will be."

Jethro spat on the ground in anger as Ling San continued. "We Chinese have a word for it—joss. You speak of it as luck. The Gods control all joss, Sum-mer. As long as we trust them, all will be well."

"You don't need me then, dammit!"

"Oh yes, Sum-mer. We need you very much. It is best not to trust one's joss to always be good."

———•◦•———

Jethro felt especially queasy the next few days. Wherever he went, hostile looks and furious mutterings were his lot. Tiny knots of angry whites gathered along the perimeters of his tracklaying gangs, mouthing obscene curses and threats. Though such knots broke apart when Jethro approached, they soon formed again at the far end of his scattered crew, shouting more curses and threats.

Jethro dared not ride from the end of track to check on his grading crews for fear an explosion would occur in his absence. He tried several more times to persuade Ling San Ho to quit the camp with his Chinese in tow, but the Oriental obstinately refused.

———•◦•———

"Damn it, Dick!" Jethro shouted. "You promised me you'd split 'em apart when we caught up to schedule."

"What makes you think we've caught up?" George Dickerson asked.

"I've got eyes. I can count. We caught up a couple days ago, and you know it."

Dickerson moaned. "Summers, I've got a road to build. Hell, if we pulled the chinks off the rails, we'd be behind again in two days."

"That's a problem you've got with the other crew. They're the ones pulling the work slowdown, not my men."

"It sure as hell is a problem. I'll give you that." Dickerson rubbed furiously at the back of his neck.

"Why take it out on the Chinese?"

"I'm not taking anything out on the Chinese, Summers. We're merely getting the best work possible out of our men."

"But you promised."

"I did no such a damned thing. I said I'd see what I could do. I can see now that I can't take your Chinese off tracklaying or we'll fall behind again. Dammit, man, it's into November now. We're living on borrowed time before winter sets in. I want to finish the year ahead of schedule, and I want to be in Leadville by next July. The only way we can do that is to keep the chinks on the iron. Surely you understand that."

"All I can see is we're just seconds or hours or short days away from a blowup. And when that happens, men are going to get hurt. Then where'll your precious god-damned roadbed be?"

"Summers, you're tired," the trackboss said. "We're working you too hard. You're beginning to see things that ain't there."

"Meaning what?"

"Meaning there ain't goin' to be anything happen like you think."

"You mean those little bunches of men out there cussin' and throwing rocks at my Chinese, are harmless little boys having fun?"

"I mean there will be no trouble."

"There already is trouble, dammit. Open your eyes."

Dickerson again rubbed his neck. "Summers, those men work for the D&RG. As long as they work for this railroad, there will be no trouble. Take my word for it."

Jethro shrugged in resignation. "Will you at least talk to your other foremen and get them to control their men?"

"I already have."

"Then they're doing a damned poor job of it."

"Why don't you go back to your tent and rest, Summers? Take a nap. Hell, I'd give you a day or two off, but I just can't spare you this close to winter."

Jethro's laugh was hollow as he strode toward the office car door. "You sure as hell can't, Dick. But the damndest thing is, you don't know the half of it yet." Taking Dickerson's advice, he headed for his tent.

Living in transient tents proved far less convenient than life in the boarding cars of the white crew, but Jethro had suggested the practice as a way of reducing tension by keeping the two groups apart. Jethro's small, spartan wall tent contained a sleeping cot, tiny coal stove, a few scattered clothes and an extra pair of boots. For a table, he propped his battered cardboard suitcase on end. The tent also stored a saddle and bridle used when he rode the gray to the grading crews.

The young man pulled out his pocket watch. It was two hours before his crew was to begin laying track. He sprawled upon his cot, hands clasped behind his head. He thought of the pulsing hatred of the whites; knew some was directed at him because Indian blood coursed his veins, and some because he championed the Orientals. Would it never end?

———•·•———

Jethro Spring sensed trouble the instant he left his tent. The first shift had just ended, but the white crew stood around their work stations, talking among themselves. The Chinese huddled to one side, silent, making no move toward the track or the roadbed and flatcars.

Jethro sized up the situation, and strode to the foreman of the first shift. "What's going on, Jonesy?"

"They're just waiting for the chinks to take their places," Jones said. His voice had a nervous catch in it.

"In a pig's eye. They never did that before. Why do they have to be relieved personally now?"

"I don't know, Summers. All I know is what they say."

"Do something, Jones. My Chinese are not going on the job until they leave."

"I'm not sure anybody can do anything," Jones muttered. "I don't like the way things are going here."

"That makes two of us." Jethro walked back to Ling San and the knot of Chinese track men. All looked expectantly to him.

"Are you ready to strike for higher wages now, Ling San?"

"No, Sum-mer. It is an evil thing they do. To let them frighten us away would be wrong."

"Trying to begin work now would be wrong, too," Jethro said.

"That is so, yes. But what will we do?"

"I don't know about you, Ling San, but I believe I will

have some tea. Things always look brighter after a cup of tea. Would you ask the boys to bring up the tea cans, please?"

"So sorry. But ..."

Jethro cut in—his voice stinging, "Goddammit, Ling San, that's an order!"

Ling San chattered in Cantonese. Soon, two coolies, their queues bobbing, ran forward carrying big cans of tea.

By twos and threes, the Chinese squatted around holding their metal cups. The servers moved through them, ladling each man a generous serving of the dark liquid.

"Another day," Jethro said. "Perhaps two. That's all we have, my friend—if we survive today."

Ling San squatted beside him, sipping from his cup, dark eyes restlessly sweeping the sullen men standing along the track. "Perhaps," he murmured. "It is the will of the Gods."

Jethro saw Dickerson's bald head jut from his office car. Then the trackboss leaped down to trot to the Chinese. "What's going on here, Summers?" the panting man demanded.

Jethro gestured toward the track. "When they leave, Dick, we'll go to work."

Dickerson glared at the white crew still standing at their work stations. He stomped off to find the foreman. Soon he was back, Jones in tow. "Jones says they'll leave when somebody takes their places, Summers."

"Uh-huh. Tell them to leave now and we'll go to work."

"Look, Summers, and you too, Jones," Dickerson said, his voice rising, "I don't know what in hell is going on here and I don't rightly give a good goddamn. But I do know we're building a railroad to Leadville, where there's tons of silver to freight. Maybe neither of you knows what that means, but I do. It means this railroad will be built no matter what the cost and despite whatever petty jealousies crop up to stop it!"

Jethro and the Orientals waited patiently for Dickerson to continue. He spluttered for a moment, then turned to Jones.

"Jones, goddammit, get your men off the tracks!" Then he spun back to Jethro. "And Summers, you get those goddamned chinks out on the tracks! I'm warning you!"

Jones started away. Jethro took another sip of tea and leaned back on an elbow.

"Summers, I'm not warning you again!" Dickerson raged. Then the trackboss turned to Ling San and said, "Chinee go work, chop chop. Be hokay. Trackboss see, makee makee all right. Hokay?"

"So solly," Ling San said. "No speakee 'melican."

"Oh shit!" Dickerson returned to Jethro. "Summers, can't you please get these men moving?"

Jethro watched Jones talking to several ironmen, saw the workmen shake their heads. Jones shuffled back to Dickerson. "They said they'll only leave when the chinks replace them, Dick. I don't know what's got into them, but I can't do anything about it."

Jethro broke off a dried grass stem and stuck it in his mouth.

"Summers! Didn't I warn ..."

"I got an idea, Dick," Jethro said. "But you'll have to come along with me. What do you say?"

"Do I have any choice?"

"Not really, if you want us to work." Jethro clambered to his feet and led Ling San to one side, where they conversed quietly for a few moments. Ling San nodded.

"Okay, Dick, I'm ready," Jethro said. "You and me,

we'll walk out to the tie-setters first."

As Jethro and the trackboss started walking, a long line of coolies formed up single file behind them. The man at the far end of the roadbed failed to meet their eyes as Jethro and Dickerson approached.

"Okay, mister, you're relieved," Jethro said, reaching for the man's shovel. The man hesitated, knuckles turning white on the handle, then he relinquished it and stalked away.

Jethro handed the shovel to a coolie. Then he walked to the next man, an indolent laborer sitting on a stack of ties. "You're relieved."

"Who says?" the man asked.

"I do."

"You're not a chink. I'm being replaced only by a chink."

"You'll get up and get out, by God!" Dickerson roared. "Or you won't have a job!"

The man held his ground for a moment, then slunk away. Jethro waved another coolie to his place. The next man left at their approach, and Jethro picked a replacement from the shuffling line behind him.

But the next crewman stood his ground belligerently.

"You're replaced," Jethro said, measuring him.

"Go to hell, half-breed. Over my dead body."

Jethro's straight right came from nowhere, smashing against the man's jaw, laying him out with one blow. "Help me roll him away, will you, Dick?"

The next man also stood fast, although he actually cringed with fear. Jethro slapped him twice, spun him around, grabbed his coat collar and the seat of his pants and tossed him face-down into a pile of gravel. Then Jethro waved another Chinese forward and the single-file column inched along.

The next three men melted away at their approach, then Jethro had to knock another one down. Gradually, Jethro and Dickerson and the shuffling line following them worked their way past the chair spacer, through the tie-setters, up to the ironmen. They stopped before the two five-man rail-setting crews, who clustered together for strength.

"All right, men," Dickerson said, "break it up. Let these chinks go to work."

Jethro searched their faces to pick out a pink-cheeked youngster with a weak chin. "You're relieved," he said.

The youth's eyes fell away and he shuffled his feet uncomfortably. A black-bearded, brawny fellow shoved forward. "They want our jobs, let 'em come take 'em," he said, pointing a finger at the Chinese. Other ironmen inched forward.

"You're relieved," Jethro said.

"Let some chink tell me that," blackbeard said. "I don't take orders from you. You're not my foreman."

"Then take orders from me," Dickerson snarled.

"Only a chink can relieve me," blackbeard said stubbornly.

"Ling San!" Jethro called, his stare fixed on the blackbeard's face.

Ling San pushed forward.

"This gent says he won't be relieved by anybody but a Chinese, Ling San."

Ling San stepped up to the bearded man and said, "You are relieved, sir."

Blackbeard swung. Ling San shifted, caught his arm and pulled the man on around. A swift, hard chop at the base of the man's neck laid the assailant on the ground. It had taken but a second.

Another man roared, but Ling San's boot smashed into

his belly, cutting short his cry of outrage.

At Ling San's first blow, Jethro was on them, laying two men out before they knew what happened.

A gun roared once, then twice more. Jethro and Ling San whirled to see Dickerson holding a small, smoking revolver pointed skyward. "Get out of here! All you bastards!" the trackboss roared.

The ironmen picked up their fallen comrades and hurried away. Other workmen held their ground only until Jethro and Dickerson approached. Then, after exchanging barbs, they melted away.

At last, near the rail-loaded flatcars, none of the first shift remained.

"You still think there isn't trouble brewing, Dick?" Jethro asked as the two men watched the industrious Chinese at work.

"An hour and a half we lost, by God," the trackboss muttered. "An hour and a half we'll never make up."

"Let the Chinese go back to grading, Dick. That'll pay off next spring. Let's split the crews or there'll still be hell to pay."

Dickerson shook his head. "There won't be any more trouble. I'll see to that."

Jethro took his saddle and bridle from his tent, carried them to the rope remuda corral where he caught and saddled his big gray. Then he patrolled the tracklaying crew, a double-barreled twelve-gauge shotgun across his saddle pommel.

CHAPTER SEVENTEEN

Jethro Spring was up before dawn, saddling the big gray amid driving rain. He wore a floppy, wide-brimmed felt hat and a drab poncho that had seen better days as Confederate Army issue. His boots sucked mud with each step. He slipped the hackamore bridle on the big horse, then threw his wet gloves away in disgust. "Goddamned rain," he muttered.

Jethro led the gray a few steps from the corral, twisting the stirrup before mounting. He swore again as he settled his rump onto the wet saddle. "Mud, mud, mud," he muttered. "Two days of steady rain and the mud gets you. Never can figure this damned weather. Should be cold and snowing by now."

Jethro jogged past the worktrain and heard the noises of the first shift readying for the coming day. *That's one good thing about the rain,* he thought. *At least it's put a damper on white anger.*

He'd not checked on the grading crews for a week, but with the rain drumming against his tent again, he knew conditions there had to be bad. "One thing about it, old hoss," Jethro said to the darkness, "it's only four, five miles out there now."

It was bad—*really* bad. Jethro rode by a fresno and saw the big scraper's wheel spokes solid with sticky gumbo mud. Two double-hooked mule teams struggled to move the half-full, barrel-shaped, open-sided scraper forward. He watched the teamster trip the fresno handle to drop its load, then curse because the clinging mud wouldn't dump. The man whoaed his team and a young Oriental ran through the slime to pry clinging mud from the scraper's concave surface.

The teamster slogged to his sweating mules, whip curled in one hand. He petted the leaders and adjusted their collars. On his way back, he noticed Jethro and spat a stream of tobacco juice, then shrugged helplessly. "One team cain't hardly move 'em none empty, let alone with a load in the goddamn fresno," the man said. "We ain't gittin' a whole hell of a lot done, Summers."

"I know, Hank. I also know you're doing your best."

The young Chinese still worked feverishly at the mud clogging the metal wheel spokes. Beyond the near fresno, other double-hooked fresnos jerked to the direction of cursing, floundering men of two races. Jethro shook his head as a harnessed Oriental dragged a loaded wheelbarrow through the mud while another Oriental pushed mightily from behind. Soggy-clothed men struggled through sloppy, boot-top mud amid a muted babble of English and Cantonese. Pride flooded through Jethro at the efforts of his poorly supervised roadbed crew.

One dark little Chinese ran through the rain and mud, muttering at the fuses and dynamite sticks he held in both hands. The man saw Jethro and turned away, embarrassed. Then, with a hesitant smile, he turned back and bowed to Jethro. He held up the sticks of dynamite and fuses and said, "Boom-boom no good. Alla wain makee wet." The smile vanished and the little man seemed on the verge of tears.

Jethro remembered the man had been with him since Portland. He smiled and murmured, "It's all right." But the man wheeled and plunged away on his mission—whatever it was. Jethro turned toward end-of-track.

Tracklaying was at a snail's pace, Jethro saw as he and the big gray jogged by. A heavily laden tie-wagon was off to one side, buried to its axles in mud. Another had several teams hitched to it merely to pull it where tie-setters waited miserably in the driving rain. Riding past, Jethro was conscious of hate-filled stares from the white workmen.

Jethro slipped into Dickerson's office car. He shrugged from his dripping poncho and shook water from his sloppy hat. "Mornin'," he said to two surveyors who glanced up from maps spread across the trackboss's overflowing desk. "Mornin', Dick."

"How are things going with the grading crews?" Dickerson asked.

"Slow."

Dickerson grunted. "Back up to the stove, Summers. Dry off. We'll be through here in a minute."

Jethro made for the little pot-bellied coal stove. He ignored the others and considered how best to approach the trackboss....

The surveyors rolled up their maps, struggled into

their slickers, and left. Rain still pelted down.

"Bad up there, huh?" Dickerson asked, looking up from his desk.

"Yeah," Jethro replied, staying at the stove, talking across twenty feet of rail car. "They're pretty well bogged down and there's not a damned thing we can do about it."

Dickerson shrugged. "Freeze-up I expected. Not this."

"Dick, we'll catch 'em in a few days. They're only a little over three miles out. Sure to God we'll catch 'em in a week, what with this weather."

Dickerson nodded, staring at Jethro, aware his foreman had more on his mind.

"Let me take my Chinese tracklayers and go help 'em, Dick."

The trackboss said nothing, so Jethro plunged on: "Hell, we've only got eleven hours of daylight now. Even starting in the dark and stopping in the dark, the best we're getting is twelve hours work out of both crews. You know that."

Again, Jethro paused for Dickerson's reply. The trackboss merely rubbed his neck thoughtfully.

"You can put your old crew back on ten hours, or a daylight-to-dark schedule and they should get as much done as two crews are doing now. I can move my Chinese up with the rest of their kind and we'll stay ahead."

Still rubbing his neck, Dickerson said, "The hole in that theory is, the first shift can't catch the roadbed crew we've got out there now, no more'n they've been putting out lately."

"They'll do better when we get the Chinese away from 'em, Dick. That's what's sticking in their craws. Out of sight, out of mind."

"Summers, I got a mind to fire the whole lot of them bastard first-shifters. That'd teach 'em."

A chill ran through Jethro. He said just loud enough to carry, "Do that, Dick, and we'll have a war on our hands for sure."

"I don't like somebody else running my railroad, Summers; you or a bunch of pig-whelped ironmen who think they got a God-given right to lay every damned rail on this road."

Dickerson's intensity shocked Jethro. "Dick," he said slowly, "try this: let me leave one Chinese crew working on grading, just like now. But let me take the other one up to that cut we got coming up near the Granite stage relay. It won't pay off until next year, but looking at the long haul, that's the best way to get the most out of the men—both Jonesy's crew and my Chinese."

"We'd lose too much time," Dickerson growled. "It'd take too long for you to pick this bunch of chinks and move 'em lock, stock, and barrel to Granite. We'd lose three days."

"No it won't, Dick," Jethro pleaded. "We can move the forward grading crews to Granite, then move the track crew up to the roadbed. That way, we can do the whole damned thing in one day."

Dickerson stared at the potbellied stove. "Hmm. You might have something," he said at last.

"Let's do it, Dick. It'd be better for everyone. I'll ride up early in the morning to the grading crews and tell 'em what's in the wind, then we'll make the switch the next day."

Dickerson stopped rubbing his neck, staring blindly at the stove. Abruptly he pounded his chair arm and said, "All right, Summers. You win. Go to it."

Jethro exhaled, his eyes closed. He snatched up his hat and poncho, bolting for the office door. "I'll get right on it, Dick!"

He nearly collided with Jones as he rushed out the door. The first shift foreman wouldn't meet his trackboss's eyes when he entered. "They're slowin' down more, boss. It's rainin' like hell out there, but they're doin' so bad they can't even use that for an excuse. It's a slow-down sure. It's deliberate and I can't do a damned thing with 'em."

"I can," Dickerson growled. "If it's true, I can fire the whole damned bunch."

Jethro was up at four a.m., fighting weariness. He struggled into his damp clothes and boots and peered outside. The rain had turned to light snow and the temperature was dropping. "Storm's over," Jethro muttered, taking up a heavy mackinaw.

Half an hour later, Jethro led the saddled gray to the edge of camp, hunched against the snow and cold. He twisted a stirrup, slipped a toe in and swung into the saddle just as Ling San Ho materialized out of the darkness. "I bring evil news, Sum-mer."

"Huh? What kind of news?"

"The enemy of Sum-mer is here."

"My enemy? What enemy? What are you talking about?"

"The one whose face was on fire."

A chill washed over Jethro. He checked the dancing gray until the horse settled. Then he asked, "How do you know?"

"We have watched for this man since the day we learned he was the enemy of Sum-mer. He comes on the supply train. And he stays as the supply leaves."

Jethro heard the supply train engine huffing into the distance.

Ling San said, "We are sorry for Sum-mer to leave, but you must ride with the wind."

"Joss," Jethro murmured. "Where is this man now?"

"He crouches by a small fire, away from work train. Perhaps he does not wish others to know he is here until day begins."

"The move!" Jethro exclaimed. "I was going to start the roadbed crew moving today, then move your people tomorrow. Ling San, we must move our Chinese away from the whites. Otherwise ..."

Ling San smiled and placed a hand on his friend's knee. "No, Sum-mer. Danger to Chinese is not so great as danger to Sum-mer. You must go now."

Jethro nodded, then paused. "Ling San ..."

"Yes, Sum-mer?"

"We can shift the move up a day. Dickerson needn't know until it's too late to stop it. I can go out by way of the roadbed crew and start them moving before I ride on. You can ready your crew and shift them today without me. With luck, nobody'll know I'm not overseeing the whole thing until it's all done."

Ling San bowed. "It will be as Sum-mer wishes."

"Well," Jethro grinned, leaning down to thrust out a hand, "you're one fine man, my friend. Give my regards to Che'n Wei and Tse Deng."

Ling San grasped Jethro's hand in both of his. Tears welled in both men's eyes. "Do you wish nothing from your tent?" asked the Chinese.

Jethro shook his head. "Nothing there I can't do without."

"I will gather what is there, my friend. And I will keep it against the day you may return."

Jethro touched heels to the gray, trotting away into pre-dawn blackness. "Go with your God," Ling San softly called.

Jethro and the gray arrived at the roadbed camp while the men were still at breakfast. He called to the two English-speaking Chinese and gathered all the men together to explain the move they were to begin that day. Then he waited while the interpreters passed on his instructions.

The grading crews accepted the new orders philosophically, actually happy to be leaving the deep mud of the Arkansas River bottom to begin work on a rock cut. As well, the Chinese were delighted to a man that the other Oriental crew would work apart from the angry white tracklayers.

Dickerson rolled from his cot while Ling San was still bringing his message to Jethro. The trackboss cursed aloud as he stubbed his toe on a cot leg while fumbling to raise a lantern shutter. He twisted a knob and the pungent odor of raw kerosene filled the car. The trackboss then struck a sulphur match against the metal sidewall and held flame to the lantern wick. The lamp flared amid rolling black smoke, its flame settling at last into dancing flickers.

Moments later, Dickerson sat upon his cot, pulling on heavy boots, lacing them methodically, thinking of the move the Chinese tracklayers would soon be making. *Summers is right,* he thought. *Things will run smoother with the chinks gone. I should have listened to him before.* The trackboss reached for his greatcoat and wool cap with earflaps. It felt drafty in the big office car. *The damned stove went out again.* He carried the lantern to the far end of the car, where his desk lay burdened under papers and overdue reports.

Next year, any damned white crew we got will produce, goddamn 'em, he thought. *Next year I won't let this bullshit get started.*

Dickerson dropped from his car and felt the fine snow. Like Jethro, the trackboss thought the storm would soon be over, and his spirits lifted. He whistled tonelessly as he walked along the worktrain to the kitchen car. There, he poured himself a cup of coffee. "Mornin' Jonesy," he murmured.

The lanky foreman glanced up from the table where he sat alone. "'Lo, Dick."

"Weather's improving, eh?"

"Yeah. Maybe we'll get something more out of the crew today."

"We better," Dickerson said. "We better or we'll get us another crew."

Jones nodded, staring into his empty cup.

Other foremen trickled in: Darby, in charge of livestock; Heineken from rolling stock maintenance; Betters of the surveyors. Dickerson was soon immersed in a multitude of small problems. Jones was gone by the time the trackboss ate the last of his ham and flapjacks. He swallowed his fourth cup of coffee and came to his feet just as the work crew began crowding into the car. Dickerson nodded to a couple of ironmen as he left. He received only blank stares in return.

There was a faint light flickering from the worktrain engine as the fireman shoveled coal into the firebox, bringing the boiler to temperature for the day's work. Dickerson began whistling again. He whistled while he rekindled a fire in his stove, and actually smiled as he settled behind his desk.

But when Jones pushed open the office-car door a few minutes later, he faced a furious trackboss. "What the hell's the matter now, Jones? This train's moving at a snail's pace!"

The foreman shrugged helplessly. "Still a slowdown, Dick."

Dickerson glared at Jones and a vein began pulsing in the trackboss's neck. He started to tell Jones about tomorrow's move of the Chinese, but perversely decided against it. "Fire them!"

"But ..."

"No buts about it! I'm through with the whole goddamned lot of 'em."

"I'm not sure ..."

"Nobody's telling me how to run this road," Dickerson fumed. "We'll build the whole goddamned thing with chinks. I've gone far enough with them white bastards. I'll fire the whole damned bunch and next spring, any of 'em want work, they'll damn well work on my terms."

"Don't you think we ought to talk ..."

"Damn you, Jones! You got sandbags for ears?" Dickerson's face was turning beet red. The trackboss pushed his chair back, half-rising.

"But ... but what'll they do?" Jones stammered.

"I don't give a good goddamn what they do. They can pick buffalo bones for all I care!"

"I mean, don't you ... aren't you afraid they'll ..."

"Jones, dammit!" Dickerson roared, livid, going beyond logic. "Shut that crew down. Get 'em to hell off this right-of-way. Then turn out the chinks and get them yellow bastards to work. You do that now or damn you, you don't have a job! Hear?"

Jones stared at his apoplectic boss for a moment, then

shrugged and turned for the door.

Dickerson settled back into his chair, still seething. He picked up the report he'd been preparing and stared unseeingly at it for a moment, then crumpled and threw it aside. He reached for another sheet of foolscap and picked up a pen to stab jerkily at the inkwell. At last, the trackboss settled down and began writing.

Minutes ticked by, then Dickerson paused, listening. Shouting came from the distance. The pen scratched on....

The door to the office-car crashed open. Sutton stumbled in. "Dick! We got trouble! They're tearing up the track!"

"Who's tearing up the track? What the hell are you talking about?"

"Jones fired the track crew," Sutton panted. "Said you told him to."

"That's right."

"Some of 'em are goin' after guns. Set the tie-stacks on fire. Tearing out the rails."

"They're what?"

"Dick, they're going to wipe out the chinks!"

Dickerson lunged to his feet, shoved Sutton aside and leaped from the car. He saw groups of angry men buzzing randomly along the worktrain. Flames danced from a stack of creosote-treated crossties, inky smoke billowing aloft. Dickerson broke into a lumbering run. White faces peered down at him from the locomotive as he passed. Beyond the worktrain, a knot of men labored with crowbars and sledgehammers, ripping up rails and just-laid crossties.

"You there! You men stop that!"

A bearded man spat as the trackboss rushed up. "Go to hell," he said, his face twisted in fury. "I don't work for you no more."

Dickerson grabbed the arm of a man who was prying

on a rail with a crowbar. The man snatched his arm away and backhanded the trackboss across the mouth. Two others came toward Dickerson, their fists bunched. "We'll teach you to hire chinks and take our jobs away from us," one growled.

Dickerson backed away, step by grudging step. The men continued ripping us his track. He wiped a trickle of blood from his mouth. "I'll see you all in jail!" he shouted.

They laughed.

Dickerson whirled and lumbered back the way he'd come. Jones ran toward him, meeting the trackboss at the engine. "They're goin' crazy, Dick," Jones gasped.

"I got eyes," Dickerson snarled. "Are they tearing up track behind the train?"

"No, I don't think so."

The engineer jumped down beside them. "Want I should back the train away from here, Dick?"

The trackboss stared along the train, biting his lip. More angry men rushed by, two of them brandishing guns. Carmody, an ironman overseer, ran up. "They're goin' for the chinks," he shouted.

Someone grasped Dickerson's elbow. He jerked loose, only to be spun around by a stranger. "Get the hell out of my way," the trackboss snarled.

"I'm looking for a man named Summers," the newcomer said, flipping open a leather case with a badge pinned inside. "Where can I find him?"

Dickerson knocked the billfold to the ground. "Are you crazy!" he shouted. "Don't you see what's happening?"

"Summers?" the man said, bending to pick up his wallet.

Something about the man—perhaps his scarred face—made Dickerson pause. "How the hell do I know where he is?" he snapped. "Try the chinks."

Sutton and another surveyor hurried up.

"The train," Dickerson snapped. "We got to protect the train and the track behind it. Jones, you and Carmody get down to my car and dig out the rifles. Round up anybody you can trust to help. Then get to the back of the train and keep anybody from ripping up track behind us. Shoot if you have to. Sutton, you and Keefer go with Jones and bring a half-dozen rifles back here. We also got to keep the bastards away from the engine."

"What about the chinks, Dick?" Carmody asked.

Dickerson glared toward the distant Chinese compound. He leaped aboard the coal tender and stretched his neck to get a better look. A swarm of angry whites marched toward the Chinese. "Do as I told you!" he roared down at his group.

The men hurried away, leaving the engineer standing alone on the ground. "Keep the fire up, Sneddar," Dickerson said. "We may need it."

The engineer nodded and clambered back into the locomotive.

The unruly white mob continued to grow. The men who'd been tearing up track ran to join them. Dickerson climbed higher on the tender. He could see a group of Chinese clustered before their camp.

Sutton and Keefer raced up, each carrying three repeating rifles. They handed two up to the engineer and his fireman.

Dickerson heard a far-off roar. He saw men hurling rocks at the Chinese. Sutton climbed beside him to ask, "Why don't they run?"

Dickerson bit his lip and shook his head. Flames licked through a loaded tie wagon a quarter of a mile uptrack. A gunshot popped in the distance, then another.

"Summers should be here," Sutton murmured.

"That's it!" Dickerson blurted. "He's at the roadbed crew. Sutton, get a horse from the remuda and fetch him!"

"I'll try, Dick."

Another gunshot—ominously nearer this time—rang out. In the distance an Oriental fell. The mob surged forward.

Chapter Eighteen

A bright sun peeped cheerfully through wispy clouds while Jethro was still at the grading camp. He attended to a myriad of last minute details prior to the encampment's move up the Arkansas River to the rock cut. At last he mounted the gray and pointed him upriver to the unknown, waving a last time to those men of the roadbed crew who saw him leave. The day was one of glorious promise. Sparrows flitted among scattered pinion and juniper. Ravens called from a distance while high overhead, a golden eagle rode unseen air currents.

The man rode so deep in thought through the soft white land that it was his horse, pausing to turn its head, ears forward, that alerted him to the pursuing rider. The man came at a gallop, flogging his horse. A cold chill washed over Jethro as he recognized the surveyor, Sutton.

"SU-M-M-M-ERS!" the rider shouted from afar. "SUM-M-M-M-ERS!"

Jethro spun the gray and jammed heels into his ribs.

Sutton slid his horse to a stop as Jethro bore down upon him. "Dick fired the whites and they're going crazy! They're butchering your chinks!"

Jethro jammed his heels even more savagely to the big gray, bending low over the horse's neck, holding the saddlehorn with his right hand, pushing bridle reins forward with his left, as if willing the animal to greater effort.

Goddamn you, Dickerson. I told you a blow-up was coming!

Horse and rider thundered through the grading camp as men scattered like quail.

Hell no, Dickerson, you wouldn't listen. You and your goddamned railroad. To hell with anything else! To hell with the chinks! To hell with the palefaces, too. Your railroad, that's all that mattered!

He ground his teeth, lips pinched into a brittle line.

No—hell no, Dick, you bastard. You sit behind that desk and you don't see anything. That goddamned desk, piled high with letters and maps and blueprints and wage sheets. That desk is your throne. But you don't have a diddle-dee fart of an idea about what's going on, do you? Long as the iron goes down, you don't care, neither.

A mile and a half out, Jethro heard the shooting. He slashed rein-ends against the gray's sides. A pall of smoke rose ahead, blurring the azure sky.

Why didn't I take the Chinese out? To hell with Ling San. To hell with Dickerson. I could have done it. Ling San, you obstinate slant-eyed bastard. I could lick you now. I could've licked you and got you safely to Che'n Wei and Tse Deng, even if I had to carry you. And if I won you over, all your goddamned double-rotted Chinese would come along. Why, God, didn't I do it?

He saw blue-clad figures darting through river-bottom

willows as the gray pounded toward their encampment. Every tent blazed. Closer now, Jethro could make out men darting back and forth through the smoke. None wore the blue cotton pantaloons of the Chinese.

Ling San, damn you! If anything's happened to you....

A man wheeled at the sound of the pounding hooves, surprise mirrored on his face. He threw up his rifle just as the maddened horse plowed into him, knocking him sprawling to the mud, galloping over him.

Why? Why? What in God's name is wrong with these animals? Can't they see, all the Chinese wanted was to be left alone?

The gray hammered into the burning camp, carrying a savagely screaming Jethro Spring. Blue-clad bodies lay scattered about like tree limbs after a windstorm.

Another man whirled at the gray's thundering approach. He flung a burning torch. The horse, half-crazed from his rider's wild beating, careened into the obstacle before him. A far-off shout and guns began banging in earnest. A bullet whipped flesh from Jethro's upper leg; another spun the big floppy hat from his head. In the distance, Jethro saw the worktrain huffing backwards down the track in retreat.

Run, Dickerson. You bastard! Run away from your legacy to the ones you called chinks!

A bullet slammed into the horse and Jethro felt him falter. Other bullets plucked at Jethro's loose-fitting mackinaw coat. He heard men shouting and more shots firing. And he saw men running from him.

Where are you, Ling San? You ugly, slant-eyed, yellow fool! Where are you?

The gray's pell-mell rush carried him another hundred feet before the beast collapsed, throwing Jethro over his head. The man rolled as he struck the ground and quickly came to his feet. He saw his tent directly ahead, saw the flames, the blue-clad bodies and more men running. He fumbled for the Barlow knife in his trousers pocket and began slashing wildly at the guy ropes. Down one side; up the other. The tent collapsed into a heap and Jethro grabbed its ridgepole, casting flaming remnants aside. He beat about his smoldering possessions, stamping out the fire, tossing aside bits of burning canvas, oblivious to searing burns on his hands.

Please, God! Let it be all right!

He found the old battered suitcase—charred and smoldering, but still mostly intact. He fell on his knees among the embers, fumbling for the still scorching metal clasps, thinking of a Texas Ranger's parting words:

"Just don't bury your gun too deep, hear?"

Sobbing, Jethro threw back the lid and frantically dug under scorched clothing.

"You keep it, boy. You keep it. Who knows? Your luck might hold and you might get a chance to dig for it before all hell breaks on you."

Jethro's hand closed over the butt of the Colt. The gunbutt was scorching to the touch, but he ignored that, as he had earlier burns from the flaming tent. He jerked gun, holster, and belt free.

A fool's wish, boy. Come time you need it, you'll not have time to run home and dig it outta no cardboard suitcase."

Jethro yanked the leather thong from the hammer and flung both the holster and belt from him. He leaped to his feet and spun, ready to fire.

The anguished man made another, slower circle. He staggered a few feet toward end-of-track and stumbled upon the familiar figure of a blue-clad Oriental lying across the body of a Caucasian. A great wracking sob burst from his as he rolled Ling San over, saw his friend's crushed skull, the arm at a grotesque angle, the bullet hole in his chest.

"God, nooo," he moaned. His mouth tightened into a thin line and he crawled to his feet and swung around again, searching for something to shoot, someone to kill!

There was no one in sight; no one upon whom to wreak vengeance. The riot was over, its slaughter ended, the blood lust sated.

Dazed, Jethro staggered a few feet, staring wild-eyed about. His horse lay a few feet away, kicking feebly, eyes glazing. Nothing else moved—no man, no animal; not even a bird fluttered near end-of-track.

Stumbling back to his friend, Jethro squatted between Ling San's body and that of the dead white man. Slowly his eyes cleared, focusing on the Caucasian. *One*, Jethro thought. *One lousy sonofabitch-of-a-killer among the dead. A goddamn poor trade-off if ever there was one.*

The man lay face-down in the snow and mud. He was stocky and broad-shouldered. Then it registered that this dead white man wore clothes that, though mud-spattered, were a cut above those of a common workman. He rolled the man over and the head flopped at a weird angle. The exposed side of the dead man's face was slick and shiny pink, scarred from a long-ago fire. Jethro peered more closely and saw the crushed larynx. And it came to him in a flash that the dead bounty hunter was Ling San's final legacy; a parting gift to his friend, Bar-ry.

Jethro pushed himself upright. Tears streamed. He staggered round, waving the revolver, and moaning, "Ling San!" over and over. Finally, overcome by his consuming grief, the distraught man sank beside the body of his friend.

What now? he wondered. *What of Che'n Wei and Tse Deng? What will become of them? What of Tse Deng, my lit-*

tle black-haired darling? How will she fare in a strange land that spawns such hatred? Will the survivors ever stop running? Tse Deng ... Che'n Wei—how will I tell you of this terrible day? This cruel end to your father and husband? My friend? "Oh, God!"

With Ling San's limp body clasped to his own, Jethro began to rock, staring sightlessly, tears continuing to wash his twisted face. Smoke wafted, bringing a faint pungency to his nostrils, carrying with it the sickening stench of burned flesh. The only sound was of fires crackling as they inched their way through nearby tent poles.

Except for an eerie, far-off whistle from the retreating worktrain's locomotive.

The sound drifted into distorted memories of Montana; of calliope calls from rutting elk or the floating, hollow mockery of a lonesome loon. It was the tune of a lonely man following a long, long trail across the endless horizon that was America and the trackless West....

Watch For

Bloody Merchants' War

An exciting sequel to *Echoes of Vengeance.*

Set in southeastern New Mexico amidst the Lincoln
County War.

You'll read of Billy the Kid, John Tunstall, Jimmy
Dolan, Charlie Bowdre ... and the beautiful
temptress, Susan McSween, wife of one of the chief
players in this sweeping saga.

They're all there.

And so is Jethro Spring, innocently caught in the
midst of this bloodiest of merchants' feuds in all
western history.

Turn the page for a scene from
Bloody Merchants' War

(due for release September, 2002)

From *Bloody Merchants' War*
Pages 19-21

Wanted fugitive, Jethro Spring, is using the alias, Jack Winter:

... No one replied. Instead, Riley said, "Mr. Winter, Jimmy and I would like a word with you. Do you mind?"

"Guess not. Here? My room? Or your place?"

Dolan stood. "I believe it would be more appropriate if we met in my office."

Jimmy Dolan, John Riley, and Jethro Spring trooped across the street from Wortley's Hotel to the huge, two-story brick building of J.J. Dolan & Co. It was Riley who unlocked the door and held it open. Dolan led the way down narrow aisles, past shelves laden with merchandise. They entered a rear office where Dolan drew blue print window curtains aside for more light. His partner entered and closed the door. The small man spun from the window and in his high-pitched voice asked, "How long do you propose to stay in this country, Mr. Winter?"

Jethro shifted to place his back to a wall and flicked the thong from the hammer of his Colt. He took some satisfaction that Riley and Dolan exchanged glances. "Why?"

"Because if you remain, we'd like you to work for us."

"Doing what?"

"We really haven't decided. We do have a wide assortment of work: stock ranches, the store, a freight outfit. We make cattle drives ..."

"Because of last night? Because I slapped a couple of drunks and took their toys? You're joking."

Riley's deep voice cut in, "I assure you, we're not."

Dolan nodded and said, "Can't you just accept the fact we'd like to have you associated with Dolan and Company?"

Riley added, "We admire your courage and decisiveness, Winter, and we'll pay sixty a month and what you need from the store at cost."

Jethro shook his head in wonder. "I've been in town one night and already I've picked up two job offers."

"May we inquire as to your other offer?"

"Sure. Chisum. Last night. Said if I wanted ..."

"We'll pay you eighty dollars per month, Mr. Winter."

Jethro caught his breath, then exhaled audibly. "That's war wages, Mr. Dolan. I already told Mr. Riley my gun's not for hire."

The small man's smile held as much warmth as an open door on an empty stove. "We have no intention of hiring your gun, Mr. Winter. Our only concern is that we retain able, hardworking men. We both agree that your demonstrated ability to think and act clearly and courageously warrants prime consideration.

An awakening bluebottle fly tapped and buzzed at the window. All three men swiveled their head to stare in silence at the intrusive tapping. Finally Jethro asked—so softly it was almost a whisper, "And if I say no?"

Dolan's head whipped back and his high voice was harsh, "Then we must ask you not to stay long in Lincoln County."

Jethro's thoughtful nod hid the sudden rush of anger. "And how long might I consider your proposal, gentlemen?"

Dolan's reply came too quickly: "We want it now."

"Jimmy!" Riley exclaimed. "We can give him some time."

Jethro Spring's gray eyes narrowed as they swept the dapper Jimmy Dolan from head to toe, then the younger man brushed past the lanky John Riley to stride down the narrow aisle to the front door, and on into the dusty street.

Echoes of Vengeance 256 pgs. 5-1/2 x 8-1/2 $14.95 (postpaid)
The first in a series of six historical novels tracing the life of Jethro Spring, a young mixed-blood fugitive fleeing for his life from revenge exacted upon his parents' murderer. by Roland Cheek

Chocolate Legs 320 pgs. 5-1/2 x 8-1/2 $19.95 (postpaid)
An investigative journey into the controversial life and death of the best-known bad-news bears in the world. by Roland Cheek

My Best Work is Done at the Office 320 pgs. 5-1/2 x 8-1/2 $19.95 (postpaid)
The perfect bathroom book of humorous light reading and inspiration to demonstrate that we should never take ourselves or our lives too seriously. by Roland Cheek

Dance on the Wild Side 352 pgs. 5-1/2 x 8-1/2 $19.95 (postpaid)
A memoir of two people in love who, against all odds, struggle to live the life they wish. A book for others who also dream.   by Roland and Jane Cheek

The Phantom Ghost of Harriet Lou 352 pgs. 5-1/2 x 8-1/2 $19.95 (postpaid)
Discovery techniques with insight into the habits and habitats of one of North America's most charismatic creatures; a guide to understanding that God made elk to lead we humans into some of His finest places.   by Roland Cheek

Learning To Talk Bear 320 pgs. 5-1/2 x 8-1/2 $19.95 (postpaid)
An important book for anyone wishing to understand what makes bears tick. Humorous high adventure and spine-tingling suspense, seasoned with understanding through a lifetime of walking where the bear walk. by Roland Cheek

Montana's Bob Marshall Wilderness 80 pgs. 9 x 12 (coffee table size) $15.95 hardcover, $10.95 softcover (postpaid) *97 full-color photos, over 10,000 words of where-to, how-to text about America's favorite wilderness.* by Roland Cheek

Telephone orders: 1-800-821-6784. *Visa, MasterCard or Discover only*

Visit our website: www.rolandcheek.com

Postal orders: Skyline Publishing
P.O. Box 1118 • Columbia Falls, MT 59912
Telephone: (406) 892-5560   Fax (406) 892-1922

Please send the following books:
(I understand I may return any Skyline Publishing book for a full refund—no questions asked.)

Title	Qty.	Cost Ea.	Total
_____	_____	$ _____	$ _____
_____	_____	$ _____	$ _____
_____	_____	$ _____	$ _____
		Total Order:	$ _____

Ship to: Name_____

Address_____

City_____ State_____Zip_____

Daytime phone number (_____)_____-_____

Payment: ☐ Check or Money Order

Credit card: ☐ Visa ☐ MasterCard ☐ Discover

Card nunber_____

Name on card_____Exp. date___/___

Signature:_____